WILLOW'S WAY

AN EROTIC URBAN TALE OF LOVE, LOYALTY, LIES, AND REVENGE

Also by Pertelle Gilmore

*THE UNFOLDING: EVOLUTION OF
THE APEX PREDATOR:
Autobiographical poems and short
essays of a former gangster.*
***

**AVAILABLE ON
Amazon & Kindle
pgilmoresolutons@gmail.com**

WILLOW'S WAY

AN EROTIC TALE OF LOVE, LOYALTY, LIES, AND REVENGE

Pertelle Gilmore

P. Gilmore Solutions & Publications
In Association with
NATTIC RUEMAN INTERNATIONAL
And Kindle Publishing

This Book is
Dedicated to
Daryl Jennette Allen
(Raheem)

I certainly believe this: that it is better to be impetuous than cautious, because Fortune is a woman, and if you want to keep her under it is necessary to beat her and force her down. It is clear that she more often allows herself to be won over by impetuous men than by those who proceed coldly. And so, like a woman, Fortune is always the friend of young men, for they are less cautious, more ferocious, and command her with more.
— Niccolo Machiavelli

BOOK ONE

Of mankind we may say in general they are fickle, hypocritical, and greedy of gain.
—*Niccolo Machiavelli*

Chapter One
SHEIK

Make mistakes of ambition and not mistakes of sloth.
Develop the strength to do bold things, not the strength to
suffer.
—Niccolo Machiavelli

Jasmine's nude body moved like hot lava.

She was a sexy Colombian chick with smooth skin the color of peanut butter. Her long silky black hair was piled loosely on her head, a few strands effortlessly dangling in her angelic face. Laying on my back, I was relishing the moment as Jasmine rode my erection, her hips stirring as patient as a summer's sunset.Caught in an intense gaze, our starving eyes devoured each other. Struggling to hang on to my control my eyes flicked down her shapely figure, marveling at her perfection. Her skin was misted over with sweat and with every thrust, an orgasmic sound rolled from her full, sweet lips. Breathing in large pants, her French manicured nails gently grated my chest as she braced herself, obviously enjoying her ride.

We were in my luxurious bedroom on a cloud soft sleigh bed. Dozens of candles were lit, casting an enchanting glow over the huge room. Expensive French perfume, the

3

fruity scent of burning aromatherapy oils, the lingering sweetness of marijuana smoke, and the distinct aroma of sex all fused together, producing a uniquely pleasant fragrance in the cool air. Bob Marley's reggae classic "Is This Love," oozed from the surround sound speakers, mingling with the sloshing noises of Jasmine's womanhood. All my senses were being blitzed with pleasure. This was my heaven.

I glanced down at where my mahogany brown skin met her golden flesh. Suddenly her vagina contracted, squeezing my hardness so tight that it forced a groan from me. Obviously pleased at my reaction, she flashed a seductive grin.

Suddenly the bedroom door opened and in came Rosa like a stalking lioness with a big fat joint in one hand and my Iridium Satellite phone in the other. Her abundant curves sway with a rhythm so sensual, so hypnotic, that it caused an ache deep down in my manhood.

The flowing cranberry-red silk-and-lace robe that Rosa's wearing is open, revealing glimpses of a body identical to Jasmine's. Rosa shared another coinciding trait with Jasmine. Their faces were spitting images of one another. Together, they were my Gemini seducers. Twin sisters with a raving appetite for freaky sex and a fetish for my ebony loving.

Rosa breezed over and eased onto the bed. She took a long drag of her joint and handed me the phone, informing me with a whisper, "The caller said it was urgent." The accent of her homeland is as thick as her thighs.

Placing the phone to my ear I exhaled a frustrated, "Yeah. What's up?"

"What's up homie?" It was Crook, my best friend and business partner. She asked, "Why in the hell is both of your cell phones going straight to voicemail?"

I responded, "Because I'm a foot deep in something really good, so can this wait?"

"Nah." Crook cleared her throat, her voice serious. "We need to talk."

"About what?"

"That thing that you wanted done is finished."

She had my full attention.

Snapping my fingers I signaled for Jasmine to get off me and when she ignored me, I pushed her, sending her tumbling sideways. Laughing at her sister Rosa scooted over so that I could slide off the bed.

Running a hand over my short wavy hair I strolled over to the French doors that led out to the balcony. Pushing the doors open, I stepped outside. A gentle, summer night breeze brushed over my sweaty skin. Standing at the balcony's marble rail gazing out at the sparkling lights of the city's nighttime skyline I asked Crook, "How did it go?"

"Smooth as a baby's bottom."

I glanced back at the twins. They were on the bed sharing a joint. Quietly I told Crook, "Good job."

"I need to see you face to face."

"For what?"

"We need to talk."

Staring at the twins I asked Crook, "Is it that important that it can't wait?"

"Very important."

The urgent tone in her voice alarmed me and I asked, "Where are you?"

"In the hood."

"I'll be there in half-an-hour."

Ending the call, I stretched my arms to the sky and exhaled a deep breath of satisfaction. A triumphant grin graced my face. For a moment I tried to recall all the faces of the people I had sent to early graves. I couldn't. There were far too many.

Gazing at the city I was in awe of my view from atop of the majestic Lewis and Clark Building. Just a few months ago I had bought the penthouse that sat in the heart of downtown. I had it completely renovated to my liking, adding several amenities that made my home the most extravagant and costly piece of real estate downtown.

Sometimes I found it so hard to believe that I had to pinch myself to see if I was dreaming. Coming from a rundown South First Street Housing Project apartment to a 4,700 square foot crib overlooking the entire city was enough to make anybody question reality. I had come up majorly and by the view I had in front of me the city was mine.

"Sheik," one of the twins called out. "Is everything alright?"

Without looking back, I replied "Yeah. Everything is cool."

"Well darling, come inside before someone sees that big black anaconda between your legs and calls the cops."

They both laughed and I cracked a smile.

Turning on my heels I headed inside, went over to the mini-bar, and poured a stiff shot of Grey Goose, downing the smooth vodka in one gulp. This was a celebratory drink to the end of a nagging problem.

My attention went to the exquisite couplets relaxing on the bed. Both of their eyes were on me, obviously wondering what was going on.

Rosa teased, "That was your little girlfriend, huh?"

Smiling I told her, "I don't have one of those."

"We're his girlfriends." Jasmine laughed as she slipped from the bed and quickly closed the distance between us. She stood directly in front of me, my six-foot-two frame towering over her. She gazed deep into my eyes, studying every nook and cranny of my soul. Then she raised up on her toes and kissed me, her hand moving to my nether region, massaging the object that she worshipped. A smile grew on her face as I grew rigid in her soft hand. She purred, "Can we resume sharing our birthday with you?"

I planted a quick kiss on her forehead. "Something important came up and I'm gonna have to leave for a little while."

Jasmine griped, "Why is everything always business with you?" She planted a few kisses on my chest. "Poppi, you are the hardest working Black man that I have ever met. Take a break sometime. Relax." She snuggled into my embrace.

I gently brushed the back of my fingers over her cheek. "Work hard, play harder." Then I kissed her lightly and stepped away, but she tightened her hold, keeping me from moving.

She tucked her arm possessively through mine. Pursing her mouth in an exaggerated pout she whined. "We came all the way to the United States for you." She planted a few more kisses on my chest. "Not to have you taken away by your work."

From the bed Rosa teased, "Sheik does what he wants while everyone else do what they can."

Jasmine purred, "Yes, he does." Then she eased to her knees and her experienced mouth was on me before I could resist. She relished me with a slow groove. Intense. Made me feel so good my toes curled, foot cramped, while I mumbled a few curses of how someone had robbed God and stashed heaven in her mouth.

As much as I wanted to continue, I fought my desires and fled before my arousal led me to experiencing more of her velvety mouth.

Following a quick shower, I returned to the bedroom where I found the twins relaxing in bed chatting in their native tongue.

Rosa came over and massaged my entire body with lotion while she sang along with Bob Marley's "Waiting in Vain." She admiringly commented, "You have a beautiful body. Lean muscle like a swimmer."

Jasmine called out from the bed, "When are you going to take us on a tour of the historical Charlottesville?"

"Tomorrow," I replied. "All day we'll go hang out, beginning in the morning."

Jasmine clapped her hands excitedly, "Wonderful! I will get to see the University of Virginia's campus and Monticello and the famous Rotunda!"

Rosa whispered in my ear, "I want the three of us to have sex on the roof by the pool, under the stars."

I patted her bare ass and chuckled. "We will party later. Be patient. We have an entire week to enjoy each other. Right now, duty calls."

Jasmine commented, "Rich and powerful running

out handling business on your leisure time." She giggled. "I thought a Don delegate his responsibilities to his soldiers while he relaxes."

I smiled. "If I was a Don like your father then that would be the case, but I'm not."

Rosa planted a few kisses on my chest. "Daddy says that you are the son that he's never had."

"Your dad is an exceptionally good man. He's blessed me tremendously."

Jasmine said, "Daddy says he'll retire soon, and you'll take over the business."

"Not interested." I told her. "I have a goal to reach. After that I am through." I clapped my hands and spoke a no nonsense. "Enough chatter! I have to go!"

They both knew when enough was enough and scurried off, returning a few moments later with my clothes. Valentino cream-colored linen slacks with a Gucci cream and taupe short sleeved silk shirt. Tan Louis Vuitton loafers with a matching belt. My jewelry consisted of gold and sparkling white diamonds, a watch, bracelet, pinky-ring, and a chain.

Jasmine placed the Sig Sauer P226 MK25 nine-millimeter handgun in the belt holster on the small of my back, while Rosa slipped the snub-nosed Smith and Wesson J-Frame .38 revolver in the ankle holster.

After a sweeping inspection, I was satisfied with the dignified man reflected in the full-length mirror on the wall.

Rosa nodded her head in approval. "You're the sexiest man alive." Her delicate fingers stroked my neatly trimmed goatee. "Sexier than any movie star or model."

I thought to myself how I hear that all the time.

Chapter Two
SHEIK

Everyone sees what you appear to be, few really know what you are.
—*Niccolo Machiavelli*

Sitting behind the wheel of my black 760 BMW, I was cruising with Jay-Z's throwback classic album, *Reasonable Doubt* whispering from the Bose speakers. His words were my thoughts. The soul of a hustler bleeding on each track.

Navigating through the maze of downtown streets, I smoked a blunt. The high caused my thoughts to slow down to a snail-paced stream so that I could thoroughly analyze each one individually. My life demands constant observation of the world around me, and short-range reflection on who is who and what is what. Nothing does that better than good weed. I gotta stay on point, because when you are the top dog, everyone is gunning for your spot. So, it's either stay a few steps ahead or get buried by the competition or some up and coming youngster with aspirations of being the man.

The ride was peaceful. Insightful. My thoughts were on the many lessons I had learned over the years. Namely, how most men are ruled by their emotions. I can honestly say that

I had mastered the art of distancing myself from the present moment, never allowing my emotions to influence my plans. Every decision I make is about furthering my business interest, making me wealthier. My life is about making money, stacking my paper, then riding off into the sunset. Nothing else really matters.

Trust no one....The world is a jungle....It's kill or be killed....Master your emotions....Those who smile in your face and hug you eventually stab you in the back....Distance yourself from the moment and think seven steps ahead....Death is the only thing that people truly respect..... Because the strong rule the weak, but the wise rule the strong.

Lesson after lesson scampered through my mind.

Creeping up the main strip of the South First Street Housing Projects my eyes attentively scanned the landscape. As usual for a summer night the 'hood was a beehive of activity, people everywhere.

The red-brick apartment buildings that had birthed and raised me had not changed much over the years. Those of us who had spent most of our years there often joked that South First was carved in eternity and if a nuclear bomb ever hit the city, our projects would be the only thing that would remain after the smoke cleared.

I parked behind Crooks cocaine-white Infiniti QX80 and hopped out. Late night cook outs were everywhere. Chicks in skimpy clothes pranced around in flocks while rowdy thugs and deep pocket hustlers were out shining like stars. Men, women, and children of all ages were doing what ghetto folks do best; running from the reality that they were truly living in hell on earth.

People rushed me from all directions treating me with the reverence of a king. Eyes of admiration, respect and fear watched my every move. Mingling through the crowd I made my way towards Crooks apartment building.

I stopped momentarily, chatting and flirting with a hopeful crowd of female admirers sitting in lawn chairs under a tree. They told me that Crook was not home and pointed up the block towards Lankford Avenue.

A candy-apple red Ducati motorcycle was speeding down the main strip of South First. The front end of the bike was up as Crook rode an impressive wheelie the entire length of South First. She ended the risky joy ride right before she reached the bustling traffic of Elliott Avenue. Then she zoomed over to me and parked the motorcycle right at my toes.

Her intense face relaxed into an easygoing smile. "What's up, nigga," Crook said as she climbed off the motorcycle.

I dapped her up and we shared a quick embrace. I told her, "You need to wear a helmet when you ride."

Her hearty laugh floated. "Fuck a helmet. If it ain't rough, it ain't right!"

"You sound stupid."

"And you look high." She giggled. Her eyes did a quick scan of my body. A trace of a smile flashed on her face. "Do you ever come outta the house not dressed like a king?"

"Gotta dress the part, right?" I chuckled.

Nodding, she was silent for a moment, watching me closely. Then she blurted out "Who was the chick that answered your phone?"

"That's none of your business." I playfully plucked her earlobe. "Now what was so important that it couldn't wait until tomorrow?"

"Wait a sec. I got something for you." She turned and hurried to her apartment building, smacking a few broads on their asses as she passed them.

While I waited, I eased over to a large dice game on the corner and watched the large cash flow go from hand to hand. It was a big money game full of top-tier hustlers. Every one of them worked for me.

A moment later, Crooks big mouth yelling threats seized my attention. I turned and saw her a few yards away throwing a fit, surrounded by five of her workers, all of them focused on their bosses every word. She was chewing them out because one of them had parked a big Yukon rental in the parking spot that she had designated as mine. It wasn't a big deal to me, but she was beefin' hard, shouting and cussing,

11

threatening to chop someone's head off.

The more she yelled the more riled up she got. I laughed to myself watching her hot-headed ass hop around. She packed a hefty energy. When she punched one of the guys in the face, everyone watching cracked up laughing.

Pointing her finger at the guy, Crook scolded him for not paying attention to her. Slowly shaking my head, I watched her closely. She had on all black from head to toe. Givenchy fleece shorts, a V-neck *Melanin Is Life* T-shirt, Dior D-Connect sneakers on her feet, and a Billionaire's Boys Club baseball cap cocked on her cornrowed head. Her limbs were decorated with a grand display of black diamonds.

Under all those loose-fitting clothes was a thick curvy figure. She was a six-foot Amazon of a woman. Ass, thighs, hips, and tits for days. She had a very pretty face and was often mistaken as Puerto Rican. But her Latina look came from the union of a Black mother and a White father.

After I had seen enough, I yelled, "Crook!" I impatiently pointed to the Audemar on my wrist.

Crook ranted. "These fucking idiots make me want to bust their ass!"

She lived for the thrill of the battle with anybody. She had always been a brawler, her reputation as a fierce fighter going all the way back to elementary school. She could beat the average man. Needed to be in the boxing ring somewhere making millions of dollars.

I spoke calmly, "You're giving something that has no significance too much power."

After a prolonged, thoughtful moment, she nodded her head, exhaled a deep breath, and came over to me, grumbling something under her breath as she rubbed her fist.

I told her, "Calm down. You always make insignificant things large when they don't need to be."

She vented "These niggas know my rules, without law there will be no order. You taught me that."

Nodding I said, "I sure wish you'd take heed to all of the pearls of wisdom I give you, rather than picking and choosing what benefits you when you wanna be justified to act a fool."

Leisurely, we migrated up the block away from the thick of the crowd to discuss business. As we strolled, Crook seemed to be preoccupied with something.

I stared at my comrade. She was beautiful, her only flaw was a scar that trekked from her earlobe to her chin, the result of a straight razor that some dude had sliced her with in a fight when she was fourteen years old.

I asked, "What's on your mind?"

"Stressed." She sent a strained look toward me.

"About what?"

She didn't reply so I left it alone for a moment.

We ended up on the backside of the projects, near the recreation center, chillin' on the steps that led down to the caged in basketball courts. Sitting side-by-side we were quiet for a few moments.

She asked, "Who was that bitch that answered your phone?"

"One of Tito's daughters."

She gasped in shock. "Tito's daughter? One of the twins?"

I realized I was smiling. "Both of them are at my crib right now."

She laughed. "Un-fucking-believable. Your slick ass is fucking the plugs daughters. Are you crazy? If he finds out, he will kill you."

"He won't find out, he's way in Caquetá, Colombia." I chuckled. "And he trusts me. He asked me to chill with them for a week for their birthday. Take them to D.C. and New York City to site see."

"You better hope that he doesn't find out that you're fucking them girls." She laughed while shaking her head, "Pussy is gonna kill you."

"Nah. Too smooth for that."

She asked, "Is the pussy good?"

"The best."

"Both of 'em?"

I nodded. "Freaked out."

Grinning, she said, "Share with your lil' homie."

"Thought you were gonna be faithful to Asia." I resisted

a smile.

"Hard thing to do…" she took off her hat and scratched her head. "…when I got every bitch in the city throwing pussy at me." She watched me silently for a few moments, her face revealing her curiosity. She asked, "How is it that you keep international chicks, and I get stuck with gutta rats?"

"Because I travel and expose myself to new cultures. There is a world outside of South First."

She defended, "South First is what made us who we are."

"Crook, we are sitting on the top of the world. You gotta think bigger than the hood."

She exhaled a deep breath. "The 'hood is all I know. You're smart. You have class. You can go anywhere and fit in, but I can't. The 'hood is the only place I feel comfortable."

"Crook, you still live in an apartment in the projects." I asked her, "Where's the logic?"

"What's wrong with living in the 'hood?"

I told her, "It's stupid. We risk our lives for this money to leave the 'hood. Resting your head in the jungle is a setup for failure."

She said, "I was born here, and I'm gonna die here."

"And you think a nigga won't kill you and make you dying here a reality?"

She raised her voice, her face balling up in a mean scowl. "I wish a nigga would try to bring drama my way! Toe tags and body bags are what I'm giving out!"

I nodded, understanding perfectly. Crook was a stone-cold killer. Her murderous reputation preceded her wherever she went. She had no regard for the lives of others and would gun a muthafucka down in the blink of an eye. She had become a legend in the streets because over the years she had taken three murder charges to trial and beat them all. Witnesses kept accidentally bumping into bullets or catching amnesia.

Her phone chimed and she glanced at the number before she answered. Her aggravation dwindled as she obviously spoke to her girlfriend. Her frown was replaced with a dreamy smile full of tenderness.

I smiled at my only friend in the world as she went into sugar daddy mode, dishing out promises of a shopping trip and a candlelit dinner tomorrow night.

Crook was a loyal friend. As devoted and reliable as a friend could be. She was the only person I trusted. The only person I loved. Even though we disagreed a lot, our love bond was genuine and unbreakable. Our friendship had been tested by a lifetime of hardship.

We were complete opposites, but our differences complemented each other and made us whole. We were an unstoppable entity when it came to handling business in the streets. Without her at my side I would have never obtained the soaring heights I have achieved with my business. I was the brains, and she was the engine that did all the legwork.

After a few minutes she finished her call and sighed. "Bitches love to spend a nigga's money."

"And you love to spend it on them."

"Fuck you." She giggled and punched my arm. "Don't get mad because I get more pussy than you."

I laughed. "If you do it's because you pay to play."

She stood up and punched me twice in the chest. "You're not gonna keep fuckin' with me."

Rubbing my chest I laughed. "Got a lil' power with them blows don'tcha?"

"I've been working out." She said proudly as she pulled off her T-shirt and draped it on my knee. She asked, "Whatcha think?" She began doing bodybuilding poses.

I watched her closely, laughing as she acted silly. I tried not to be too obvious as I allowed my gaze to drift down below her face. The fabric of her figure-hugging wife-beater was molding enticingly around the curves of her ripe and round volleyball sized breast. Her big nipples were at full attention trying to burst through the wifebeater. The sight forced a few unwanted thoughts to run through my mind.

I asked, "How long have we been best friends?"

"I'm a year younger than you, so I guess like thirty-two, maybe thirty-three years."

"Since the cradle, right?"

"Most definitely." She asked, "Why?"

"Our mothers were best friends. We inherited their friendship, right?"

"Of course."

"Then is it fucked up that my dick is getting hard as hell looking at your tits?"

We both cracked up with laughter.

She punched me in the arm, "Don't start that again."

"I'm just joking, nobody wants your dyke ass."

"You keep talking shit and I'll fuck you up."

"Can't beat the one that taught you everything."

She boasted "I came into the world weighing two pounds, addicted to coke and heroin. I was not expected to live past the first night. I'm a fighter, I beat the odds because I'm a warrior. I will fuck you up."

More laughter.

She sat beside me and exhaled a deep breath. "Damn, we've come a long way."

"Yes, we have. Kids of crackheads and dope fiends. We had it rough."

My thoughts took me back many years to a time of poverty and despair. The memories of my youth were painful and extremely difficult to think about. We grew up in an environment of complete desperation.

She said, "I remember many nights we ain't have no food. Nothing."

Shaking my head I said, "We had to go to the store and steal a meal."

"Both of our moms out selling their pussy for their next high." She spoke soberly, "Life is crazy. Neither of us knew our fathers. Our moms were drug addicts who died early deaths."

"We made a way outta no way."

"Nah. You made a way. If it weren't for your intelligence we would be fucked up," she said as she fidgeted with my diamond bracelet.

"We are a team, right? It's an us thing. Not an I thing."

"You know what I mean." She placed a hand on my knee.

"I ain't too sharp when it comes to thinking things through. It's your mind that saved us."

I reminded her, "It's always been a team effort."

"Yeah, you're right." She pulled a cigarette from behind her ear and fired it up.

We were silent for a long moment. Finally, I said, "Tell me about the hit."

She drew the smoke deep into her lungs and held it in for a long time. As she blew out the smoke, she said "Ain't nothing to tell. I caught him and his wife in their driveway about to leave. Pumped two slugs into their heads."

"What about the son?"

Her eyes met mine calmly. "I don't kill kids."

Struggling with annoyance, I said "But I told you to take care of them all."

A deep frustrated exhale escaped her frowned up lips. She growled, "The lil' boy was in a car seat. He was only like two or three years old."

"Doesn't matter. I told you specifically to leave no one breathing."

She snarled at me, "I ain't killing no kids. I don't care what the fuck you said."

Attempting to keep my cool I said, "Don't ever leave witnesses. Don't ever leave ghosts that can come back and haunt you."

"I had a mask on." She grimaced. "And even if I didn't have a mask on, what toddler can be a witness?" Her voice was heavy with sarcasm.

Nothing infuriated me more than disobedience. Anger rose in my throat and a mounting wave of frustration came over me. I studied her face. There was no room for the agitation that I felt, and my heart warmed at the sight of Crook's apologetic expression. I gave a slight nod of surrender.

I said, "Look, forget it." I stood and stretched and speaking in a calm voice I told her, "The years have taught me that if you ain't built for the life you chose then you should walk away."

She blew out a cloud of smoke and spoke softly. "Three hours ago, I killed a high-profile lawyer and his cop wife and you're talking about I ain't built for this."

She stood and stepped up on the step behind her so that she could be eye-to-eye with me. Then she snarled, "Every muthafucka you have ever told me to kill I've done without question. I've killed more muthafuckas than cancer. I'm certified and proven. Tried and tested. I creep in the shadows, blow a niggas brains out and go home, strap on my dildo, fuck my bitch and bust a nut strictly from the memory of murder." She took a hit of the cigarette and blew smoke in my face. "If you want it done your way, then next time do it yourself muthafucka."

Shaking my head slowly I said, "Dumb bitch."

My words did not please her one bit. She warned, "Call me dumb again."

"Or what?"

She didn't reply and smoked her cigarette to the filter while staring into my eyes. I had a mind to fuck her up, but I knew that I would have to kill her because she would not take kindly to an ass whipping. She would have that Glock that was holstered to the back of her shorts in her hand so quick, squeezing off shots I would never have a chance.

I told her, "Always crush your enemy totally. In chess, little pawns grow up to be queens, then come back to checkmate you."

I gave her a few moments to process my words.

She finally said, "I don't know what the fuck that means, but it sounded good."

We cracked up with laughter.

She spoke gently, "Please never ask me to kill kids."

"When kids die, people get frightened." I told her, "A little fear in the hearts of men goes a long way. If that crooked lawyer had really feared us, then he would not have stolen all that money from us."

She nodded and said, "That crooked muthafucka stole a lot of money from us, didn't he?"

"Yeah."

"Wondered what he did with all of that money."

"It doesn't even matter." I told her, "Charge it to the game. It is a major setback, but we will bounce back."

I sat down on the top step and Crook came and stood in front of me, a few steps down, our eyes level. She dug in her pocket and handed me a small felt box. Grinning, she spoke bashfully, "I hope you like it."

I opened the jewelry box and smiled. Inside was a diamond encrusted custom-made Zippo lighter.

She spoke proudly. "It's platinum and yellow gold. It has six karats of white diamonds. Three carats of yellow diamonds." She pointed to the backside where it had SFC, the initials of the name of our organization, The South First Commission, in small green stones. She giggled, "Those are green diamonds. These muthafuckas are rare."

"What did I do to deserve this?"

She grinned reflectively. "Today is your ten-year anniversary."

My brow lifted. "Since I got outta prison?"

"Yeah." She eyed me for a moment then laughed. "Ten whole years of freedom. That's a big accomplishment for a nigga from the 'hood."

"Yeah, it is." I dapped her up and told her, "I love it."

"I knew you would." She smiled broadly. "Now you can light them big blunts in style." She plucked my forehead, "And don't lose it."

"Never." I promised.

We were silent for a long moment, sharing a tender gaze.

Finally, I stood and stretched, "I'm about to go."

"Sheik, I gotta tell you something."

She looked nervous and I watched her with a sense of unease.

I asked, "What's up?"

She eyed me apprehensively for a long moment, then said, "Please don't be mad at me."

"Spit it out."

She hung her head and muttered, "I'm pregnant."

"What?"

She blurted out, "I'm pregnant!" She ran her head over her head, "I can't believe this shit."

"Pregnant? How? I mean…. what the fuck are you talking about?"

"I missed my period two weeks ago. Tested myself three times this morning. I'm pregnant." A frustrated exhale escaped her lips. "It happened that night after the club at your crib. That night we were real drunk."

"Shit!" I griped. "You're telling me that the first time I ever fucked you, which was a big mistake, you get pregnant?"

She nodded slowly, "Yep. Ain't that a bitch."

"This is some Jerry Springer shit." I shook my head. "A go-hard butch dyke gets pregnant by her lifelong, childhood best friend."

She spoke in a meditative voice as if she were speaking to herself. "This shit is crazy."

"Are you sure you're pregnant?"

"Yeah."

I raised my face to the full moon and released a scornful chuckle. I told her "We did some foolish shit."

She watched me in a deep guarded way, and I stared at her long and hard. She was unaware of the conflict that lived in my heart. I had been careful since the night we'd had sex to keep some space between us because I had no understanding of what had happened between us. What had we been looking for when we had searched each other's passions so deeply? What had we expected to discover? We had swept it under the rug, but deep down both of us needed an answer.

She had a somber look on her face, but I was certain her eyes were smiling when she asked, "So what are we gonna do?"

"Next week we visit the clinic."

"Abortion?"

"Of course."

"Thought that you might wanna be a daddy." Her face broke into a smile. "I could be your baby momma." She cracked up, laughing.

I shuddered at the thought of that.

She looked at me and saw that I was perfectly serious. Suddenly she looked remorseful and embarrassed.

Rolling her eyes she spoke with a dismissive wave. "Stop looking at me like you wanna fuck me up. It takes two people to fuck."

Shaking my head in exasperation I said, "All of that drinking got me slipping. Reminds me of this verse in the *Bible*, Proverbs chapter thirty-one, verses four through seven. It says, *it is not for kings to drink strong wine nor prince's strong drink. Lest they drink and forget the law…. Give strong drink to him that is ready to perish.*"

She listened, her face serious and intent.

I told her, "That shit can't ever happen again."

"It won't." She asked, "What's up with you quoting *Bible* scriptures?" She said, "Is there anything that you don't know?"

"I *know* that I have to polish my flaws."

"Damn nigga, it's just a minor slip up."

"Slip ups get niggas six feet deep!"

"It's not that serious. In a few days it will be a done deal."

She cocked her head to one side and studied me for a moment. I looked deep into her eyes. Saw her confusion. There was no questioning the depth of my bond with her. I still could not believe what I had done with her. The fragrance of her arousal had not left me since that deluded night that we had fucked. The thoughts caused an immediate tightness in my groin. I forced aside those unprofitable thoughts determined not to become entangled in an unwise affair with my best friend.

She spoke softly, "I love you baby-daddy."

"You're trippin."

"Charge it to my heart." She paused making sure I understood. "You're all I got."

I stood. "I gotta go."

"Are you scared?"

"Of what?"

"Magic."

"What?"

"We make magic together."

Walking away I told her, "Intellect over emotion."

She laughed as she followed me. "First time I ever seen you run from something."

I whispered to myself. "Won't be the last time."

Chapter Three
WILLOW

She is more precious than rubies: and all the things thou canst desire are not to be compared unto her.
—King Solomon

I sighed irritably. "Mom, I really do not want to talk about it. So please stop asking about me breaking my engagement to Lamont."

She spoke sharply, "Willow Hope Harrison, don't you dare take that tone with me!"

I was behind the wheel of my week-old 328i BMW heading home after Sunday morning church service. Cruising west on the 250 bypass, a gospel hymn whispered from the speakers while my mothers nagging was pulling hard at me through the phone.

I interrupted with a frustrated, "Mom, I'm nineteen years old. I am no longer a child." Stopping at a red light I wound up the window and turned the A.C. on low. "Please stay out of my personal life."

She snapped, "You don't have a personal life when it comes to me."

Closing my eyes I tried to stop my tears, but they leaked

past my shut eyelids. "Mom I really don't need your controlling personality making matters worse. I am already going through a lot."

"Are you crying?"

Ignoring her question, I told her, "I moved out of your house because I was tired of being a slave to your will."

Sarcasm gushed from her when she told me, "You moved out because you wanted to live with your whore-of-a-sister and be a whore just like her."

"How could you say such vicious things about your own daughter?"

She snarled, "I stand on truth, backed by the Good Lord and I call it like I see it. She's a slut. An embarrassment to Jesus and her family."

A car horn blared behind me. The light was green, and I pulled off. "Mom, you act like you are perfect. The Word says in Romans chapter three verse twenty-three that we all have sinned and fall short of the glory of God."

She grew silent.

I added, "Judge not, that ye be not judged. For with what judgment ye judge, ye shall be judged: and with that measure ye mete, it shall be measured to you again."

With an angry growl she told me, "I'm the mother in this relationship. I don't need your ungrateful ass quoting scriptures to me. I am okay. You need to take a look at yourself."

Shaking my head in disappointment I exhaled a deep breath. "That devil deceives and so destroys. We must take heed of having too great an opinion of ourselves. The Lord gives grace to the lowly. I love you and good-bye mother." I hung up the phone and tossed it on the passenger seat, my tears gushing like Niagara Fall.

On the ride, my sister Re-Re called and asked me to stop by the grocery store and pick up a couple of steaks so that we could throw them on the grill for dinner. As soon as she heard me sniffling, she knew that I was weeping. I am her only sibling, her Baby-girl as she affectionately calls me, and she is extremely protective of me. Immediately, she began inquiring about the cause of my sadness. I told her about the bothersome conversation that I'd had with mom. That combined with the breakup with Lamont was weighing heavy on my spirit. As she always does when I am down, she talked me through it. Gave me good soul food. By the time we finished our conversation, I had a smile on my face.

It was around one o'clock when I entered the woodsy suburbs of Greenbrier. Sitting in the northern neck of the city, the predominantly white, upper middle-class community is an awe-inspiring landscape of rolling hills spangled with luxurious homes. Peaceful, serene, and secluded from the hustle and bustle of the inner city it was like living in heaven on earth.

A couple of years ago, Re-Re purchased a charming Cape Cod cottage and I had been living with her since my eighteenth birthday. I made the move my first year of college because I had to get from under the same roof as my oppressive mother. I loved my mom dearly but the many years of being governed by her self-righteous tyranny had taken its toll on me. Additionally, I wanted my dad to see that I could be responsible without being under his watchful eye every second. And so far, I had been nothing short of excellent.

Pulling into the garage, I could not wait to see Re-Re. Her conversation in the car brought me back from frustration and her presence would do even more.

The door to the patio was open and I could hear smooth jazz coming from the pool. With a grocery bag in tow, I ambled out the back door and was immediately caught by the sight of Re-Re by the pool relaxing on a chaise lounge. Engaged in a phone conversation she did not notice me, and I paused for a moment and took in the full measure of my favorite person in the world.

Clad in a pink bikini, her green eyes were shielded by designer shades, her smooth honey-toned skin glistening in the sun. She had it all. Brains, beauty, and personal power. Everybody always says that we favor each other, but inside I knew it was not true. Sure, I'm not ugly, but I am far from being the goddess that she is. Her flawless skin drapes a tall bikini model frame that men revere. While most of the attention I receive is based on a man's lust because of my curvy voluptuous figure. Unfortunately, being blessed with athleticism also comes with a thick athletic body. I guess I should stop comparing myself to her. Everyone says I'm pretty. It's just that I don't have what she has.

Even at twenty-six years old she has perfect B-cups. The kind of perky boobs that aim at the sky. While mine are in-the-way Cs and bounce when I walk. And if it were not for our faces being similar, especially our emerald-green eyes, my light skin would betray any family resemblance.

Rather than interrupt Re-Re, I headed inside and put up the groceries, then changed into a pair of comfortable grey track shorts and a powder blue bikini top. I lubricated my skin with sunblock, slipped on my flip-flops then headed out back with my big sis.

Upon seeing me walk out of the house, she flashed a warm smile and signaled with a finger that she would be off the phone in a moment. I sat down at the foot of the chaise and toyed with the diamond tennis bracelet that decorated her tiny ankle.

A moment later she finished her call. Gazing at me with eyes full of concern she asked "Baby girl, how are you feeling? Better?"

"Yes, better." A faint smiled curled my lips. Switching the subject I asked, "What was that phone call about?"

"Big trial. My client is accused of murdering her husband. She's a little worried."

"Shouldn't she be?"

Grinning she replied, "Not with me on the case. Her acquittal is guaranteed."

"How can it be guaranteed? That's impossible."

She laughed knowingly, "It's all about *who* you know and how much money you can afford to throw around. My client is wealthy. That buys a whole lot of souls."

Pondering her words, I slowly shook my head. "You're so wicked."

"Wicked pays the bills." She laughed. "Wicked paid for that pretty silver beamer that I bought you for your birthday."

I shrugged with a smile. "Don't have a comeback for that."

Three empty Heineken beer bottles and an ashtray with a half-smoked blunt sat on the small glass table beside the chaise.

I raised a brow and pointed to the table. I said, "I thought that you couldn't make it to church because you were sick."

She grimaced, "I am sick. Feels like I'm coming down with the flu."

"What kind of symptoms are you having?"

"I've been fatigued, waking up in night sweats." She coughed. "Fever, chills, and a little muscular pain."

I nodded, "Yep. Sounds like the flu. You should make an appointment with Doctor Walsh."

"It will pass over." She flashed a smile. "The good Doctor Marijuana is doing a mighty fine job."

"You are so crazy. Need to see a psychologist."

"Well, the sooner you get your degree the sooner I'll have my own in-house psychologist."

I reached over and eased off her shades. Her eyes were glazed and slightly reddened.

"Dad was upset that you didn't make it."

Slipping her glasses back on, she told me, "He will get over it. I'm sick. God forgives so why shouldn't he?" She reached over, picked up the blunt and asked, "So what did our handsome daddy, the good reverend, preach on today?"

"Friendships. The title of it was 'Show me your friends and I'll show you the future'."

She took a thoughtful moment, then blurted out with a smile, "I betcha he preached out of the book of James, chapter four, verse four."

With a nod I giggled, "Yep."

In unison, mocking our fathers deep voice, we quoted the scripture, "Ye adulterers and adulteresses, know ye not that the friendship of the world is enmity with God? Whosoever therefore will be a friend of the world is the enemy of God."

We both cracked up with laughter and did a high-five.

As her laughter dwindled, she asked, "You mind if I smoke this right here?" She pointed to the blunt. "Or are you going to make me walk across the yard?"

I whined, "Nooooooo, Re-Re. I'm not going to let you bring your demons around me."

With a mischievous grin she said, "Pray them away." Then she playfully went into a professional, heated court room argument supporting her need of marijuana.

Re-Re is so crazy. Laughing at her I reluctantly submitted. "Go ahead." I moved over to a chaise on the other side of the table. I asked, "Why do you smoke that garbage? Partaking in the devil's playground like you were not raised as a good Christian lady?"

She chuckled and lit the blunt, deeply inhaling the stinky smoke. "This is my peace. I deserve this euphoria. It eases the accumulated stress of my hectic life."

"Well, the Lord doesn't like it."

"Shit! Baby-girl you need to wake up." She blew out a cloud of smoke. "In Exodus chapter three verse two when Moses was dealing with the burning bush, what do you think it was?" She took a long drag of her blunt and said, "It was weed. He was getting high."

Laughing I told her, "You are insane."

"Insanely genius!"

We laughed.

I loved Re-Re so much. Whenever I was around her, she made me laugh. She was smart and sassy and had one of those care-free spirits that made life a lot less harsh. Her raw in-your-face personality always expressed what was in her heart, no matter if it was at the expense of other people's feelings.

We both were silent for quite awhile. As she smoked her *burning bush*, I was silent watching her closely, wondering why she loved sinning so much.

When she finished her blunt, she gave me a curious glare. "What's going on with you and that half-witted ex-fiancé of yours? Have you heard from the bitch?"

Grimacing I complained, "Re-Re your language does not

have to be so graceless."

She responded calmly, "Fuck that want-to-be white, sneaky, inconsiderate motherfucker. I do not know what you saw in him anyway. Besides his imminent multi-million-dollar NFL contract he has absolutely nothing to offer you!"

"There's more to him than what you think!"

"You're defending that idiot?

Exhaling a deep breath I said, "Let's not talk about him."

"If it's over." She pointed to the engagement ring on my finger, "Then why are you still wearing that?"

Glancing at the ring I sighed but didn't reply.

She gave me a hard glare. "You need to get rid of all his belongings. Anything that reminds you of him."

I began crying. "It's hard. Trying to get him out of my system isn't as simple as I hoped."

She came over sat beside me and hugged me while I cried on her shoulder. With a tender tone she expressed, "I hate what he did to you. If I had my way he would be castrated and forced fed his balls."

In between whimpers a faint giggle came through the pain. "You're so crazy!"

"And you are so beautiful." She kissed my forehead. "It's his loss and your gain."

"Then why do I feel so bad?"

"Because you're in love with him."

I sniffled. "What am I going to do?"

"You're going to be strong." Squeezing me gently she gave me a hug. "You are going to make it through this. We will do it together."

"But how?" I took my palms and wiped tears from my cheeks. "It's like I don't want to live anymore."

"You have so much to live for. You have Jesus. You have a wonderful life, a bright future." She kissed my cheek. "And you have me your big sis who's going to make sure you're all right."

I vented. "He said that he loved me…. that he'd never hurt me. Why?"

With a matter of fact tone she replied, "Because he is a

stupid testosterone-fueled bastard, and he is not worthy of your presence. You are a gorgeous queen." She guided me over to the sliding glass door that led into the house and stood me directly in front of her.

Staring at our reflection in the glass I wiped away my tears with the back of my hands.

She spoke cheerfully, "Look at how beautiful you are. This is the face and body of the stunning beauty that reigned as Miss Teen Virginia two years ago."

Staring at my reflection with a critical eye I studied myself. All my life everybody always ranted and raved about my extraordinary good looks, but I could never see what they saw. To me, I was just a regular Plain Jane who just so happened to have green eyes.

Re-Re told me, "You're every mans fantasy woman." She giggled and squeezed my buns. "And probably quite a few women's fantasy too, with your sexy ass. I wish I had this big, beautiful Cardi B booty of yours. I would have kings eating my asshole as I am bent over counting my motherfucking millions."

A laugh escaped my mouth, and I squirmed from her clutches. The doorbell chiming captured both of our attention stealing our playful moment.

Re-Re asked, "Are you expecting someone?"

I shrugged. "No." I asked, "What about you?"

The doorbell chimed again.

Re-Re cupped her hands around her mouth and yelled, "We're around back!" She told me, "It's probably Walter coming over for a quickie of my goodies." She giggled. "Well, I definitely don't need any part of that little dick."

I eased inside to freshen up a little. Crying had me looking like a hot mess.

I went into the bathroom, washed my face, and pulled my hair back into a tight ponytail. Staring at my reflection in the medicine cabinet mirror I forced a smile. Tried to make myself feel better by acting as if my smile was sincere. Pain was in my eyes. I prayed for peace and joy to fill my heart. Prayed for the Lord to remove the ache from my soul.

I headed outside and heard a voice that made me cringe. My breath escaped me, and it felt like my heart was about to stop. I started to sweat at the thought of having to see him. Gathering myself I knew it was now or never.

As I came to the door there he was standing toe-to-toe with Re-Re. The silhouette of his 6'4" football frame could have swallowed hers, yet he was being swallowed by the fire of her anger. There she was, saving me from more pain. My valiant sister-warrior in battle for me again.

I waited there for a few minutes while he became smaller and smaller. I grew stronger with each moment knowing that I could do this. I could finish this for the last time, seeing that he was completely defeated by Re-Re, to the point where he was starting to look tinier than her. This was my moment. I walked out of the house boldly. With a determined step and my head held high I walked straight to him. He turned his head and looked at me and it was with that one look that I could see he was finished.

It was my turn.

"Why are you here?" I asked with authority, my anger simmering.

Lamont went to respond but Re-Re cut him off with a cold. "He need to leave before I go inside and get my gun and target practice with his head!"

Lamont shook his head and grimaced. "Yo Re-Re with all due respect, mind your business. I'm here to talk to Willow."

I told him, "I don't have anything to say to you."

Re-Re tried to push him but he did not budge.

Pointing to the back gate I commanded. "Leave right now!"

His eyes begged while the defeated tone of his voice yanked at my soul. "Please Willow just hear me out."

Re-Re barked, "No way! Fuck you, Lamont! You need to go step in front of a speeding train!"

I exclaimed "Re-Re please! All of that is unnecessary!"

With her hands on her hips, she sucked her teeth and with attitude rolled her eyes at me.

Lamont spoke a stifled, "Please Willow."

Exhaling a deep breath, I gazed deep into his eyes. Saw regret swimming in the depths of his soul. I sighed. "Come on Lamont, we'll talk as I walk you to your truck."

Re-Re shouted angrily, "Willow no!"

In a calm yet firm voice I told her, "Can you please let me handle this the way that I need to?" My piercing stare demanded that she leave it alone.

In response to the question she shook her head, mumbled something under her breath then stormed away.

I told Lamont, "Lead the way."

Following behind him the combination of my nervousness and anger had my hands trembling. Neither of us uttered a single word, our tense steps reciting the tidings of our hearts.

When we reached his black Ford Explorer, he rested his back on the driver's side door, his long arms crossed over his chest. Silence ruled the moment. We shared a gaze, my thoughts on how much I loved him.

My thoughts traveled back to the good old days when everything was splendid between us. Everyone had labeled us the picture-perfect couple. He was the charming star quarterback of the University of Virginias football team, and I was the first-year captain of the cheerleading squad and a fledging track and field star. Voted as the homecoming King and Queen our lives were destined for prosperity. We shared love and it was that love that was our motivation to become the best people we could be for one another.

Lamont was in great shape, his body adorned with the lean muscles of a man that was dedicated to physical fitness. His light skin always was glowing, and his cute boyish face and short curly hair gave him an innocent look that made any heart melt. He had never been able to grow much facial hair, but he had adorable little peach fuzz growing on his chin and over his top lip.

Standing there silent, felt like an eternity.

Lamont was in his usual garb, sneakers, baggy gym shorts, and a white T-shirt. Everything adorned with the University of Virginia's emblem.

He asked, "What can I do to make this right?"

My anger would not let me respond. I simply stared at. Mr. Lamont Carrington, the guy who had given me so much heartache these last couple of weeks. The guy who I was to marry after graduation and spend the rest of my life with. The guy who had severed our bond of fidelity.

He cleared his throat. "Look I uh …. I apologize. The last thing I intended to do was hurt you."

Annoyed I spoke sharply, "But you did hurt me, and the entire ordeal has been extremely embarrassing."

"Willow…." He took a step toward me. "I messed up and know that you're angry, but I repent. Doesn't the *Bible* say something about forgiveness?" He asked, "Why can't you forgive me?"

Anger engulfed me. "Lamont don't try to use the Lords good word as a tool of your deceit. You hurt me. You lied. And I cannot trust you anymore."

He spoke with a calm determination. "All I ask is for you to give me another chance."

"Give me one reason why I should?"

His voice sounded strained. "Because I love you and I know that you love me."

"So, why Lamont?" My sadness nearly choked me. "Just tell me why?"

He made an impatient sound, "We've been best friends since we were nine years old, and we've been dating since we both were sixteen." He paused for a moment then told me, "It is so difficult being around a woman I am in love with and not being able to express my love in an intimate way. At least try to understand I'm a man. I have needs."

"Lamont you're aware of the principles that I live my life by, and you know that I am saving myself for marriage. That's God's Law. You said that you accepted that part of me."

"Willow its just that…."

With a hint of bitterness in my voice I cut him off. "It's just that you allowed your carnal desires to take full control. You allowed your lust to override the so-called love that you claim to you have for me."

He sounded sincere when he said, "Willow I'm sorry, I'm so-so-so sorry."

I almost felt sorry for him. I took a deep breath, gathered my thoughts then laughed sadly. "You cheated once, and I forgave you because people make mistakes. I understand that. Then you cheated again. My God, that hurt me so much, but we worked through it. We weathered the storm. But three times. Lamont, I caught you in the bed with another woman. Do you have any idea how traumatizing that was? You broke my heart. And its clear that trampling on my heart is something that you are enjoying in some sordid way."

Silence prevailed for a moment.

My head was beginning to ache. I told him, "Proverbs chapter twenty-six verse eleven says, *as a dog returneth to his vomit, so a fool returneth to his folly.*" I closed my eyes for a moment then said, "I think that sums it up."

With frustration he vented. "You're always throwing the *Bible* into our relationship."

His response irritated me. I told him, "It is always about the *Bible*. Proverbs chapter three verse five says that I must trust in the Lord with all my heart and to not lean on my own understanding in all my ways acknowledge him and he will make my paths straight."

He adamantly protested, "Stop it with the bullshit!"

A disappointed breath escaped my mouth. "The fact that you cannot accept Him as your personal Lord and Savior is enough for me. I want you to know that I will pray for you." I turned to walk away.

Lamont grabbed my arm and pulled me to him. "Wait.... Willow.... I can't lose you."

I wiggled free from his grip and told him, "You're heartless and selfish."

"You know that isn't true." He hesitated and reached for my hand. Reluctantly I gave it to him. Gently toying with my fingers he said, "Our love has the strength to endure anything."

His touch melted the ice around my heart. I admitted, "You were my future, my hopes, my dreams, my everything."

"How do I restore your confidence in me?"

I shrugged. "The question is how do I restore confidence in myself." Exhaling a deep breath, I told him, "You shattered my dreams, and I feel sick to my stomach.... to my soul."

He spoke gently, "I miss my bright and bubbly Willow. I've been walking around in a daze. Can't even function at football practice. Our season opener against Miami is this Saturday and I haven't even learned half of the plays because I can't stop thinking about you."

I asked, "What happened to you?"

"What do you mean?" He raised my hand to his lips and planted a few kisses around my knuckles.

I took my hand from him and replied, "I'm talking about your integrity, faithfulness, and lack of loyalty."

"I got caught up in all the hype. The limelight blinded me. Being a Heisman Trophy candidate my first year in college and everybody building me up. I lost sight of who I was. All of this is so new."

I said, "I have much to ponder. I need time to step back and reflect."

He tilted his head sideways and gave me a sad, puppy-dog look. "I want our relationship to be like it was when we were in high school."

Speaking in a near whisper I said, "Back then you were thoughtful and very doting."

"I'm still that same person."

Slowly shaking my head, I told him, "Over the years your unconditional friendship made so many priceless and precious contributions to my life."

"Willow it's a matter of bad judgment."

I let silence hang in the air for only a breath then I said, "At one time we had both chemistry and compatibility."

"And we still do."

"No, we don't." I glanced up at the clear blue sky and sighed. "Your life is centered around living the party life and Lamont to be honest, a shadow of distrust dims our chances of being nothing more than casual acquaintances. It's sad but true."

"Truth is whatever we accept as reality and Willow, I am telling you now that is not our reality. We can resuscitate this relationship."

"Drunk in Love" by Beyoncé and Jay-Z ringtone blared from the cellphone in his pocket. Hearing the melody of love and passion assigned to someone's number other than me piqued my curiosity and because he refused to answer the phone it really seized my attention. His slightly nervous eyes were a dead give away. Lamont was not a good liar.

I asked, "Why aren't you answering the call?"

"It's not important!"

"Who is it?"

"My sister."

"Answer it. I want to talk to Latrice. Haven't spoken to her in quite a while."

Before he could respond I snatched the phone from his pocket and answered it with silence.

The caller, a female, kept calling Lamont's name. I knew the voice very well. It was Amber, the girl I had caught him in bed with. My stomach turned as a flood of destructive emotions washed over me.

The look on his face told it all.

With as much calmness as I could muster, I handed him the phone and said, "I've been exposed to a painful truth."

"She uh…."

"Wait Lamont." Holding back my tears I said, "The poison of betrayal chokes the heart, slowly slaying the capacity to trust and love unconditionally." A single tear fell from my eye. "I have a bitter distaste that disgusts me to the point of hating you …. but I do not want to hate you. God does not like hatred. The admiration, trust, and respect that I once had for you is canceled."

He went into a grand speech about how much he loved me. With every word he spoke it felt like someone was stabbing my heart with a sword.

Standing completely still, I absorbed his words as my tears increased to the point that the floodgates were completely open. Over the last six months I had developed a tendency to accommodate him even if it was at the expense of my emotions. But not this time.

I spoke softly but sternly. "That's not a satisfactory explanation. I hope you have a wonderful life. I will keep you in my prayers. Good-bye." Then I turned on my heels and headed towards the house.

Lamont repeatedly shouted my name, but I did not reply. I kept my eyes on the front door., the tears rolling full stream.

Re-Re was standing in the doorway. I instinctively knew she had been there all along. As I passed her to go inside, she told me, "Good job!"

I caught a glimpse of that big gun in her hand, snugly tucked beside her leg. Without a word I headed up to my bedroom and stretched out on the bed. I cried and I cried and I cried.

A broken heart is a pain so great that it makes you feel like you cannot go on. When you genuinely love someone and they do not reciprocate the love with equal or greater passion and dedication, it is very disappointing, almost devastating. And when they take it a step further and violate the bond of trust and loyalty that all meaningful relationships are built on then sorrow becomes your best friend.

It is a grueling process to make it through the storm and grow whole again. Healing comes in the form of tears, regrets, and anger. Yet, I know, on the other side of the garbage is hope and faith. The Lord places situations in our path for us to endure for reasons of making us wiser and stronger. I know this and I accept this because the Lord is my shepherd.

Chapter Four
SHEIK

Victorious warriors win first and then go to war, while defeated warriors go to war first and then seek to win.
—*Sun Tzu*

Crook and I owned a little corner store a few blocks away from the hood, on Hinton and Avon, right behind Garrett Square Projects. *S and C Market* is what we called it. The modest establishment got a lot of business from the surrounding neighborhoods. I had a few people from the hood running the spot for me and I kept an office in the back where I hung out during the day meeting with people and taking care of business. I usually juggled time between there and a sports bar I owned as my central base of operations.

It was early Thursday morning and Crook, and I had been locked in my office counting cash all morning. We were packaging the cash into cardboard boxes preparing for my Saturday morning meeting with our supplier. Cocaine was low and it was time to re-up.

The air conditioner was on high, the 100-inch flat screen television on the wall was on ESPN's Sports Center while the surround sound speakers pumped out Tupac's old school classic album, *All Eyes on Me*.

Crook was on the black leather couch placing the last batch of cash in a box while finishing of a blunt. She was bobbing her head to the music while rapping along with 'Pac on "Hit 'em Up." I had my feet up on my desk, phone to my ear, chatting with a little sexy Ethiopian chick that worked at the spa that I frequented for massages.

After Crook and I finished we loaded the boxes into a U-Haul and locked the truck in a rented storage garage down the block. We ate lunch at Mel's Café, ran a few errands, and were back at the store by four o'clock.

Sitting behind my desk I was sipping on an ice-cold Corona watching a rerun of Oprah. It was a show about sex and Oprah had a bunch of experts talking about diverse ways to pleasure a woman. Crook was relaxing on the couch cleaning her gun, her attention being divided between me and her weapon. Something was on her mind.

She asked, "What time is this nigga Goldie supposed to show up?"

I glanced at my Rolex. "In about twenty minutes."

"Whatcha, think he want?"

I shrugged. "Don't know. Maybe he wanna talk business."

She owned an unreadable expression as she stared at me. Her mind was churning, tryna figure out dude's motives for coming to see me. She was my self-appointed pit bull, a guard dog trained to protect me and my interest to the death. She'd lay down her life to safeguard me. The bullet lodged in her back is evidence of her fierce dedication to keeping me safe.

It intrigued me that Goldie, an old school hustler from back in the days wanted to see me. Dude was fresh out from a seventeen-year stint in the Federal Prison System. From what I had gathered he had only been home for about two weeks.

Crook gave me an uneasy look. "I don't trust it."

"Me either but outta respect for this niggas history we'll see what he's talking about."

"Ain't nobody worthy of my respect but you." She grumbled something under her breath and rolled her eyes.

"Respect his history."

She smirked sarcastically. "Fuck respect. We ain't gotta respect nobody!"

"Respect all until they prove they're unworthy of it."

"Ain't nobody worthy of my respect but you." She grumbled something under her breath and rolled her eyes. Took her attention back to the gun.

Goldie Johnson was the official "Father" of a well-organized outfit based uptown in Westhaven Projects. They called themselves The Johnson Family Mafia or JFM for short. Goldie had started the organization back in the 70's, starting as a budding, small gang of family members who sold a little weed and trooped around town rumbling other rival gangs. As the years passed, and times changed the once loose knit band of relatives become a large movement. They become organized. And in the 80's they took over every illegal enterprise in the city.

With a campaign of brutal murders and ferocious acts of violence they ruled the streets. Became wealthy. Superstars. Legends in their own times. They ended up catching the attention of the feds who came down hard on them. Locked up most of them on the federal Racketeering Influenced and Corrupt Organizations or (RICO) law. The reign was over. At least that's what everyone thought.

When Goldie got locked up in the early 90's, his three children took over the business which had crumbled due to the hierarchy being incarcerated. Using the same type of violence their forebears exercised they rose from the ashes bringing JFM back to the top. Once they had a stronghold on all rackets, they finessed the entire game by running their business like a major corporation. The siblings became like a board of directors each one respectively running a facet of the business, while they sat at one table and voted on all major decisions. The official C.E.O. of the empire was Rita, the oldest child and only female of the clan.

With the JFM in Rita's hands the violence died and like a well-oiled machine their business ran smooth while they got filthy rich. And now their dad, the King, had returned. He had come home to an empire that was a hundred times larger than what he had left. Marijuana, heroin, ecstasy, meth, gambling, prostitution, bootlegging, and stolen goods. They had a lock on it all. The only market that they had not monopolized was cocaine. That was my domain, and I had no rival.

I asked Crook, "What's on your mind?"

"You." She sighed. "Always you."

Crook got up and came over to me. She sat down on the arm of my chair and gently ran her hand over my head. She said, "My gut is telling me that this ain't no good thing with meeting with dude."

"There's nothing wrong with talking."

"If you say so."

I checked her out from head-to-toe. My heart smiled. Crook had on all-white. Linen slacks, silk button-down shirt, tan Gucci loafers, platinum framed Cartier glasses, her gold and diamond jewelry sparkling.

I looked at her gorgeous face and said, "We are the exception. Not the rule."

"Whatcha talking about?"

"We are gonna leave this business on our feet. No jail cells. No caskets."

She gave me a puzzled look. "There you go talking that retirement shit again?"

"If all goes according to my plan, we can bow out filthy-fucking-rich and go somewhere tropical and live out our days in paradise."

"Gangsters don't retire. We live it up and die young." She laughed.

I shook my head at her ignorance.

My sole motivation was abundant wealth. With that I could insure and assure an exceptionally good life free from the stress of the working man. I did not want the glory or the fame. I simply wanted to leave this business with my health, sanity, and a bank account full of zeroes.

Crook saw no end to this journey. From day one she had been caught in the glamor of being a celebrity. Blinded by the here-and-now she could not see past the women, cars, clothes, clubbing and the jewelry. Now do not get it twisted, all that stuff is good in moderation. The fruits of our sacrifices were supposed to be enjoyed. But *excess* with no plan of *exit* leads to your *extermination*. Hustlers without foresight, without a plan to get out, without a goal, will be destroyed by a game with no heart. Look at all of them dudes being fertilizer for grass in the cemetery. You gotta get in and get out. The sooner the better.

I wanted the best for Crook. I wanted my vision to become hers. She was all I had in the world.

I said, "In a year or less we'll be through with this shit."

"Big dreams." She toyed with my fingers. "It's gonna be hard leaving this life behind."

I shook my head, "Not for me."

She leaned over and planted a few kisses on my forehead. I cringed every time her thick lips touched my skin. I hated when she crossed a line that we determined was forbidden. The warm smile she wore was rare. I think I am the only one who has ever seen her really splash a smile of joy. In her mind I'm the only one that deserved it.

She grabbed my beer and took a swig. She said, "You act like you ain't want to me kiss you."

I didn't reply and took my attention to the television.

She grumbled something under her breath and plucked my ear so hard it hurt. I responded with a punch to her thigh. She grimaced in pain, rubbed the spot where the blow had landed, and then she laughed.

Crook draped an arm around my shoulder. Put her face right next to mine. Cheek to cheek she asked, "Do you wanna fuck?"

"Stop being stupid." I sat up and moved away from the warmth of her body. Could not be weak. Had to remain strong for the both of us.

"Punk ass nigga." She snarled, "What nigga runs from pussy but a fucking faggot!"

That did it. I snapped. With a one hand grip I seized her neck and slammed her on the floor. I choked her while I growled for her to stop playing so much. I watched her face turn red then purple as she fought to get free. By the time I let her go she was damn near unconscious. Gasping for air the crazy bitch laughed at me and started peeling off her clothes.

I fucked her. Rage fucked her. Gave her what she wanted. Like wild animals we went at it hard for a couple of minutes. Afterwards she hurriedly got dressed and ran from the office. Both of us had felt shame and embarrassment. Could not even look one another in the eye. I was glad that she had left, and I was angry with myself for being so weak, going against my word. For reasons beyond my understanding my appetite for her had evolved into an addiction. And I found that I could not control the compulsions. Neither could she. That alarmed me.

At exactly five o'clock Goldie walked into my office smiling, his gold teeth bright and shiny. He was sporting a blood-red pinstripe suit, red gators on his feet, and a red derby cocked on his head. Standing tall and thick like an NFL lineman, his skin was the color of tar, his ugly bulldog face full of deep wrinkles. His eyes were hidden behind a pair of designer shades, and he had one of those elaborate gold and wood pimp canes. I thought to myself, *Certified Grade-A Clown.*

He spoke with a deep raspy voice. "Young Sheik I finally have the pleasure to meet you."

I walked over to him and greeted him with a firm handshake. "My pleasure and honor to be in the presence of a legend."

He chuckled. "Legend hunh? Dudes with them titles are dead."

We shared a laugh.

I asked, "Can I get you something to drink?"

He nodded. "A cold Heineken would be nice. It's hotter than a Tonsler Park whore's pussy outside."

I laughed at his choice of words and got him a beer outta the fridge. Then we both took a seat at my desk.

He surveyed my body and said, "It is good to see a young man like yourself dress casually in linen, silk, and hard bottoms. My sons are in their thirties, and they still walking around wearing jeans and sneakers most of the time.

Tasteless. Especially for men with money."

I smiled. "Maybe now that you're home you can teach them a thing or two about style."

"That's damn sure on my to-do-list."

I asked, "So to what do I owe the honor of your visit?"

"Straight to the point ain'tcha?"

"I'm a busy man."

"No need to rush."

"Patience is a virtue but it ain't one of mine."

"You're an important man." He sipped his beer. "Your goons out front frisked me, took my gun, then ran a lil' metal detector over my body, then ran some type of gadget over me that they said could detect wires and bugs."

I chuckled. "Gotta be careful. It's a tricky world out here. Snakes and rats around every corner."

"Young man I ain't do all that time in prison by being no rat."

"Forgive me if I offended you but I wasn't implying that at all."

"No offense taken."

I told him, "My guys will kindly return your gun when you leave."

Nodding he glanced around the office then returned his attention to me. "Nice office you got here. Classy."

I smiled but did not say anything. I watched him closely.

"I knew your dad Big Sheik. He was a thoroughbred. The gangster of all gangsters. An original and authentic Black Panther that did not play games. And I've heard some extraordinary things about you too. A real fucking Black Robin Hood that takes good care of the entire South First Projects. It seems like the apple don't fall far from the tree."

"I ain't no gangster. I am a businessman."

"I hear different."

"Believe none of what you hear and half of what you see."

He chuckled. "My kids tell me that a couple of years ago that ya'll had a disagreement."

"I wouldn't call it a disagreement. It was merely a failure to communicate."

"Oh yeah?"

"Your family didn't approve of having a little business competition."

"A little competition?" He smirked, "From what I hear no one could compete with the quality of your product or the good prices."

"I take pride in delivering the absolute best product for your dollar."

"That's the sign of a good businessman."

"I try."

"People tell me that you got Miami prices. Got folks from D.C., North Carolina, Maryland, West Virginia, and Tennessee coming to see you."

I asked, "How can I help you today?"

"I wanna talk business with you young man."

"I'm listening."

"I'm home and before I left, I used to do things a certain way."

"And what way was that?"

"All of my friends used to bestow me with a percentage of their income as a token of benevolence."

I laughed.

Smiling at me he took a piece of hard candy from the candy jar on my desk and popped it in his mouth. Watching me closely he was trying to read me.

I finally stopped laughing and said, "Is this a joke?"

Smiling broadly, he said, "I am fifty-six years old. I don't have time for jokes. In this day and age, you young folk ain't got no respect for us pioneers who made it possible for ya'll to flourish in this white man's world. You pay homage by respecting me. You respect me by paying dues. It's all in the spirit of good peaceful business relationships."

"With all due respect, I feel like you're disrespecting me with your request."

"Do not feel disrespected. It's not personal. I am home. This is my city. Things are gonna change."

"I didn't get where I am by playing by anybody's rules but my own."

"Good thing about life is that we can learn as we go along. Take this as a learning experience."

"I'll be the first to affirm that we must live and learn so that we can learn to live but Goldie this is one lesson that I refuse to pick up."

He told me, "Think before you speak."

I chuckled. "Maybe it's time that we end this meeting."

"I'll say when this is over."

Smiling I asked, "Do your children know you're here?"

He spoke a serious. "That's not an appropriate question."

"And you're not making an appropriate request."

The door opened and Crook walked in toting a Foot Locker bag. She eyed Goldie suspiciously and headed over to the bar and poured herself a drink of Hennessy. Then she perched on a stool and watched Goldie with disdain in her eyes

I smiled at Crook. "Meet Mister Goldie." I introduced her as my business partner.

Crook did not reply when he spoke to her.

Goldie looked at Crook with lust in his eyes. "Now ain't you a beauty. A little Latina mommi. Thick as a milkshake."

Crook simply stared at him with a fuck you glare.

He cleared his throat and brought his attention back to me. "She's a silent one ain't she?"

I forced a smile. "Goldie it was nice meeting you but I'm gonna decline on the offer."

He laughed. "Young Sheik that wasn't an offer."

My tone spoke my disfavor. "Goldie now you are disrespecting me."

He said, "Either we can be gentlemen about this or barbarians."

Crooks body suddenly tensed up, her eyes narrowed, her focus on Goldie. Like a cobra she was coiled and ready to strike.

I tried to be civil and keep things peaceful. Speaking with a pleasant tone I told Goldie that we had nothing else to discuss. But the old stuck in his ways maggot refused to respect me. Refused to leave well enough alone. He was set on extorting me. Tempers flared. Egos bruised. Testosterone at dangerous levels. Both of us struggling to be the alpha male.

He said, "Youngin' it should be an honor for you to speak my name."

I spoke coldly, "Get the fuck outta my presence old man."

He stood and shouted, "Muthafucka you wanna rumble with the devil! I will make sure that you touch all parts of hell!"

I warned. "Old man don't ever threaten me again!"

Crook slipped off the stool.

"You young punk ass nigga disrespecting me like I'm a clown! I will bury you my muthafuckin' self!" Goldie snarled then spit in my face. "Bitch ass nigga!"

Before I could react, I saw Goldie's head fall from his shoulders, hit the floor with a loud thud and roll a couple of feet away. His headless body stood there for a couple of seconds, blood squirting everywhere, before it hit the floor.

Crooks' violent reaction shocked me into stunned silence. It was like time had stopped.

Crooks touch brought me back to reality as she took a napkin and wiped the spit from my face. Speaking tenderly, she asked, "Are you okay my nigga?"

I looked at her. She was holding a machete in her hand its sharp blade with a long, small thread of Goldie's blood near the tip.

We both were silent for a couple of seconds sharing a gaze. I was trying to make some sense of what had just happened.

Warmth was in her eyes when she smiled, "That chump ain't know who he was fucking with did he?" She laughed. "Now who's the bitch ass nigga?"

Reality began sinking in and I spoke just above a whisper, "Why did you do that?"

"Fuck that old ass muthafucka!"

I looked at Goldie's lifeless body resting in a rapidly growing pool of blood. "You've started a war."

Crook glanced at Goldie's body, then looked at me. She must have recognized the anger in my eyes because she hung her head and stared at her feet. Guilt blanketed her face.

She mumbled. "Dude disrespected you."

"You were impulsive!"

She walked over to the bar, dropped the machete on the floor and drowned her drink. Blankly staring at me she was silent.

I asked, "Do you have any idea what you have done?"

"Nigga I ain't stupid. I know what the fuck I done!"

A deep sense of distress washed over me. The repercussions behind killing Goldie made me nauseous. A war was not something I needed right now. Too much was at stake. I had entirely too much to lose. Absolutely nothing at all to gain.

She said, "I do you a favor and you get mad?"

I dropped my head so she could not see the disgust in my eyes.

She spoke sarcastically, "You was gonna let that muthafucka' spit in your face and do nothing about it?"

I growled through clenched teeth. "We don't move reckless. We plan."

"Well, I planned myself." She pointed at me. "Planned and executed his Black ugly ass!"

"Stupid bitch!"

She argued passionately, "You are getting soft! I did what you were scared to do! Gangsters don't tolerate disrespect. Gangsters take respect!"

I grabbed the Meyda Tiffany lamp from my desk and hurled it at her, but she ducked. The lamp hit the bottles on the bar and knocked them to the floor, the sound of shattered glass ringing loudly.

She screamed, "Do you wanna piece of me muthafucka!" Her gun was in her hand.

I stormed over to her and pushing my finger into her forehead I shouted, "Use your fucking mind!"

She screamed, "I did what I was supposed to do!"

"You reacted from emotion instead of thinking."

She cursed me out. Called me everything under the sun. Threatened to put a million bullets in me.

I back hand slapped her so hard she fell back into the bar.

Stunned, she glared at me rubbing her cheek, her eyes moist.

I growled, "Bitch, don't you ever talk to me like that again!"

"You ...."

I cut her off, "Or next time it'll be your head on that muthafuckin floor!" I shouted, "Am I understood!"

She didn't respond.

I shouted louder, "Am I understood!"

She nodded, her face holding a grieved expression. Her voice was frail. "Yeah.... understood."

Standing with my hands on my hips I stared at Goldie's head trying to figure out what in the hell I was gonna do with this situation.

I mumbled to myself, "I'm always cleaning up your fucking messes."

Like a spoiled child she grumbled something then stomped over and kicked Goldie's head. Like a ball it rolled across the room. Then she plopped down on the couch and pouted, staring at the floor.

Rubbing my chin, I tried to gather myself. I needed to be composed. Had to figure something out.

Crooks voice was low. "Why are you so mad at me?"

I sat down in the chair and tried to collect my thoughts. I willed myself to calm down. I hung my head and muttered, "Our plans are gonna crumble."

"Tell me whatcha mean."

"Crook, what do you think these JFM niggas are gonna do when they find out that their dad is dead?"

In a soft weary voice she replied, "We can bury the body. Ain't nobody gotta know about it."

I shook my head grimly. "We don't know who he told about this meeting or who saw him come in here."

"We can say that he ain't show up?"

I massaged my throbbing temples. "Crook, you fucked up big time on this one here."

She snapped. "You ain't gotta keep reminding me."

I asked, "How did he get here?"

"There is a red Cadillac Escalade sitting in front of the

store."

With my thoughts brewing I sat there staring at the mess on the floor.

Crook sighed. "Let me clean this up."

"Fuck no. Leave it to the pros. Get our best two capos on it." I told her, "Call Buck and Denny. They just got back from Dubai. Get them on it. They are on South First right now trying to squash that beef between Taneak and Lil' Ru-Ru, some wild nigga from uptown on Anderson. You just let them lead and you play the background and learn something from them. We gotta make that Escalade disappear, and this body disappear as soon as the sun goes down. Nobody should ever find him. Call big Holsapple from Belmont and tell him that we gotta pig eating job for him. Pay him fifty grand. I still owe him twenty-five for that other thing. Take the cash outta the safe at your house."

She asked, "What about all of this blood?"

"After Buck and Denny clean it up really good, they'll torch the store." I glanced around the office. "Yeah. Burn this muthafucka down."

"Burn the store?" She asked, "Are you crazy?"

"Nah. I'm smart. Too much DNA has seeped into too many nooks and crannies of this office. Too risky. Insurance will pay for everything. We will build another one."

"Damn!"

"That's the price of making foolish mistakes."

After I gathered all the important things from the office, I took the back door exit and left her alone. As I drove away my gut told me that this situation would snowball into something that I did not want to face. Something that would strip me of a lot of what I've built.

Always expect the unexpected.

My mind was on war. Death was lurking. Hopefully not mine. Hopefully.

Chapter Five
SHEIK

Who can find a virtuous woman? for her price is far above rubies.
—King Solomon

It was a humid Saturday morning, and I was shirtless loitering on a wooden pedestrian bridge in the heavily forested section of McIntire Park. Ten feet below me was a winding creek and I was leaning with my elbows resting on the railing of the bridge. Not a soul was in sight and the many sounds of nature was a soothing song.

I had drove to the park for some much needed separation from the chaos that was my life. Every Saturday when I was in town I would pay an early morning visit to the bridge, smoke a blunt and gather my thoughts. The atmosphere was calming. Over the years many of my most burdensome problems had been resolved while I stood alone on the bridge.

I had a lot on my mind. Primarily my approaching retirement from the cocaine business. I had been on top for almost ten years, and it was time to gracefully bow out. I was tired of the everyday stress of my lifestyle, and I could not stomach the bullshit much longer. If my exit plan goes smoothly, in a year or so, I should be leading a quiet life in a tropical climate. Hopefully with a beautiful woman that I can learn to love so that I can start a family.

I was also thinking about the JFM situation. The streets were talking and word around town was that I personally had something to do with Goldie's disappearance. So, it was only a matter of time before someone from the JFM would be visiting me searching for answers.

Lastly, I was brooding over a dilemma involving me and Crook. Last night we had sex again. And after it was all over instead of parting ways, she had spent the night. Naked we had slept together and when I woke up this morning, she had been all snuggled up on me like I was the love her life. The shit had felt so weird that I'd slipped outta bed, showered, got dressed and left the house before she woke up. That had been an hour ago and I had been at the park ever since.

It was obvious that Crook and I shared some type of passionate affection for each other because last night hadn't just been a simple case of fucking. It had been slow, sensual love making, full of kisses and caresses. The more I thought about it, the more my stomach turned. What in the hell had our relationship become? One minute we are sitting around joking about all the chicks we had ran through, and the next minute she's riding my dick moaning that she loves me.

We could not afford to sabotage our friendship or business relationship over the complications that came from some lovey-dovey bullshit. Too much was at stake.

But who knows, maybe our entire lives had been preparing us for this moment in time. Maybe it was an inevitable fate that we had no control over. Or maybe I'm just trippin' tryna rationalize something that I know is a step towards failure. I had a decision to make. Either I could nip it in the bud or accept the evolution of what we had become. I knew that either way somebody would end up with their feelings hurt. And I was 100% sure that it was not gonna be me.

A feminine scream came from my right, jarring me from my contemplative moment. I turned and to my surprise spotted a woman about forty yards away. She was laying flat on her stomach, sprawled out on the asphalt trail that led down to the bridge. She struggled to get to her feet, and it appeared as if she was injured.

Curiosity compelled me to see what was up with her.

On the walk over I watched her roll over and sit up. She wrapped her arms around her folded legs and buried her face in between her knees. Muffled sobs came from her as she simultaneously mumbled something about wanting God to take away her pain.

She did not notice me walk up to her and for a long moment I stood over her watching her.

She had on a pair of tight grey track shorts, a form hugging T-shirt, and a pair of white and grey Nike Air Max. Her knees were scraped up badly, the bloody wounds caked with dirt and gravel.

"Excuse me." I asked, "Are you okay.?"

Obviously startled she jerked her head up and gasped when she saw me standing there.

Our eyes met.

She was crying hard, her cheeks drenched with tears.

For a few moments I was speechless. She was breathtaking. Completely stunned I gazed at her in blatant adoration. I found it hard to believe that a woman could be so gorgeous.

She had smooth skin the color of butterscotch. Her long chestnut-colored hair was pulled back into a loose ponytail. Her face had gentle features and was accented by a set of bewitching green eyes and pouty luscious lips. She had the face of a woman destined to be on movie screens. In all my days I had never seen a more beautiful broad.

Bawling like a baby she eyed me, longing for something I could not pinpoint. She was young, perhaps eighteen or nineteen, maybe a little older.

I cleared my throat. "Do you need me to help you?"

She nodded but not a single word came from her mouth. Only sobs.

I said, "If you let me know what you need, I'll help you."

She sniffled. "I twisted my ankle."

"Let me see." Crouching down beside her I inspected her

ankle. When I touched her, she shivered. I asked, "Do you think that you can walk on it?"

"Maybe." In a soft weary voice she said, "Please help me stand."

"Sure." I hoisted her to her feet. Her clothes were drenched. Sweat was raining from her skin.

With one hand she gripped my arm using me as a crutch while the back of her other hand wiped the tears from her face. I watched her closely. I could tell that her tears had not been a result of her fall. Nah, it was obvious that she had been crying because of emotional pain. I would bet my life on it that her distress was a by-product of a broken heart. I'd been a donor of such heartbreak countless times to women, and I knew that look very well. The eyes told it all.

Her T-shirt had grey calligraphy letters across the front that read *JESUS LOVES YOU*. Small diamond studs were in her ears and a tiny silver-toned necklace with a small diamond cross around her neck.

I told her, "You're gonna need your wounds cleaned."

She looked down and grimaced. "Gosh. That looks nasty."

"My car is parked up near the softball fields. I have some anti-bacterial wipes in the glove department."

She looked at me as if she were unsure whether to accept my aid. Like there was the possibility that I could be a rapist. The lessons of her youth came flashing in her mind; *never talk to strangers* and definitely never go anywhere with them.

I smiled. "You're safe. I'm not a serial killer."

"Your help is appreciated. I'm sure that the Good Lord will bless you for your kindness."

"Do you think that you can walk?"

She tried to take a step but almost fell. I caught her.

I told her, "I am gonna carry you……if you don't have a problem with that."

"No, I could not allow such a thing. I'm sweaty."

"A lil sweat ain't never hurt nobody."

She took a moment then nodded. "Okay, but first…." She extended a hand. "I'm Willow Hope Harrison."

Shaking her hand, I told her, "And I'm Shakur Andrews. All my friends call me Sheik."

"Nice to meet you Sheik and again, thank you so much."

I took a quick moment to take in her full measure. She was about five-foot-eight and had an hourglass shape. Long toned legs, wide hips, a slender waist, flat tummy, and a pair of big tits bulging in her shirt. She was well put together. Built like a track and field athlete.

I scooped her up in my arms and she wrapped an arm around my neck. Her moist skin was slick against my body, her damp clothes giving my belly a slight itch. The odor of her perspiration inter-blended with hints of her strawberry scented perfume, forcing thoughts of sweaty sex sessions into my mind. I tried my hardest to force those thoughts out, but they refused to leave. I was glad that she was in my arms above my waistline and could not see the bulge in my crotch area. My dick was hard as cold steel.

Walking up the hill I commented, "You were jogging hunh?"

"Yes." She told me, "I had jogged from Jefferson Park Avenue, came down Harris Road, down Fifth Street, took a right on Elliott, a left on Avon, shot through downtown, crossed the Belmont Bridge, then High Street took me to Two-fifty which led me here."

Her proper speaking and perfect pronunciation of each syllable revealed that she was educated. Had come from a good home. Good schools. Cultured.

"Long run." I asked, "Where were you headed?"

"Was going to Brandywine Drive in Greenbrier."

"Tough trek."

"Was trying to run something out of my system." She looked at me in a way that suggested that she is on the brink of giving up on life. Like she is losing the courage and strength to fight for her sanity. I see despair.

I spoke a gentle, "Dude hurt you really bad, didn't he?"

She gave me a puzzled look but didn't reply. Her expression told it all. I was right.

Peering deeply into her eyes I told her, "He must be a fool

55

to have hurt such a beautiful woman."

She asked, "What are you talking about?"

"I am talking about the cause of your sorrow."

"What sorrow?"

"The sorrow that's choking your heart."

"I never said anything about sorrow or a man."

"Didn't have to."

"I suppose you're a psychic."

I smiled. "Nah. Just a man who has experienced his share of grief."

She was silent for a few moments, then admitted, "Yes, you were right, I've been going through some minor stuff."

"Minor stuff don't make you cry as hard as you were crying."

With a slight nod of her head, she did not reply. She stared at me like she wanted to know me. Needed to know me.

I asked, "You wanna talk about it?"

"You've been kind enough. Wouldn't want to burden you with my issues."

"It wouldn't be a burden."

She smiled. "Thanks, but I'm okay." She switched the subject. "Splendid morning."

"Yeah, it is."

"When I was running down the path, I saw you standing on the bridge." She asked, "Do you come here often?"

"When I'm stressed out or need to clear my mind I come and hang out on the bridge. The scenery and atmosphere gives me a soul satisfying tranquility."

"It's good to have a place of solitude where you can experience tranquility."

"In a world of chaos, you gotta have that space."

"Jesus gives me the ultimate peace."

"Woman of faith?"

She flashed a sincere smile. "I love the Lord with all of my heart." She quoted a few Bible scriptures and elaborated on each one. She knew her stuff. She asked was I a believer.

"Nah," I replied. "Faith in the unseen seems a lil' too far-fetched for me."

"You should taste and see that the Lord is good"

I smiled. "I'd like to taste quite a few things to see if they are good." My eyes raked her body.

She blushed and cleared her throat then averted her eyes away from me. Neither of us spoke another word until we reached my BMW.

I opened the front passenger door and sat her on the seat with her legs outside of the car.

She said, "Nice car." Her eyes inspected the interior.

Reaching past her I opened the glove department and told her, "I need to take it to the car wash."

"My uncle owns a carwash. Speed Clean on Pantops."

"Yeah, I know the spot," I said as I grabbed the box of anti-bacterial wipes and a bottled water.

She said, "If you like I can hook you up with a free car wash. It is the least I could do."

"Nah. I'm cool. I gotta guy from the 'hood who details my vehicles."

"The hood?"

"South First Projects. That's where I'm from."

"Small world. My father is the pastor of the church across the street from South First Projects."

Crouching in front of her I said, "Yeah, small world."

She looked directly into my eyes. "Never seen you in church."

Pouring a little water on her wounds I told her, "Not too fond of religion."

"Christianity is not a religion. It is a way of life."

"Same thing." I told her, "These wipes have alcohol in them. This is gonna burn a lil' bit."

"It'll be fine. I have a high threshold for physical pain. It's the emotional stuff that I don't handle well."

When I wiped her knee, she hissed. I said, "Preacher's daughter hunh?"

"I've been in the church all of my life."

"Are you one of them church girls that gotta pair of red horns under that long hair?"

"Not at all." She spoke proudly." My life is dedicated to

doing Gods Will."

She had uttered those words with so much conviction that I believed her.

I told her, "Stop twitching so that I can clean it good."

Grimacing she said, "Its burning more than I expected."

"A lotta things in life burn more than we expect."

"Amen to that. Yes, they do."

We shared small talk while I thoroughly cleaned her wounds. She was raised in an upper middle-class home in Ivy. She had always had the best that life has to offer. With all the benefits of being well-off she seemed genuinely humble. I gave her the surface story of my life. Left out details of like that I had been to prison, been shot twice, and the delicate subject of the death of my family.

I have never been a man that forced myself to conform to others. Nah, not one bit. Either you attune your life with mine or get the hell outta my way. But with Willow, I found myself toning down my aggression, my profanity, my personality. That was unusual for me.

Willow gazed at me in amazement. "You do not look you are thirty-four. I would have put you at twenty-five at the most."

I smiled. "Thanks for the compliment." I told her, "Let me get this shoe off so I can look at your ankle." Then I slipped off her shoe and sock. Examining her ankle, I informed her, "It's a lil swollen. Ice it when you get home."

She had cute feet. French pedicured, pretty toes.

She said, "Let me try to stand on it."

"Suit yourself." I helped her to her feet.

With one shoe on she limped away from me. Leaning on the car I enjoyed the scene. My curiosity was aroused and my lust surging as I observed her plump perfect ass bounce with every step that she took. A generous portion of her shorts was wedged in the crack of her ass, dishing out a sneak peek of her golden buns.

She hobbled over to the sidewalk and took a seat. A moment later I was sitting beside her.

Willow said, "If you weren't on that bridge, I'd be in a

world of trouble right now."

"Everything happens for a reason."

"It's all Gods purpose."

I didn't respond. Left that alone.

Willow stared off into the distance for a few moments. Then she spoke softly, "I was trying to run my fiancé out of my system."

"Why would you wanna do something like that?"

In a depressed tone she replied, "I don't want him to rent space in my heart any longer."

"So, evict him from your heart."

"He refuses to leave."

"What you own is yours, make him get out."

"Issues of the heart aren't that simple."

"Our problems are as simple as we choose to make them."

She sighed. "If only they were."

We were silent for a long moment sharing a gaze. She had the most beautiful eyes. Magical eyes. The green like a sparkling emerald

I sensed a deep and sorrow-stricken loneliness coming from her. I asked, "You wanna her a joke?"

"Sure."

"Why did the crackhead cross the road?"

She shrugged. "I don't know. Why?"

"Because the guy across the street had some good crack for sale."

She was silent for a few moments staring at me then suddenly she cupped both hands over her face and cracked up laughing. In between laughs she said, "That was so corny."

Smiling I said, "But it made you laugh."

"Yes, it did." She giggled.

"Good."

We were silent for a few moments.

Willow spoke in a defeated voice. "My soul is fatigued."

"Sounds like you've been in a long battle."

"It has been." She looked at me curiously.

Her eyes scanned my body. She examined my tattoo covered torso, her attention lingering on the hefty Tiffany

Titan gold and diamond bracelet designed by Pharrell Williams that was sparkling on my wrist. Next was the matching chain around my neck that held her attention for a moment. She raised a brow when her eyes rested on the massive pinky ring. Next was my Ferragamo belt, the Louis Vuitton jogging pants, and the Giuseppe Zanotti sneakers, the diamonds in my ears, and the two iPhones resting next to my thigh.

She asked skeptically, "Are you a drug dealer?"

I laughed. "Nah. Why would you ask something like that?"

"Because you look like one."

Smiling I asked, "What does a drug dealer look like?"

"Like you."

"Stereotyping is the bastard child of ignorance."

She nodded. "I agree." Then she asked, "But are you a drug dealer?"

I laughed "Shorty you're trippin.' Nah, I ain't no drug dealer."

With a look of concern she asked, "Why do you have that gun in your glove compartment?"

"Very observant." I chuckled. "Or just plain old nosey."

She smiled. "Couldn't help but notice something as out of place as a gun in a glove compartment."

"I carry it everywhere I go."

"Why?"

"Protection."

She spoke with a shy smile. "Jesus should be your protection."

I joked. "Jesus is what I named my gun so technically he is."

We both laughed.

I said, "It seems like you're feeling better."

"I am." She stared at me as though she was studying every detail in my face. She told me, "Crying is good for the soul. It cleanses. Heals."

"You sound like an expert on grief."

"I am. I had many years to master the science." She giggled. "So many lessons."

"You're not old enough to have mastered anything in life."

"How old do you think I am?"

"Nineteen, maybe twenty."

"Good eye." She smiled invitingly at me. "I'm nineteen."

"Young and beautiful."

She smiled. "The Good Lords time is not like our perception of time."

"What does that mean?"

"It means that the lessons that we think would take years to learn God can bestow upon us in a second if He chooses. It is all about His purpose and His Will."

I said, "You sound like a preacher."

"It's the spirit of my dad. As a child I wanted to be a preacher."

"So, what happened?"

"My wants conflicted with the Lords plans."

"When you said you had many years to master grief what did you mean?"

She sighed. "It's a long story."

"I don't have anywhere to be."

"Maybe some other time."

"Sounds like you're asking me on a date."

She laughed. "You are slick."

"Nah. Just observant."

A smile rose on her face. I considered her an interesting young lady. Sunny and lighthearted. Distinctly feminine.

Her eyes were smiling. "I can't believe you live across the street from a church and never visited once."

"And I can't believe your church has never come across the street and helped the poor."

That caught her off guard. She did not have a reply for that one. Her dumbfounded expression told it all.

Finally, she admitted, "You're right."

"I know."

"I've been trying to get daddy to start some programs over there."

"Maybe you should take the initiative."

"Yeah, maybe you're right." She asked, "What's it like

living there?"

"I don't live there anymore. I was raised there."

"But you still visit, right?"

"Yeah." I told her "It's grim in the hood. Hard times for the people."

We both grew silent for a few seconds, gazing into each other's eyes. Next thing I know she began talking about Jesus and how he wanted me to be a part of his family. She kept going on and on about his mercy, love and grace. Ol' girl had transformed into a mini preacher quoting scriptures and all that stuff that preachers do. I was not paying much attention to her words. My eyes were on her big tits.

She laughed. "The Lord doesn't like lust." She playfully crossed her arms across her breasts.

I laughed. "I was daydreaming about something."

"I'm not going to ask about what." She told me, "Keep that to yourself."

We shared a laugh.

Gradually our laughter dwindled, and we were left with a few moments of thoughtful silence. Our eyes were locked in an intense gaze. I had been with an enormous number of women. Some of the most beautiful women on the planet. But this was my first time being interested in the inner person of one of them. I had an intense desire to know who Willow was.

She confided. "I've been hiding behind my emotional pain by eating and shopping."

"Best way to deal with trying situations is not to medicate but confrontation."

"Spoken like a true man. Opposition cannot solve every problem."

"Never said that it could." I explained, "But medicating the ailment only soothes the pain for a little while then it returns and you gotta medicate it again. That's like taking an aspirin for the discomfort of a splinter in your finger. Best way to end the pain is to remove the splinter.

"Very wise words."

I smiled.

"I need to remove the splinter," she said firmly.

"What did he do to you?"

"He cheated." She paused a moment then asked, "Why do mean cheat?"

I shrugged and said, "Lust and selfishness."

"And why do us women tolerate it?"

"Only you know the answer to that."

"Why do you think we put up with it?"

"Emotions cloud people's judgement."

"Blind love leads us into a pit of stupidity."

"Or maybe it ain't love at all."

She was silent for a few minutes then said, "I find unfaithfulness disgusting."

"The longer you live you will see that disloyalty is the norm. No one is trustworthy."

"You say that like you've been hardened by treachery."

"I have dealt with many people of all backgrounds. All have proven to be dead to honor."

"You have lost faith in man. Gods people are not like the people of the world."

I smiled. "The *Bible* says in Proverbs, Chapter 28 verse 21 that a man will sell God out for piece of bread."

"It does not."

I chuckled, "Check it out for yourself when you get the chance. Read Jeremiah, Chapter nine, too."

"I surely will." She spoke with a curious expression. "Thought you didn't know Jesus."

"Jesus and the Bible are not the same thing."

"Jesus is the Bible."

"In your eyes he is." I told her, "Jesus was nothing more than a wise man. And the Bible is merely a book of history. Several diverse historical events mixed with the abracadabra of man's imagination."

She was silent for a long moment then she asked, "How are you familiar with those Bible verses?"

"I've studied the Bible extensively."

"For what purposes?"

"I had a period in my life where I had a lot of spare time

on my hand."

"Why study the Bible?"

"It wasn't just the Bible. There were other books."

"What other books?"

"*The Quran. The Art of War* by Sun Tzu. *The Prince* by Niccolo Machiavelli. *The 48 Laws of Power* by Robert Greene. *The Tao Te Ching.* Just to name a few."

"You're a man who studies conflict." She said, "Your God is power."

"Why do you say that?"

"The books you have studied, your luxurious car, your gaudy jewelry. You are a powerful man. Your toys are expressions of your power."

"Is that so?"

"And your swagger. You are a boss."

I chuckled.

She asked, "What kind of work do you do?"

"I own a banana import business and a few small businesses in the city. I'm part owner of a pharmaceutical company and I am a venture capitalist. I bankroll a lot of risky upstart businesses that banks usually by-pass."

She pointed to my Rolex. "That would explain the extravagant costly jewelry." She flashed a grin. "I really thought that you were a drug dealer."

"If that was the case then why did you remain here with me?"

She grinned. "Why not?" She told me, "Drug dealers do not scare me. When you got Jesus there is no need to fear anything."

I asked, "What do you do?"

"Just began my second year at the University of Virginia. I am pursuing a degree in psychology. I'm thinking about being a counselor."

"You wanna help people hunh?"

"Yep. That is the purpose that God placed on my life."

I sensed that she genuinely loved people. Really cared about humanity. I did not detect any faking with her. She was authentic. Loved life. Loved the human spirit. It gushed from her entire being.

She said, "I love to help others. It brings me joy."

"The helpers need help sometimes too."

"I agree."

"You need help?"

"Maybe."

"Talk to me."

She cleared her throat. "My fiancé's beguiling ways almost destroyed me."

"How?"

She lowered her eyes and sighed. "I was suicidal for a short period of time."

"You tried to kill yourself?"

"No." She looked at me. "Just had the thoughts. The devil whispering in my ear."

"Never quit. Never give up."

"I know." She sounded deflated. "Lamont and I have been best friends most of our lives. We began dating when I was sixteen. He has been by my side through some extremely trying situations."

I nodded understanding perfectly.

She said, "Repeatedly he cheated and repeatedly I forgave him and set out to make amends."

"Do you ever think that a romantic bond should have never been added to the relationship? Like maybe you two should have remained friends instead?"

"Absolutely. And if I could rewind time I would. But I cannot and I have to live with what we have created."

"Something that ultimately afflicts you."

"Yes, and it's hard because even though we won't be romantically involved anymore I don't want to lose his friendship."

"You're stuck between a rock and a hard place."

"Yes." She asked, "Do you have a special someone in your life?"

"Nah."

"Why?"

"Never met anyone that makes me wanna never leave the

comfort of their soul."

"Scared of exploring the depths of your heart?"

"Nah. I just have never met that special lady."

"Do you want love in your life?"

I told you her, "I think deep down everyone wants love in their life."

"Yes, I agree." She sighed and was quiet for moment then said, "Love is supposed to be inspiring. It should be considerate and kind." She asked, "Right?"

"I guess." I told her, "I imagine that it calls for a lotta personal sacrifice."

"All he's ever done was trample my heart." Tears welled in her eyes.

"You're a sensitive soul." I reached over and pulled her to me. She rested her head on my shoulder and cried softly.

Through her quiet sobs she chuckled. "You must think I am cuckoo. All this crying."

"My past keeps me from being judgmental of anyone's personal journey. I have no right to judge others based on their reactions to the cold world that is all around us. This wild jungle that we call life is a place of hardship and suffering. Everyone reacts differently."

She sniveled, "What do you mean?"

"Let's just say that I have no shortage of regrets. I have lived a life trying to escape my demons. I have come to believe that we all have our own demons, and I refuse to condemn the next man by how he deals with his."

"What are your regrets?"

"Mainly lost dreams. A whole lotta mistakes. Misjudgments."

"We all have those."

"And as you get older, they begin to pile up, forming mountains. But you cannot let them dictate who and what you are."

She raised her head and made a little space between us. "Sorry for crying on you." She smiled. "Can't believe that I was just nestled up on a stranger."

"We're not strangers. We know each others name."

She laughed and I smiled.

She exhaled a deep breath. "Life has many paths, and you have to choose one."

"Where did that come from?"

"Thinking about life…...love. I am wondering what's in store for me."

"If you are uncompromising, you'll receive the best that life has to offer."

"I hate Lamont."

"You are angry. Emotions cloud rational thinking. Tomorrow you may feel different."

"Tomorrow I will be set on never experiencing the misery of love again."

"Do not be so settled on running away from love. With love you gotta find some middle ground within yourself that accepts alotta bullshit without fully compromising your principles."

"But love isn't supposed to be difficult and trying."

"Love is whatever the unique situation calls for."

"We have vastly different ideas of what love is." She told me, "Love should be sympathetic and understanding. It is supposed to be benevolent and induces adoration and fondness. It's full of joy. Delightful. It's supposed to be blissful."

I laughed. "That sounds good in theory but life in real time tends to contradict a supposal derived in a classroom at some university by some quack professor who never experienced life outside of his books."

She stared at me attentively.

I told her, "Where I am from love is hard, tough, nasty, grimy, and downright ugly. Love is not even an emotion at all. It's a supreme understanding shared by two people that transcends all life can throw at you. Love is being there for your family member when he is locked away for twenty years. Accepting his collect calls, visiting him when you can, writing letters, sending him pictures and money. Love is never turning your back on your crackhead aunt who has proved that she has no good in her. But you never let go of the hope that things can turn around. And during the meantime you still treat her like a human being. Love is taking over the responsibility as a father to your dead homie's children. Love ain't pretty but it is real. It's unconditional and when we begin to place *why's* on it, then we prove that it really ain't love at all because the *why* makes it conditional."

She stared at me in thoughtful silence.

I told her, "We can conjure up all these different definitions of what we think love to be. But love is love. It does not change. It's the only entity that remains the same always and forever."

Without a word she stared at me. Curiosity beamed from her twinkling and alert eyes.

I told her, "Your eyes are enchanting."

She blushed. "All glory goes to God."

I spoke gently. "It would be impossible to ignore and not cherish a woman as beautiful as you. Every second of my life would be centered around expressing the privilege of having such a magnificent creature like you at my side."

She smiled and lowered her head in obvious embarrassment. She giggled. "You're making me blush." She fanned her face with her hand in a mock gesture of overheating.

My voice was low and serious. "I can make you do more than blush."

With a sheepish grin she asked, "What do you mean by that?"

"It means exactly what you think it means."

She laughed and cocked her head to the side as if she were amused by the game. "You're serious, aren't you?"

"I say what I mean and mean what I say."

Fidgeting with her fingers she stared at me with a serious expression on her face. Then she looked away and gazed across the park. When her eyes came back to me, she sighed, then nibbled on her lip, her mind obviously churning.

When I leaned over to kiss her, she shied away and giggled.

She spoke softly, "That wouldn't be lady like."

I leaned over again and this time she accepted my mouth.

The kiss was gentle. We kissed for quite a while.

Finally, she pulled away, gave me an embarrassed look, and spoke just above a whisper. "This is so unlike me."

I kissed her lips with a quick peck. "Every exit is an entry somewhere else." I placed my hand on her thigh.

"I think it's time for me to go home." She asked, "Do you mind giving me a ride."

"Of course, come on."

The speakers in the car were hissing out Mary J. Blige's classic album, *My Life,* and Willow was quiet gazing out the window. I gave her space and let her deal with what she had to deal with.

After a few minutes I broke the silence with, "Hard lessons are the most valuable. Those are the ones that we cherish the most."

"I wish I had not learned this one."

"But you did."

"And it was the worse pain that I ever felt."

She lived in an elegant stone exterior house in Greenbrier. I parked in a driveway behind a champagne-colored Range Rover and a silver Beamer.

I opened the door to get out and help her, but she stopped me.

"No. I can make it." She sighed. "Thanks for everything."

"No problem." I said, "I would like to see you again."

"I don't know if that's a good idea considering my situation."

I smiled. "No is not an option."

She giggled. "Demanding."

"A man gotta fight for what he wants."

"No, he does not. All he must do is ask."

I smiled. "Can I see you again?"

She nodded. "I'd like that." She gave me her phone number as she climbed outta the car. Standing in the door she said, "I'm going to keep you in my prayers."

"Please do."

"Maybe you can accompany me to church one day."

"That's cool. Set the date and I will be there front and

center."

She glanced at the house, then brought her attention back to me. She took a deep breath and smiled. "Shakur. That is Arabic right.?

"Yeah."

"What does it mean?"

"Thankful to God."

She raised a brow. "Interesting."

I told her, "My father was a Black Panther. He named me that because he said that I was God's gift to the world. Used to preach to people that I was the chosen one, a messiah to my people. I was something that the White man could never take away or destroy."

We smiled at each other.

She said, "Shakur is a beautiful name. Where does Sheik come from?"

"The streets named me that when I was a youngin. Another gift of my dad. It's an inherited nickname. It's a long story."

"Promise me you'll tell me when you call."

"I promise."

"Good." She smiled. "Thanks again for your help."

"Anytime." I smiled at her. "You ain't gotta die to experience heaven."

"What?"

"I can give you heaven on earth."

"Call me." She giggled. "Good-bye." Then she shut the door, my eyes were fixed on her phat ass. Couldn't wait to pound it. Could not wait to give her what I know she needed. Couldn't wait to fuck her so good that she would catch amnesia and forget that lame nigga forever.

Chapter Six
WILLOW

For out of prison, he cometh to reign, whereas also he
that is born in his kingdom becometh poor.
—King Solomon

Thursday evening around 6 o'clock I was in mid-town at Mel's Café. The modest eatery was packed with Black people of all ages, chowing down on the best soul food in the entire city. I was outside settled at a corner table on the small patio, watching the bumper-to-bumper traffic of West Main Street. A crowd of rowdy teen-agers were loitering in the parking lot, their chatter and laughter mingling with the booming sounds of hip-hop blaring from their car stereo systems. It seemed as if every male around had their attention focused on me. Quite a few of the guys, both young and old, had approached, flirting. Most of them offered to buy me a meal and I had politely declined their bold advances informing them that I was waiting on my date.

After class, this afternoon I had headed home, took a bath, then curled up in the bed and watched television. Then I received a surprise call from Sheik inviting me to dinner. Without hesitation I had gladly accepted. We both had the taste for soul food and agreed to meet at Mel's.

I had quickly jumped out of bed and slipped into an ankle-length sea blue skirt, a sleeveless white button-down blouse, and a pair of cute, jeweled leather sandals.

I am sick and tired of being depressed and it is time that I do something other than wallow in my sorrow. I am fed up with crying myself to sleep. I need a breath of fresh air in my life. Sheik's thought-provoking words that he'd uttered so convincingly were stamped on my heart. Especially the piece about how he could "give me heaven." It was unreasonable, borderline insanity, that I was actually hoping he could back up those words. My curiosity was aroused. A broken heart my motivation.

My eye caught a metallic grey Ferrari dipping in and out of traffic then zoom into Mel's parking lot and park in an empty space.

All eyes were on the extravagant sports car. A moment later Sheik climbed out of the Ferrari. He spotted me just as he closed the door and flashed an adorable smile. Butterflies fluttered in my stomach.

Smiling I waved and enjoyed the sight of the handsome heart throb making his way in my direction, his long slow strides emanating a majestic air. It seemed as if everybody knew him, going out of their way to speak. Even the mean-mugged thugs cracked a smile, their eyes sparkling with what seemed like admiration. He was like a celebrity, and I was fascinated by his detached demeanor, like he could care less of their adoration.

Sheik stopped to talk to a guy and signaled to me with a finger that he would only be a moment. Today he was dressed stylishly in a crisp white button up tucked into a pair of beige slacks, his feet adored with a pair of tan loafers.

Feeling a tad bit self-conscious I took my hand and smoothed out a tiny wrinkle in my blouse. I raked my fingers through the thick waves of my hair making sure that my do was in place. I even glanced down at my feet making sure that I did not have a minor case of ash.

As Sheik and the guy shared conversation, I took a

moment to study him. The Good Lord had blessed him. The more I took in his details the more I realized that handsome was an understatement. Breathtaking was more befitting. His face was chiseled with sharp features. Coffee with a dab of milk best described the hue of his smooth skin. Thick eyebrows, long eye lashes, and deep cleft in his chin gave him a distinguished look. But what I absolutely adored was those thick full lips encased in a neatly trimmed goatee.

"Hey there beautiful," Sheik spoke as he stepped in from of me. His bright smile revealed a set of perfect, pearly white teeth. "You sitting there looking all sexy."

Grinning I stood to shake his hand, but he surprised me by pulling me into his arms. We exchanged a hug that made me wish that I could get lost in his big arms forever. His touch warmed me with an awesome intensity and quickened my heart rate, inspiring thoughts of grade school crushes. His cologne was enchanting. Savoring me with those magnetic eyes he talked smoothly about how beautiful I was and how glad he was to see me again. Said that he loved my outfit and that my perfume was heavenly. I stood there blushing and grinning bashfully.

We took our seats, and he apologized for being late. Sheik's deep voice was melodic. He had a distinct way of speaking extremely slow. God, I adored his voice.

He asked, "How are the knees and ankle?"

"Knees are scabbed. Ankle is fine. Thanks for asking."

"And what about your heart?"

"I'm better." I shrugged, hesitated, then told him. "Lamont and I had lunch yesterday."

"How did it go?"

"Horrible. We ended up getting into a big argument."

"Wanna talk about it?"

"I gave him the ring back."

"And how do you feel after doing that?"

"Like a weight has been lifted from my shoulders."

"I think it's for the best."

"Yeah." I considered soberly. "It is."

We both ordered the fried chicken platter. As we waited,

we shared a steady flow of conversation, mostly about a couple of new movies that had just hit the theaters. We had the same taste in film. That was quite refreshing.

I admitted. "Your wisdom, your advice, helped me get through some rough days."

"Glad that I could help."

I took a deep breath, smiled, and switched the subject. "The BMW when we first met and now the Ferrari. Exquisite taste."

"I'm fortunate."

"A Black man taking care of business in a major way." I smiled. "That's inspiring."

"I try."

I asked, "Do you own any other vehicles?"

"Yeah, I gotta Range Rover too."

"Why so many vehicles?"

"Gotta sports car for when I am feeling frisky. The luxury sedan for when I'm getting my grown man on. And the SUV for those rugged get-outta-my way days."

I chuckled. "Interesting."

Sheik asked, "What kind of counseling are you gonna do after you graduate?"

I told him, "I'll probably be a counselor at the city jail where my father is superintendent."

"Your father is a pastor, and he runs the jail?"

I smiled proudly. "Yes. He is a remarkably busy man."

"I imagine he is."

I confided. "While I work at the jail I am going to pursue my Masters, then my Doctorate. Eventually I will be a psychiatrist. That is what I am leaning towards."

"Ambitious."

"The Lord has also placed the desire in my heart to start a number of programs in the community."

We talked and he dished out pieces of his past. His life had been full of unfortunate circumstances. When he was only two years old his father had been gunned down in the street. Eighteen years ago, his mother had committed suicide by ingesting a bottle of sleeping pills the same day that a hit-and-run drunk driver killed his twelve-year-old sister. I felt so sorry for him. He told me that he had no living relatives. His only family was his lifelong best friend, a girl named Crook.

I asked, "What kind of a woman was your mother?"

He spoke in a quiet, serious voice. "My mother was a crack addict."

"Sorry to heart that."

"It's ok."

"It must've been hard on you."

"In the early years it was because me and my sister ain't have no one to provide for us. We would not see our mom for days at a time. And when she'd come home, she would sleep for a couple of days then head out again."

"So sad."

"Left me a young boy taking care of my toddler sister."

"How did you manage?"

"I did what I had to do. I made a way."

"But how?"

"Shoplifted, robbed, hustled, had a little help from neighbors who didn't wanna see us get lost in foster care. My best friend Crook who shared the same reality helped." He paused. "We helped each other."

"So much responsibility at a young age."

He said, "That was normal for everyone in the hood when I was growing up. Most of us lived that reality."

"Crack is a devastating tool of Satan."

"It's a two-edge sword."

I raised a brow in interest. "What do you mean?"

"It got rough at one point and if it were not for the crack-cocaine trade ain't no telling what would have happened. Once I began selling coke at the age of ten our situation improved. I could buy clothes, pay the bills, fill up the fridge and make sure we ain't want for anything."

"Ten years old, selling crack in the streets." I said, "That had to be dangerous."

"Do or die."

He told me that even though he was faced with the daunting task of taking on the full responsibilities of an adult he still managed to go to school. He had a love for learning and school was his haven away from the madness of project life. In his teen years he made a good living selling crack. He also was a high school football star, a quarterback, and he had graduated at the top of his class.

Impressed, I asked, "What college did you attend?"

He laughed. "College won't in the cards."

"Why? You must've had tons of scholarships."

"The hood has a way of placing unexpected pits in front of you."

"What do you mean?"

He sat back, smiling, fiddling with the thick diamond encrusted bracelet on his wrist. "If you stick around long enough maybe I'll tell you all about it."

I placed my hand on top of his and spoke earnestly. "I'll be around as long as you allow me."

His eyes smiled while his face remained serious. "My life is extremely complicated, and I don't think you're ready for the ride."

I spoke tenderly, "I see a man committed to becoming the best that life has to offer."

He smiled. "Believe none of what you hear and half of what you see."

I chuckled. "Stop being so pessimistic."

"Hardened by reality."

"With the opportunity to be softened by what I can offer you."

"Show and prove."

"I will." I met his gaze with a joyful smile. "I promise."

By the time our food arrived I had a better understanding of who he was. Raised in the projects he had made a way out of no way. Through the storm of his past, he had persevered and became immensely successful. The adversity he had encountered all his life explained his strong presence.

While we ate, we talked about our dreams and hopes. He wanted to eventually combine his time, energy, and efforts on a construction company. He had aspirations of becoming a Donald Trump-esque construction mogul. It thrilled me that he had such lofty ambitions. I wish we had more Black men with his passion for success. He listened attentively when I doled out my dreams of starting a national program geared towards helping at-risk teen-age girls and women coming out of prison and recovering from drug addiction.

Wiping my mouth with my napkin I smiled. "That was delicious."

"Yes, it was."

I told him. "You make me proud."

He gave me a puzzled look. "I make you proud?"

"You were faced with daunting obstacles, and you did not let that hinder you. A lot of brothers use their troubled past as an excuse to fail."

"A lot of guys don't know any better."

"But they have the intelligence to see that life offers more."

"What about when you've been taught that life outside of the ghetto don't exist?"

"That falls on the parents."

He laughed. "But their parents gave them the same ignorance that they were taught and they only passed on what they knew."

"A perpetual cycle." I exhaled a deep breath. "Horrible."

"People from the outside have wishful ideologies that seem right and exact on paper but the reality of the gutta is something completely different than what you learn in a classroom."

"What about you?"

"What about me?"

"You are obviously an exception to the rule. What was your motivation?"

With an easy going smile he said, "I have aspirations of being the wealthiest man in any room that I enter."

I stared him straight in the eyes. "And that's your soul motivation?"

"That and the desire to never experience poverty again."

"Interesting." I took a long look at him then asked, "You miss your mom a lot, don't you?"

"Of course. Even though she was on crack I still loved her. She was my mom." His face grew somber. He tried to hide it, but it was clear I had touched a subject that he was not too enthused to discuss. I had found the chink in his armor. The smooth handsome guy with the irresistible charm did indeed have a weakness. I promised myself that one day I would get him to talk about his past losses and pain. Help him heal. Help him deal with the distress that he had buried deep down within himself. It was going to take time. But I would be patient. He needed me and somehow, I knew deep down in my heart and soul that I needed him too.

I felt a sudden sense of pity for him. He had lived a tragic life. I wanted to hug him and tell him that I would be a friend to him. Maybe whisper soothing words in his ear.

Sheik sat across from me silently appraising me. He had a remarkable calm about him. His eyes were friendly, and he spoke a gentle. "Come here."

I asked quietly, "What are you talking about?"

He spoke with a seductive smile. "Come over here and sit on my knee. I wanna be close to you."

"No." I giggled. "That wouldn't be appropriate behavior for a lady."

He spoke soothingly, "I'm not gonna bite you," He extended a hand.

Gazing into his mysterious eyes took my breath away. He winked knowingly. When I placed my hand in his hand I felt a rush of excited anticipation.

His smile caressed and eased my apprehension. He said, "And even if I do decide to bite you it will not hurt. It will feel good." He ushered me around to his lap.

Giggling I sat on his knee, and he pulled me to his lap. Snuggling up to his hard body we shared a closeness that made me warm inside. With an arm draped over his shoulder I gazed into his eyes.

He casually held my hand, kissing my fingers as if it were the most proper thing to do. Like we had been lovers for ages. His closeness was satisfying. He watched me closely and I wonder what he sees when he looks at me. I wonder do I measure up to the many women of his past.

He asked, "This is better, right?"

I nodded.

His fingers are so soft. I glanced down at his hands. His fingernails are clean and manicured. A massive gold ring with hulking diamonds decorates his pinky. It was a different ring than the one he wore when we met at the park.

He kissed me on the cheek. "You look at me like you care about my well-being"

"I genuinely care about people."

"In a world full of selfishness that's interesting."

"It's my duty to care for and service others."

"Why?"

"The Holy Spirit that dwells in me compels me to be a living testimony of the Lord's love."

"Your entire life is dedicated to that?"

I nodded. "*The Bible* says in Galatians six verse two – Bear ye one another's burden and so fulfill the law of Christ."

"That's alotta weight to be placed on your little shoulders." He planted a tender kiss on my shoulder.

"Philippians four verse thirteen says, I can do all things through Christ which strengtheneth me."

He spoke simply. "Faith."

"Faith is the substance…."

He interrupted, "Faith is the substance of things hoped for, the evidence of things not seen. Hebrews eleven verse one."

Smiling I said, "Impressive. That is the second time you surprised me with scripture."

He chuckled then leaned over and brushed his lips against mine. My heart rate accelerated, and he sent shivers up my spine. When he kissed me affectionately, I returned the kiss. My emotions were soaring, and I am slightly embarrassed sitting here publicly wooing a pretty boy bachelor who I suspect has intentions of seducing me out my panties.

"You're interesting." He whispered, "And I'm curious."

"Curiosity killed the cat."

He smiled. "I ain't a cat."

We both laughed.

He said, "Tell me more about your volunteer work at the jail."

"I tutor GED classes and there is a mentor program that I facilitate. I work extremely hard to redefine what the inmates accept as reality."

"Brainwashing."

"Never heard it put that way."

"That's what it sounds like to me."

"Brainwashing." I shrugged. "But in a good way. For the betterment of humanity."

"Tell me more."

"I provide a forum for solving the many problems that affect our community. My hope is that individually and collectively we will learn to be successful and become a spiritually empowered people. If we can individually nurture these wayward men and women and teach them social skills and the knowledge of God, we will defeat recidivism and we will prosper."

He seemed genuinely interested when he asked, "And how do you begin to accomplish such a monumental feat?"

"It begins with refreshing the inmate's interpretations of what their purpose in life is."

He chuckled. "I would assume that their purpose is to be locked up."

I spoke a serious. "That was not funny."

Smiling he said, "It's funny to me."

"Incarceration is a disheartening, grim reality. Very discouraging. It should not be laughed at."

He stated dryly, "It's a part of life. Accept it."

I shot him a disfavored glare. "That's rather cold." I spoke passionately. "If you only knew how hard and oppressive it was for those brothers and sisters on a daily basis, you'd certainly have a little more compassion."

He laughed.

I raised my voice. "What is so funny?" He had irritated me. I was angry.

He shook his head and held a sarcastic smirk on his face,

but he remained silent.

A torrent raged in my blood. "That is typical of someone who has never seen or experienced the pain of incarceration and the struggles of that life. That is why our society is so messed up and recidivism is so alarmingly high. Brothers like you do not sympathize with prisoners of society, insensitive to their tragic journeys through the torment of incarceration. I bet after a day in jail you would quickly reconsider your attitude of indifference."

Smiling he asked, "Are you finished preaching on your soap box?"

I huffed. "It's the truth you...."

He cut me off with a very calm, yet commanding voice. "Everything you are saying sounds good if you were talking to some lily-white human activist. But a day in jail." He laughed sarcastically. "Please come better than that. I did six years, four months, and twenty-six days for something I ain't even do. So, keep that self-righteous bullshit sermon for yourself and any other chump who wanna hear it."

Staring at his serious face, something in my heart told me that he was not lying. Well, he shut me right up. I stayed silent, slightly embarrassed, feeling as small as a flea.

He looked at me, his face holding a look of self-assurance. He flashed a smile. Forgave my ignorance with a wink of his eye. "Cat gotcha tongue?"

"Six years." I gently brushed the back of my fingers over his cheek. My voice was soft with sympathy. "I apologize. I had no idea."

"It's cool. Shit happens."

His pardonable demeanor made me feel at ease.

I asked, "Are you sure we're, okay?"

A hearty laugh escaped his lips. A deep and steady sound that was pleasurable to my ears. "Give me a kiss and I'll forgive you."

I leaned over and kissed him. We shared a tender smooch. He told me that he had been sent to prison by being in the wrong place at the wrong time. A corner store in his neighborhood had been robbed and he had been walking up the block. The cashier at the store had been riding in a police cruiser and pointed him out. Black male, jeans, and a white T-shirt. Mistaken identity.

We discussed prison life. The stress, the oppression, and the loneliness. Sheik was so intelligent. He had an uncanny insight about life and people that was foreign to me but interesting. He would have made a great psychologist. He shared a whole bunch of comical stories about his life in prison and he had me laughing so hard that my stomach hurt.

We decided to leave the cars behind and take a stroll. We headed further uptown going in the direction of the University of Virginia's campus. As we crossed the West Main Street Bridge I said, "Hosea chapter four verse six says 'My people are destroyed for lack of knowledge: because thou has rejected knowledge, I will also reject thee, that thou shalt be no priest to me: seeing thou has forgotten the law of thy God, I will also forget they children.'"

He asked, "What's that about?"

"Our neglect of Gods laws curses our children, which ultimately is our future. And the ignorance is perpetuated until the curses flood generation after generation. It is apparent all around us. Especially in the Black community."

"We live in a world where pleasure is priority," he said as he smiled at me.

"Yes, we do." I sighed. "And the greatest challenge is developing our youth into responsible people of God."

He gently squeezed my hand in encouragement. "And that's where people like you come in at."

"It should not be isolated to people like me. It is a collective effort. We all have a role to play. Especially men like you who have been blessed to come from the ghetto and be successful."

He chuckled. "Willow, I ain't got no responsibility to people I don't know."

"Selfish way of looking at life."

He shrugged and didn't respond.

I said, "We have a lack of positive role models. And I genuinely believe that it takes a village to raise a child. We need collective leadership."

He stated matter-of-factly. "The only thing that these muthafuckas gonna collectively lead is like crabs in a barrel pull each other back into the barrel."

"That's not a nice thing to say."

He exhaled a deep breath. "The world is not a nice place. It is a place full of greed, envy, lust, hatred, selfishness, and violence."

"If that is what you choose to see then that is going to be your reality. But it does not have to be. Jesus loves you."

A smile grew on his face. "His love doesn't pay the bills."

I looked at him. "Why is submission to God so difficult for Black men?"

"I'm an individual and can only speak for myself."

"Fair enough."

"Submission to the will of anyone or anything other than myself is outside of my sense of logic."

"But God is not a someone. He is God."

"Your God is something that I've never seen."

"God is seen in everything. Matthew five verse eight says, 'Blessed are the pure in heart for they shall see God.'"

We stopped at Lucky Seven convenience store on University Avenue and bought a pint of butter pecan ice cream. Then we trekked a block up and sat on the steps of the magnificent Rotunda and ate out of the same pint of ice cream using separate spoons. It was quite romantic sitting there under the stars with the teeming traffic in front of us while surrounded by the awesome historical architecture of Thomas Jefferson's hands.

Being with Sheik felt like it was where I was meant to be. A unique friendship had been formed, and I valued his company dearly.

He reached over and gently stroked my hair. "What about you?"

With a grin I asked, "What about me?"

"You are so concerned with helping the world, but you are neglecting the most important person. You."

"My dad tells me that a lot." I rested my head against his

shoulder.

"You are running from something inside of you. Something you do not wanna face."

"Why do you say that?"

"I have alotta experience when it comes to understanding people." His fingers stroked my forearm. "The truth is usually seen, rarely spoken." He affectionally grabbed my chin and turned my head so that I looked him in the eyes. "The eyes are the windows to the soul. I look into your eyes and see your heart."

I wanted to look away, but I could not. Our gaze lingered. The nexus of what Sheik personified was smoothness, and the expertise to soothe troubled hearts, lulling one's soul to calm pastures.

I spoke softly, "He broke my heart and it's been extremely painful."

He gave me a kiss on my forehead. "When you endure pain, it builds character. Makes you wiser and stronger."

I gave a halfhearted smile. "I didn't ask to be stronger."

"But I'm sure it's what you needed." He paused a moment then said, "Maybe if people *fall* in love they can *fall* out."

I spoke a frustrated, "If that's the case then I wish I would fall out of it, because it hurts to still be in it with someone who isn't in it with me."

A longing was burning in his eyes. "I wanna help you through it"

I gazed into his eyes. "Are you up for the daunting task?"

"True friends bear one another's hardships."

"I didn't know we were friends."

He chuckled. "So, you're kissing strangers now?"

We both laughed.

I spoke with a shy smile. "I really like you a lot."

He slipped a hand behind me and held me close. He planted a tender kiss on my neck. "Would it be a stretch of your imagination to forget your pain and remember how wonderful you are?"

I shrugged. Looked away for a moment then brought my attention back to him.

Sheik said, "No return on your emotional investment is robbery."

"Exactly." I told him, "My auntie used to say that love is for the soul what food is for the body."

He smiled. "I think you may suffer from a severe case of malnutrition."

I giggled. "I need a well-balanced wholesome meal of good old love."

We laughed.

He spoke softly. "Being in love is a direct result of first learning to love yourself."

I looked at him skeptically. "How can a man that claims he's never been in love say that?"

"I heard a chick on Oprah say it."

We both cracked up with laughter.

I told him, "You are so knowledgeable. You have a handle on all aspects of your life."

"Nah. Not quite, I merely strive for perfection."

"You can never reach perfection."

"Maybe you're right. But when you always aim for it, you are giving every second of your life your best."

"Unique viewpoint. I like that, might adopt it."

"It'll take you far."

I said, "My sister says that when things seem too good to be true it's because they are."

"What's your point?"

"You're like the perfect man."

He toyed with the tennis bracelet on my wrist. "Is that what you see in me?"

"That's what you're presenting."

"I am just being me. What you see is what you want to see."

"Expound upon that."

"The mind believes what it chooses to believe. What it wants to believe."

"So, you're saying that I *want* to see you as perfect."

He shrugged, "Maybe."

We were silent for quite a while, both of us deep in our

own thoughts.

I kissed him and whispered. "There are those brief moments in life when everything seems crystal clear.... perfect."

"Like now."

"Yes."

He smiled. "I'm one hell-of-a-guy ain't I?"

I giggled. "Emotions are clouding my judgement."

"Embrace the pain of growth."

"It is easy for you to do that. You come from years of struggle. But I am not that strong yet."

"An excuse ain't nothing but a lie in disguise." He flashed a grin. "Thought that you didn't lie."

I smiled and nodded. Then I kissed his lips and admitted, "I'm so scared of being alone."

"Defeating your fears begins with acknowledging that you have fears."

I confessed. "I think maybe my fear of failure keeps me from being complete."

"Falling down doesn't make you a failure, but if you stay down, it does."

I asked, "Have you ever felt like giving up?"

"Plenty of times when I was young and dumb. But I learned that in trying times you cannot quit trying. You gotta keep going."

"It's so easy to stay down." I paused. Looked away then brought my attention back to him. "And it's hard to get up."

"Life is designed to be difficult."

"I agree."

"Anyone who says differently ain't dealing with reality."

"There's a lot of people who live delusional lives."

A moment slipped by.

Sheik said, "Like pieces on a chess board we all have positions to play."

I opened my heart and spoke passionately. "I just want someone to embrace the full spectrum of who I am, including my flaws."

He nibbled my ear and whispered, "Someone who will

genuinely share the trials and the triumphs. The good and the bad."

"Yes." I closed my eyes enjoying his warm breath tickling my earlobe. I spoke a hushed. "I've prayed for someone like that."

"Maybe your prayers were answered."

"Yeah. Maybe." I kissed his lips. "Thank you for this healthy and healing dialogue."

"It's my job."

"How so?"

He chuckled, "I am your man ain't I?"

"Optimistic." I smiled.

"Shouldn't I be?"

"Absolutely." I nodded with a grin.

"We both seek the same thing."

"And what is it that we both seek?"

"Understanding."

"Understanding?"

"Understanding of our desires, our heart, our past, our future, and the sometimes jumbled confusion that is our life." He kissed my forehead. "And we yearn to feel whole inside."

I reached over and ran my finger around the outline of his lips. "You are so insightful. It is scary how well you read me."

He looked deep into my eyes. "If you trust me, I will give you the secret to peace and joy."

"That's an interesting proposition." I smiled.

We grew silent for quite a while. Shared intense eye contact. I was thinking about how he makes me feel empowered and enlightened. His entire swagger was captivating. He made me feel like I could not trust myself. Everything about him had me in awe. At some point I leaned over and kissed him. Adrenaline rushing through me. His kiss said that I was the one. My kiss whispered that I wanted to drown in his affection. Our kiss was a silent, secret covenant that our hearts uttered, declaring promises of better days. He needed me as much as I needed him.

Chapter Seven
SHEIK

Never attempt to win by force what can be won by deception.
—*Niccolo Machiavelli*

After Willow and I left the Rotunda, we strolled back to Mel's Diner. She still wanted to hang out, so we decided to park her car at her house and take mine. She was so thrilled when I let her drive the Ferrari. Like a toddler with a new toy, she squealed in excitement and bounced with joy as she sped through the city. She kept ranting about how she could not believe she was driving a Ferrari. With *Songs in A Minor,* Alicia Keys album seeping from the speakers; we rode to Pantops, parked at Darden Towe Park, and walked down to the Rivanna River.

She took me to a spot where her father used to take her fishing when she was a child. Standing on the riverbank in the cool of the evening we watched the sunset while listening to the roar of the traffic crossing Free Bridge, high above our heads. We shared laughs and light conversation. Found a bunch of flat rocks and skimmed them across the water. I was surprised that having so much fun playing with rocks. The experience took me back many years to my childhood. We stayed there for hours, talking and enjoying each other's company.

I pulled in front of her house around midnight, and we sat in the car for a little while, talking, neither of us wanting the night to end. We kissed a lot, our tongues growing extremely familiar with one another. She made me feel like I was floating. High without the weed.

Willow looked into my eyes, her eyelids batting in a bashful manner. Her voice was gentle, "I really enjoyed myself. I uh…. would invite you in for a cappuccino or something but it…." She cleared her throat and paused, gathering her thoughts. "But it would not be lady-like or Christian-like to ask you in at such a late hour."

I suggested, "Maybe we can keep it respectable and have the cappuccino on the porch."

She glanced at the wicker loveseat sitting on the porch, then she brought her attention back to me. Her warm smile presented no opposition to my suggestion, and she said, "Yes, I'd like that."

A few minutes later we were relaxing on the cushioned wicker loveseat while sipping cappuccino. The front door was open, the stereo playing smooth instrumental jazz. The music was calming. The mood was easy and laid back. We had been silent for quite a while gazing at the stars. She was the kind of chick I could see myself growing old with. Those thoughts kept running through my head. I found that disturbing. I wanted to be *into* her pussy rather than *into* her personality. I was craving her juicy. Wondered what she smelled like, felt like, tasted like.

Her voice was soft. "Sheik."

"Yeah."

"Are you okay?"

"Yeah, I was just sitting here thinking."

"About what?"

"You."

"What about me?"

"I wanna touch you."

"In what way?"

"In a way that expresses my adoration for your mind, body, and soul."

She cleared her throat, "Intimacy?"

I nodded. "A longing for the softness of your body."

"Interesting." Blushing she looked away, gazing ahead.

Neither of us said a word for a couple of minutes.

Willow sipped her drink. Her attention went to my feet, curiosity gleamed in the eyes, she pointed at my ankle. She asked, "Why are you carrying that?"

I looked down and saw the .38 snub-nose revolver holstered to my ankle. I fixed my pants leg, concealing the gun.

She asked, "Why didn't you answer my question?"

I smiled at her. "It's for protection."

"From what?"

"Monsters." I chuckled.

She asked, "Isn't it against the law for convicted felons to carry firearms?"

With a smile I said, "If you won't tell then I won't."

She nodded with a smile and did not push the issue.

I reached over and held her hand in mine. "Thanks for this wonderful evening."

"You were quite the gentleman." She admitted with a warm smile, "I almost don't want it to end."

I glanced at the front door and asked, "Where are your parents?"

She giggled. "I hope they're at home." She told me. "This is my sister's home. Last year when I graduated from high school, I moved in with her. She spoils me. She bought me the BMW. Showers me with expensive high-end clothes. Between my sister and my parents, I do not want for anything."

"Your sister must be well off."

"She is very well-off. She is an attorney. Makes big bucks." She told me, "She travels a lot. She's on a trip to Aspen right now."

I sipped my drink.

She commented. "You seem like a man whose traveled a lot and have been many places."

"Yeah, I've traveled a lot."

"Where have you been?"

I shrugged. "Dubai, Tokyo, Egypt, Paris, Jerusalem, Casablanca, Rio, just to name a few."

"Impressive."

"Exploring the world and different cultures is a passion of mine."

"I want to talk about Paris." She rubbed her hands together excitedly and asked a perky, "What was it like?"

"It had a different vibe than any other city I have been to. Real cool and classy. Everybody is friendly." I smiled. "Even to a Black man."

"I have always wanted to visit. My sister says that it is so romantic."

"I guess it would be romantic if you went there with someone you cared about."

She stared off into the distance. Her mind traveled somewhere else. Probably to her ex.

I kissed her hand. "Maybe I'll take you there one day."

She laughed, "Don't play with me, because one day I really might take you up on that offer."

"No problem." I looked at the swell of her round breast and noticed the impression of her nipples on her blouse. My dick got hard.

She saw me staring and looked down at the spot of my focus. She blushed, looked away and took a sip of her drink.

I scooted close to her, trying to make our bodies one. I spoke gently, "Have you ever felt like something was meant to be. You ain't really have no understanding of it, but it just felt right."

"Yes." She smiled. She slipped off her sandals and sat Indian style while toying with her toes. "I feel like that now."

I took one of her feet in my hands and gently pulled it. "Lay back and relax. Stretch your legs out and give me both of your feet."

She did as I asked.

Gently massaging her feet, I looked deep into her eyes. "How does that feel?"

She had a blissful smile on her face, and she closed her eyes and breathed out, "Great."

"A woman like you needs to be pampered. Emotionally, physically, mentally, and spiritually. You need to be nurtured and given the treatment fit for a queen. Most dudes refuse to see that. But I see it. Recognize it. And I wanna give it to you."

She eyed me. "How can you say that? You barely know me."

"It ain't about knowing you. It's about what I feel inside. My heart knows."

She looked at me steadily. "And you think that I deserve to be treated like a queen?"

"It ain't something, I think. It is something that I know." I took an exceptionally long look at her. "I knew it from the very first moment I laid eyes on you, that you were special and quite different than the rest. But it does not mean a thing if you do not see it and realize it. A lotta times it takes a guy like me to bring it out. Don't you want me to bring it out?"

She shrugged and sighed then she moaned and flashed a cute smile. "Whoa. You hit a good spot."

"I can hit a whole lotta good spots on your body." I lifted her foot and kissed it.

Smiling she said, "You're slick." Then she jerked her foot away and sat up. "My senses are telling me that you're trying to seduce me."

"What if I am?"

"Then you're going to hit a brick wall."

I glanced over her entire body.

She giggled. "You looked at me like I was a steak, and you were starving."

"Let us not play games. I want you and I am a man who always gets what he wants."

She laughed. "Very straight forward. In a twisted way I am flattered."

"What'cha think about us going inside and I make you

forget dude forever."

"Why would I allow you the honor of taking my virginity?"

I raised a brow. "Virgin?"

She stated proudly. "I'm saving it for my husband."

"Will you marry me?"

She laughed.

I stared deep into her eyes gauging her truthfulness. "So, you ain't never had sex?"

"Never." She giggled bashfully. "I'm not lying."

"You ain't never had your pussy ate either?"

With wide mouth shock she smacked my arm. "How could you ask such a vulgar question?"

"It's just a question. Don't get offended."

She steered us away from the subject of her chastity and somewhere during our chitchat we began kissing. What started with gentle pecks quickly grew passionate, and I got really aroused. I wanted more. Needed more. I had an ache that needed to be relieved.

I took her constant means of *Nooooooo* to mean yes and when I unbuttoned her blouse and freed one her breast from her bra and began feasting, I thought her wiggles and pushing me away was her getting into it. But hey, what do I know, I was thinking with my *little* head rather than the *big* one on my shoulders.

Suddenly, she screamed that I was raping her then smacked me in the face. Stunned I sat there as she jumped to her feet, crying real tears, shouting at me. "You really know how to sabotage a good evening! I thought that you were different!" She grabbed her shoes and spoke a disgusted. "Leave before I call the police!" Then she stormed into the house and slammed the door shut. Left me sitting there looking like a damn fool.

I stared at the door for a few moments thinking maybe she was joking and that she would open the door. But she never did. I sat the coffee mug under the love seat and left. I had Willow on my mind. She had a grip on both of my heads. The big one and the little one. I wanted her and would not quit until she was mine.

Chapter Eight
SHEIK

Stolen waters are sweet, and bread eaten in secret is pleasant.
—King Solomon

With a rock-hard dick, I headed down to South First to see what was up with Crook. I had a great multitude of beautiful women on call, but something compelled me to see her. I could not find the strength to squelch the cravings of being with her.

Crook was alone in the crib, sitting on the couch playing *Madden* on the PlayStation. The room was dark with a cloudy haze of weed smoke. A half-full bottle of Hennessy was on the glass coffee table. She had Lil' Wayne's *Carter 3* album playing, her head bobbing to the beat. Judging from her expression she was fucked up.

She gave me a soft smile when she saw me walk in. She shouted over the music, "What's up nigga?"

I turned on a lamp, grabbed the remote, and turned down the music. I lightly scolded, "You're sitting in here with the music blasting and the door unlocked. I could have been a nigga coming to kill you."

She laughed and picked up the Uzi that had been resting on her lap. "I would've put so many holes in you that your nickname would've been Swiss cheese."

"As drunk and high as you look, I don't think you would've reacted in time."

Placing the gun down beside her she grinned at me. "I'm high as a mafucka."

"I can tell." I responded and plopped down on the plush recliner.

All she had on was a pair of boxer briefs and a wife-beater. She said, "I saw you tonight."

"Where?"

"At Mel's, with that pretty-ass red-boned bitch. That bitch was a dime. Fucking gorgeous."

"I didn't see you."

She giggled. "I know, I was creeping."

I smiled at her. "More like stalking."

"Won't nobody stalking you." She told me, "I was with Asia in her Accord. Stopped at the red-light on Seventh. Watched you cuddled up with that pretty bitch."

"Jealous?"

"Jealous." She smirked, "Nigga you are trippin'."

I looked her dead in the eyes. "You ain't a good actor."

"What's that supposed to mean?"

"Your mouth says one thing but your face, your eyes, your posture says something different."

"Don't give me that bullshit."

"It's the truth."

She smiled at me. "A bitch that look as good as that bitch you were with tonight either got ugly feet, funky pussy, stinky breath, or she crazy. A bitch that beautiful gotta have something wrong with her."

"Well, her feet, breath and mind are on point." I chuckled. "I'll get back with you on the pussy situation at a later date and time."

She snapped. "Fuck you!" Then she hurled a pillow at me. "I'm tired of your bullshit."

I laughed a little bit as I got comfortable on the recliner, propping my feet in on the coffee table.

Crook stood and stretched. "You think I'm a fucking joke don'tcha?"

I extend my hand. "Come here."

She whined, "Nooooooo."

I smiled and spoke a serious. "Come here."

"Nope." She headed to the kitchen." Fuck you."

As she walked past me, I smacked her big ass and grinned at her. Moments later she came back toting two cold beers. She handed me the Corona and kept the Heineken for herself. Then she straddled me, sitting comfortably on my lap. I sipped my beer and watched her watching me.

Silence hung between us.

She spoke in a quiet voice. "I bumped into a few of those JFM niggas tonight."

"Where?"

"At the Shell Station on Preston."

"And?"

She sipped her beer. "Them niggas looked at me like they know something."

"Oh yeah." I asked, "Did they say anything to you?"

"Me and the nigga Blacko talked about the Nikes I had on. He said that he liked them." She told me, "As I left, I overheard Junior tell some dude that he should bust my ass. The guy told Junior to be patient. I acted like I ain't hear it."

"Good job." I told her, "Them niggas ain't stupid. They know but they want proof."

"Well either way it doesn't matter to me."

"Peace is always better than war. If we can keep the peace, then we keep the peace."

She took a deep breath. "Our boys cremated the body and spread the ashes in the James River in Buckingham. We stripped the Escalade, sold the parts, then recycled the rest of the metal. There ain't a trace that he even existed."

I said, "His daughter Rita ain't no dummy. Once she puts two-and-two together, we are gonna have problems."

She smirked. "Fuck 'em. I will kill 'em all."

"Everybody respects death, right?"

She spoke proudly. "Not me. I have no fear of death."

"You might not fear it, but you respect it. If you didn't you would not be so willing to dish it out so freely."

After a thoughtful moment she nodded her head and exhaled a deep breath. "Are you ever wrong?"

I smiled. "Nah."

She kissed my lips with a quick peck. "That's why I'll follow you to the grave."

We shared a sloppy tongue kiss.

She asked, "What's up with your new friend?"

"You know a nigga like me don't have friends."

"I thought we were friends," she said with a grin as she unzipped my slacks. "Ain't we friends?"

I shrugged and smiled. "I don't know. You tell me."

We shared kisses while she fondled me. I did not resist when she slipped outta her boxer briefs and mounted my hardness. Didn't even take off my pants.

Like two wild animals we went at it hard. Rough. Clawing and biting. She even smacked me quite a few times. Drew blood from my shoulder when she sank her teeth into my flesh. The bitch is crazy.

When we were finished, we sat there huffing and puffing, her head resting on my shoulder. Neither of us spoke a word. She kissed my neck, my jaw.

She whispered, "You were thinking about her, won't you?"

I admitted, "Yeah." I asked, "How did you know?"

"You groaned her name." She said, "Her name is Willow."

We talked and I told her about the date. At some point, I told her I was really into Willow and that I might pursue more than just her pussy.

Crook grew silent.

I asked, "What's up with you?"

She sat up and looked me in the eyes. Her face went somber. "What about us?"

"Whatcha mean, what about us?"

She spoke irritably, "You're sittin' here with your dick in me."

"Do not start this. You are taking things too personal. This morning on the phone we agreed that we were not gonna catch feelings."

She barked, "Give it to me real! Do not sugar coat it. You cannot hurt me."

"Why do you always make shit complicated?" I placed my hands on her hips.

She leaped off me and stormed into the kitchen. I fixed my clothes while she cursed and shouted how much she hated me. She was ranting on and on as she tried to take the top off a Heineken bottle with a bottle opener.

I walked into the kitchen, took the beer outta her hand and put it on the counter. I told her, "Calm down."

She punched me in the chest. "Don't tell me to calm down."

I pulled her into my arms, gripping her bare ass. Staring into her eyes I said, "Stop actin' like a lil' bitch."

"I feel like a lil' bitch," she muttered under her breath. She twisted away from my embrace and headed up to her bedroom.

When I walked into her bedroom, I found her completely naked, laying on her back, her legs wide open. Her voice was low and husky. "Come make love to me." She chuckled.

I shook my head to clear it and said, "You're a crazy bitch."

She smiled and licked her lips. "Come make love to me. Show me what you feel for me. I know that you love me."

An hour later we lay there naked and sweaty. Her head was on my stomach as she tenderly toyed with my now limp dick.

She said, "We can't keep fucking without condoms."

"I know."

"I'm gonna buy a whole lot of Magnums and have them here for you."

I did not reply. Didn't wanna face the reality of what we had become.

She surprised me when she began rapping a song, she had written about me and her. It was a thug love song. When she finished, she looked up at me and asked, "Did you like it?"

I lied. "Yeah."

She bit my stomach, and we played around wrestling until I allowed her to pin me. Sitting on my chest she stared down at me with love in her eyes. She made me grow hard again.

She spoke with a sinister smirk, "Pretty lil' red-boned bitch gotcha horny, don't she?" She slipped my manhood inside of her.

Damn, she was so wet.

Slowly riding me, she said, "I want us to be more…. I want us to be together."

"Intellect over emotion." I pulled her to me and kissed her. Sucked her tits. Told her, "This shit ain't right."

She groaned. "But it's good…. Mmmmm…. real fucking good. Too good." She grunted, her face grimacing in pleasure. "What'cha…. damn your dick is good…. what'cha wanna do about Red and Lil Lou?"

"When deep pockets get shallow, murder begins peeking it's head around the corner."

"What does that mean?"

"Keep their pockets fat. Give 'em what they want."

She moaned. "Mmmmm….I….wouldn't…cater…. cater…cater…. mmmmm…. cater to them muthafuckas if they wanna go elsewhere to do business then let them."

"They are valuable assets. Richmond is a gold mine. And them niggas run Richmond."

"Let me kill 'em both and fuck with the next man. We can make another King of Richmond."

"Can't kill everybody."

Nibbling her lip in the most seductive way she said, "Speak for yourself."

"Your cold soul is a reflection of the deep buried pain inside of you."

She grunted with a smile. "Bootleg psychologist."

We both laughed.

She hissed as she moved in a rocking motion, a slow grind, rolling her wide hips. Her pussy was good. Glove tight. Wetter-than rain.

She groaned, her face balled up in an orgasmic scowl.

"Damn….damn…..damn! Nigga this thing soooooooo muthafuckin' good. Fuck me nigga! Fuck me hard!"

With her eyes closed and a look of concentration on her face she repeated slammed her body down on me. Her rhythm picked up to jackhammer speed. The sound of skin slapping skin was loud. Suddenly she trembled and screamed out, "Shit!"

I grabbed the hoop earrings that pierced her nipples and pulled them hard. She came hard. Stretching her arms above her head she laughed. "A beast! That was a muthafuckin beast!"

I asked, "What about me?"

"Get that pretty red chick to hook you up. She is the one you want."

"You need peace in your life you crazy bitch."

She slipped off me and sat beside me. "I don't need peace. All I need is what I just got from you."

"How do you go from bliss to anger so quickly?"

"Fuck you."

"Get outta your feelings."

"Don't keep talking shit." She grabbed hold of my rigid manhood. "Or I will cut this muthafucka off."

"You need to see a psychologist. You might be bi-polar."

"I can't keep doing this shit."

"Doing what?"

"Being second to all the rest of your bitches. Hiding this from the world. I wanna to be your number one."

I told her, "You gotta sink into your own thoughts and travel outside of the hell you've created."

"The hell is because of you. Loving you and not getting it back in return. That is pure hell."

"You receive my love every day."

"I'm your flunky."

"You're my baby." I pulled her to me. "My heart."

"That's your word?" She climbed on me. Mounted me. Let me enter her tight cove.

"That's my word."

"You love me?"

"Let me show you."
"Yeah. Show me nigga."

Chapter Nine
SHEIK

*Whosoever desires constant success must
change his conduct with the times.
—Niccolo Machiavelli*

Raptures, the posh bar downtown on Third was filled to capacity with suits from the worlds of law and corporate America. The atmosphere was exclusive, the upper echelon of their respective fields, hanging out, unwinding for happy hour.

I had come down to the bar to have a drink with Roger, my real estate agent, but he had called me just a few minutes ago telling me he would have to take a raincheck. Something about an urgent family issue.

I was perched on a stool at the far end of the bar having a beer before I headed home. I glanced around the bar. The scene before me had a surreal quality. As I sat there nursing my beer, I wondered how many present knew who I was and what I did for a living. The thought brought a smile to my face. A moment later a chuckle.

I drained my beer, sat down the bottle and glanced at my

watch – 5:43 p.m. I stood, paid for my brew and was about to make an exit when somebody said, "Shakur."

I turned around and saw Allen Rosenberg. I cracked a smile as soon as I saw him. He was a tall silver-haired man in his sixties with skin as white as ivory. His eyes were unusually large giving his face a cartoonish look. He wore his suit well, obviously Italian, and meticulously tailored as was every piece of clothing that he owned.

I said, "Allen. Long time no see."

He asked, "What brings you down to these parts?"

"I was supposed to have a drink with Roger Kirby, but something came up."

He chuckled. "Ol' Roger the millionaire real estate crook."

We both laughed.

Allen was the best criminal attorney in the city. He was a legend. A top-notch high-profile lawyer who had grown filthy rich by defending wealthy criminals. His nickname in the hood was Matlock.

I smiled at him. "How have you been ol' friend?"

He told me, "Merely trying to age with dignity and grace."

"Looks like you're doing an excellent job."

He half-smiled at me. "I hear you're at a crossroads."

"Yeah." I nodded. "It's time to walk away, retire, and go legit."

"Ahhh." He smiled. "The conclusion of your illustrious pharmaceutical career."

Before, I met my former attorney Jack Sparco, Allen had represented all members of the S.F.C. in criminal matters. He had defended Crook on all her murder charges and me on my murder case too. He had handled countless cases for the S.F.C. and they all had ended with not guilty verdicts. He had made a ton of money courtesy of the S.F.C.

I said, "I need a competent attorney to realize my vision."

"Funny you say that." He told me, "A colleague of mine just a moment ago made an inquiry about the position."

I asked, "Who?"

He patted my back and told me, "Rebekah Braxton."

"Never heard of her."

"She is the cities most talented emerging attorney. A brilliant tactician." He told me, "She has made a reputation as being a shrewd and ruthless attorney. Feared by many."

I raised a brow. "And she wanna be the consigliere of the S.F.C.?"

He nodded. "She's a far-seeing businesswoman."

"She qualified?"

He told me, "She has a degree in business management and law."

"Yeah." I asked, "But is she qualified?"

He leaned close to me and spoke in a hushed tone, "She is a villain. Definitely, your type of gal. A rebel with extraordinary legal skills who plays the game dirty. And she has ruthless business instincts and powerful friends."

"Is she clean?"

"Yeah. Never been touched by any hint of scandal."

"When can I meet this super-lawyer?

His attention to the far end of the bar. He nodded so slightly that his head hardly moved. "That's her sitting alone at the bar."

The first surprise was she looked so young. She looked twenty-five. The second thing I took notice of was her startling beauty. The look on my face must have been worth a thousand words because Allen glanced at me and laughed.

He said, "She's a beauty, isn't she?"

With my eyes glued to Ms. Braxton, I replied, "Exquisite."

"Shakur you're preparing the most significant operation of your life, and you'll need her strategic genius."

Ms. Braxton sat there lounged back haughtily on the bar stool, her gaze focused intently on me. She had honey-brown skin, wavy raven hair pulled into a tight bun. She was tall, fashion model thin but full breasted. An elegant creature.

I asked Allen, "Private practice?"

He said, "No, she's employed by Schumann, Stokes and Wallace."

I nodded. "The most prestigious firm in the city."

"Absolutely. They offer the highest salary and fringes in the country."

I studied Rebekah Braxton slowly. She had on a dark-colored pencil skirt, and a form-hugging white blouse that was open down to the second button, showing a full, firm cleavage. Pearls wound around her slender neck. She wore a strand of pearls on one wrist and a sparkling diamond Rolex on the other.

She eyed me up and down. Savored me with clever eyes. She tilted her head at a curious angle as her eyes probed mine.

Allen said, "After she graduated from Harvard law she was heavily recruited by every big firm on the East Coast."

"A person doesn't graduate from Harvard law without connections."

"Shakur, this gal made junior partner in just three years and that is unheard of at a firm ran by elitist white men. She is head of the firm's litigation department."

Ms. Braxton eased from her stool and headed toward us. She moved with feminine grace that radiated sensuality.

When Ms. Braxton came to stop in front of us, suddenly the air smelled sweet and delicious. It was the most intoxicating perfume I had ever known. Reminded me of the fragrance that Willow wore.

"Shakur." Allen said. "I would like you to meet Rebekah Braxton, junior partner at Schumann, Stokes and Wallace."

I had lost myself in watching her. I cleared my throat. Blinked my eyes. I spoke with a smile. "Pleased to meet you Ms. Braxton."

She extended a slender French manicured hand. "It's a privilege and honor." Her voice had a gentle quality, like smooth jazz. Very soothing.

I took her hand. "The privilege is all mine," I said gazing deep into her eyes.

She gave me a firm handshake. "It's a dream come true to meet such an iconic figure as yourself." Then she took my hand and raised it to her lips, her eyes never leaving my face. She kissed my pinky ring.

Her big soulful eyes were an alluring green and there was a familiarity that lived there. Like we had met before.

Her face held a serene beauty. A delicately sculpted face.

She was too extraordinary not to look at. There was not a single feature that was less than perfect.

I said, "There is something about you that strikes a chord of familiarity. Have we by some chance met before?"

She looked at me with a slow smile, as she toyed with the pearls wound around her neck, "Mr. Andrew's you are a major source of financing for the Democrats. I worked on President Obama's re-election campaign and Governor Terry McAuliffe's, along with several Senators and Congressmen. We have been at a few fundraisers together." She invited, "And please call me Re-Re, everyone does."

"Okay, Re-Re it is." I said, "I hear you've experienced enviable accomplishments in the field of law."

She passed her tongue across her lips. "I take my commitment to excellence very seriously."

I said, "Now you're looking to pursue new outlets for your ambition?"

She smiled at me. "The overall jurisprudence experience is beginning to grow stale."

I nodded in agreement. "And in your hunt for thrills you want the most vital subordinate position of the S.F.C."

"Shakur, she's not a thrill seeker." Allen said, "I assure you Re-Re's interest is solely for financial gain and the opportunity to be a part of your transition."

Re-Re added, "I've discovered that those who are loyal to you become extremely wealthy."

"How much do you make at the firm?" I asked, "Six-figure income, right?"

"Yes," She smiled. "Depending on performance bonuses, I earn close to five hundred thousand. My budding investment management firm pulls in another seventy-five before taxes."

Allen cracked a smile and told us that he had something to tend to and that he would see us later. He headed towards the rear of the bar and left me and the beautiful barrister by ourselves.

I regarded Re-Re with genuine interest. "Your accomplishments are impressive."

She spoke with a bright smile. "I'm ambitious."

"Ambition. The gift that keeps on giving." I glanced at her hand and did not see a wedding ring. "I imagine you're tireless and sleep little."

"I was born with a drive that can't be matched."

I let a moment pass before I said, "I must admit you've triggered an awful kind of curiosity in me."

"That's expected." She smiled a teasing smile. "I'm undeniably brilliant."

"With a Texas-sided ego to go with that brilliance."

She laughed at that. "My only eccentricity is my conceit."

"The evidence is clear and overwhelming."

She smiled, "You have a great sense of humor, which seems to be quite a rarity in the gangster world."

"A gangster? Where did that come from?"

She said, "That's what everyone has been whispering since you walked through the door."

"Believe none of what hear and half of what you see."

"There are also rumors which connect you to the Juarez Cartel of Columbia."

"That's a new one."

"Well, are you?"

"Absolutely not."

"You're lying." I caught a hint of amusement in her eyes.

That got a laugh out me. "I get that you're a woman who won't let something go."

She smiled the warmest smile. "Like a terrier after a rat."

I said, "Persistence, the key to enduring success or maybe the key to a shallow grave in the country."

Her eyes were thorough in their close study of me. "Spoken like a true tycoon of cocaine."

I couldn't help smiling and she stared into my eyes, holding my gaze. She was trying to hide a smile.

"Chevalier d'industries," she spoke in perfect French. Then she took a seat on one of the barstools to the right of us and I joined her perching on a stool. I watched her closely. There is a sense of almost aristocratic refinement about her.

"You speak French." I asked, "What did you just say?"

"For the record I speak five languages fluently." She told me, "And I said, *I'm one who lives by my wits.*"

The bartender came over and Re-Re told him to bring a bottle of her usual whiskey and two glasses. He left and came back with a bottle of Whistle Pig straight rye whiskey.

Re-Re poured us both a drink. We saluted each other with our glasses and drank.

She asked, "How does it feel to be a Black drug-lord in a bar full of stuck-up, snobbish, bigot white lawyers, judges, and executives?"

I laughed and she joined in, stifling a chuckle.

I asked, "Why do you say such mean things about your colleagues?"

"It's in the spirit of openness." She bit down on her lip and stared at me. She was studying me. After a long moment she asked, "Do you want to hear a secret?"

"Sure."

"I own a lot of souls in this room."

"You wanna sell a judge or a politician because I'm looking to buy?"

That made her laugh hard.

Smiling I asked, "Is it in the realm of possibility?"

"Of course. Everything has a price."

I sipped my drink. "What's your price?"

She had a smile of absolute confidence on her mouth. "I'm the best legal counseling that money can buy."

"Is that so?"

"I like to think of myself as the LeBron James of law."

The glint of amusement in her eyes cut any arrogance from her statement. I couldn't help smiling.

She leaned toward me and spoke in a confidential tone. "Allen tells me that you're trying to get out of the cocaine business and into the lucrative construction business."

I sipped from my glass then put it on the bar. "You and Allen have discussed my dilemma?"

"In great detail." She looked at me with calm, measuring eyes. "I begged him to introduce us."

"I don't take you as a woman who begs."

"Only for you." She held her glass in salute to me, then took a swallow. "I can do things for you that every other attorney you'll ever meet will find out of their range." She eyed me carefully. "I'm not your typical ethical lawyer."

She has a tremendous ease about her. Cool and confident.

She said, "We are kindred to some degree."

"How so?"

She drained her glass. "Both of us are fluent in the language of dirty money."

I told her, "So is every lawyer I've ever met."

"I'm not every lawyer, Mr. Andrews."

"What separates you from the flock?"

She leaned toward me and whispered, "I have city council members in my pocket. Prosecutors, judges, high ranking police officials, bank executives, and politicians. The list goes on and on."

I was silent, thinking. After a moment I spoke. "How does a lady gain such priceless assets?"

"Networking. Favors. Brides. Cajolery. Blackmail."

She picked up the bottle and replenished her glass and mine. She watched me with narrowed eyes, and I sense an intensity so powerful that she wills what she wants into existence.

She spoke casually, "Suck a few dicks, eat a little pussy, and secretly get those episodes on D.V.D. Great motivators to spur people to move in any direction I wish."

I said, "The more the onion gets peeled, the more fascinating you turn out to be."

"I'm a mover and shaker," she said grinning wickedly. "I've never played by other people's rules."

"A maverick."

She nodded. "Mister Andrews you are Black folk rich." She took my left hand and examined my pinky ring. "But I can make you white folk rich."

We held each other's gaze for a moment, a look of understanding.

I said, "Those are big words for a young lady."

She said, "I suggest you take me seriously."

"I do."

"I believe in absolute frankness." She paused and added quietly, "Without me on your team you will fail."

I told her, "Failure for me is a life sentence in federal prison."

A soft smile went with her reply. "Consider me your stay out of jail card."

I asked, "What kind of law do you specialize in?"

"Corporate mergers. A little international taxation. Most of my clients are corporations and banks. I do mergers, antitrust, securities, and I practice criminal law on the side for only wealthy high-profile clients."

I told her, "I have a substantial amount of dirty money that need to be funneled into legitimate accounts."

She looked over her shoulder to make sure no one could hear her. She spoke quietly, "I have an I.R.S. agent on my payroll and I represent quite a few banks. I can control any problem that may arise."

"Okay. Let me hear your pitch."

"This is the proposition in detail. You hire me as the executive head of the S.F.C. and I will flawlessly fulfill your vision. In return you pay me a six-figure salary and after I set up all businesses you that you want, I get a fifteen percent stake in every single one and you will appoint me C.E.O."

I slipped my drink and thought about it. I asked, "What's the timeline?"

"It will take me only a year to get things squared away."

"You can guarantee that in a year I'll be completely legit?"

"Absolutely." She said, "I don't make empty promises." Then she closed her eyes as if trying to gather her thoughts, then looked at me. "I am a full-fledged master of my craft. Fortune five hundred companies and wealthy high-ranking politicians seek my legal advice. I am the lawyer that the sharpest lawyers call when they need help."

I swallowed the drink in one gulp and refilled the glass. I asked, "What's your motive for wanting to make a deal with the devil?"

She hesitated and contemplated the answer. "I have an

unquenchable thirst for wealth. I love money."

I didn't say anything. Just sat there watching her. She was silent, swirling the whiskey in her glass, her gaze focused intently on me. She seemed to be waiting for me to speak.

She asked, "So what do you think?"

I thought for a moment. "I like what I've heard." I said, "But I'm not a man who makes moves rashly."

She was silent for a moment, staring at the mingling crowd. I imagined she was contemplating. We made eye contact. Stared at each other. She had the eyes of a woman who had always been a boss.

In a soft voice, right above a whisper she said, "I have powerful friends. One of my most valuable assets is having been an administrative aide to the governor. A system of payoffs can be set up so your company will receive first dibs on all the state building contracts. That connection can get you past a lot of red tape. Zoning laws, certain licenses and ordinances will all be manipulated for our benefit."

I leaned back relaxing against the back of the stool. "You are beyond a doubt sincere."

"I'm the real deal Mister Andrews."

"I'm impressed by the range of your talents and the scope of your cunning and connections."

Her tone was lawyerly. "You'd be a fool to pass on such a great asset as Rebekah Braxton."

She was right. "I have to agree."

The radiant smile on her face was bright enough to light up the room.

She told me, "It's not rocket science. It is only common sense."

"You'd make a great politician."

"I have an interest in politics." She looked at me with a proud smile. "Much later in my career though."

I said, "Political connections are priceless."

"Another incentive to hire me."

"Sweetest deal I ever heard."

"First a congressperson then a senator and you will own me. And that is just the beginning, because I will climb high up the political ladder. You are in the presence of a probable future president."

I found myself looking curiously at her. There was a seductive sexuality about her. She was so feminine, so incredibly alluring.

I said, "You are the only woman who has ever awed me."

"I'm honored and humbled." She smiled.

I had been up since four o'clock that morning. I suppressed a yawn. I told her that I was about to head home. A subtle change came into her face; it seemed almost desperate. I watched her closely, gazing into her captivating eyes, trying to decipher the emotion that burned just under the surface.

She cleared her throat. "Do you have somewhere to be?"

"Yeah." I yawned. "At home in my bed."

"But the evening is so young." She smiled at me and patted my hand.

We were silent for a long while, just looking at each other. Finally, she spoke. "You are an elegant man, and masculine, as well as intriguing. Sexy and mysterious."

I said, "You're a woman of extraordinary charm."

"A man with your good looks and wealth certainly has his choice of beautiful women."

"What's on your mind?"

She passed her tongue across her lips. "Your dick in my mouth."

"That was kind of eye-opening to me."

She downed the last of her drink, then glanced at her watch before she stood up. "Come, please walk me to my car."

We exited out the side door onto Third Street. She told me she had parked two blocks away in the parking garage on Water Street.

As we strolled, I said, "Tell me a little about Rebekah Braxton."

She chuckled and explained. "I have a liking for making money, and gourmet food and first-rate sex."

When we reached the parking garage we took the elevator

to the third level. I followed her to a candy-apple red BMW M6 convertible. She chirped the alarm off. She started the engine with the remote of her key chain. She stood beside her hundred grand ultimate driving machine with the posture of an empress.

I said, "Nice car."

She was close suddenly, and she put her hand on my arm. "I've overheard countless women talk about you." She nodded towards my crotch. "It's thick, long, huge, and you have the stamina of a triathlon athlete."

I should have moved away from her, but I didn't. I said, "You could charm a rabid wolf."

She reached behind my neck and pulled my face to hers. Before, I could respond she leisurely touched her lips against mine, then stuck her tongue in my mouth. We shared a tender kiss. Then she drew back and touched my cheek with her hand.

I gave a short laugh. "You're confusing me."

"What do you mean?"

"Do you wanna work for me or fuck me?"

"Both."

"Mixing business and pleasure is always a destructive force."

"That may be true for ordinary people. But we are two extraordinary human beings."

She radiated raw sensuality. I stared, unable to take my eyes off her. I considered what to do.

I said, "It's hard to determine just what your intentions are."

"My intentions are to serve you on all levels."

"And one of those levels is with your pussy?"

"Pussy, mouth, asshole. Whatever your fancy." She lifted her hand and gently traced the outline of my face; she stroked my goatee. She grinned and spoke in a voice as soft as a cloud. "My pussy is like delicious food. It is to be savored and enjoyed."

I told her, "We must move prudently, with discipline, not emotion."

"Mr. Andrews, when it comes to a man of your charisma that's very simple in concept, much more difficult to execute."

"You can handle it. You are a young woman of intense will."

She reached in her purse and handed me her business card. She told me. "Every pleasure in my life is yours for the asking."

I nodded.

"Where are you parked?" She said, "I'll give you a lift to your car."

"I live only a few blocks away. I walked to the bar." I turned and headed across the parking garage. Without turning I shouted, "We will do lunch Monday, so keep your schedule open."

I could hear the joy in her voice when she shouted, "Absolutely sir. Have a goodnight!"

Chapter Ten
SHEIK

It is double pleasure to deceive the deceiver.
- Niccolo Machiavelli

"Sir can I help you with something?" The attractive young receptionist smiled warmly and spoke from behind the shiny mahogany work desk.

"Yes," I said strolling towards her. "Mr. Andrews to see Ms. Rebekah Braxton."

She asked, "Do you have an appointment?"

I replied, "No ma'am."

"Ms. Braxton absolutely hates drop-ins."

"Her and I are supposed to do lunch today."

She picked up the phone and a moment later she said, "Ms. Braxton, there's a Mr. Andrews here to see you." All the while her eyes crawled over my Prada suit. When she put the phone down, she stood and came around the desk. "Mr. Andrews please follow me."

I followed the well-dressed receptionist down a sumptuously decorated hallway filled with busy lawyers and secretaries.

I said, "Busy place."

"It's manic Monday." She smiled a sly smile. "Ms. Braxton sounded extremely thrilled that you were here."

I chuckled. "What's up with that sly look that you just gave me?"

She spoke in a whispered tone. "You two are dating, aren't you?"

"That's none of your business."

"Warning." She whispered, "FYI. She is a man-eater, so be careful."

"Thanks, but…..." I glanced at my crotch. "FYI. I got a lot for her to eat. Enough to make her obese."

She blushed, gave me a wide mouth look of shock then we both shared a quiet laugh.

She escorted me to a corner office at the end of the hallway. She knocked, then opened the door and ushered me into a luxuriously decorated office. The fragrance of jasmine flavored the air. Classical music floated throughout the massive room, the harmonious sound soft and low.

Re-Re was behind her desk, talking on her phone. She gave me a radiant smile and signaled with a finger for me to give her a moment.

The receptionist smiled as she left the office and winked at me.

My gaze wandered slowly around the large office, marveling at the elegance and extravagance. The walls were oak-paneled and there was wall-to-wall Belgium carpet. Her huge solid-cherry desk was leather-topped. On the other side of the office was a living room-like area with a maroon leather couch and a few wing chairs that surrounded a polished rosewood coffee table that was glistening with mirrored brilliance. The carpet was so thick that it seemed as if I was floating.

While Re-Re spoke in courtroom jargon to someone on the phone, I strolled the room surveying its sophisticated luxury. A row of ten-foot windows lined two walls offering a charming view of the Belmont Bridge.

All around me was evidence of Re-Re's success. Museum-quality abstract sculptures, opulent fixtures, extraordinary oil-paintings, recessed bookcases filled with leather-bound volumes and a collection of elaborate framed photographs hung on the wall in the living room area.

I went over to the photos. Re-Re was in every single one standing beside a few celebrities, political leaders, and even two U. S. Presidents. I was deeply impressed.

I walked over behind her desk and looked at her gilt-framed diplomas. Underneath them were a cluster of framed awards she had received over her young career. She had achievements and accomplishments that would take the average attorney a lifetime to obtain.

"I had a high school diploma by age fifteen." Re-Re's voice came to me suddenly from behind me. "I had a bachelor's from Princeton by age eighteen. Three years later I earned a law degree from Harvard."

I turned on my heels. She was standing a few feet away in a well tailored maroon suit. She gave me a radiant smile. "At Harvard I was elected the first African American female president of the Harvard Law review."

I asked, "How did you rank in your class?"

"Top of three hundred and fifty." She stepped towards me. Stood toe to toe. She reached over and straightened my tie. "I was the youngest professor to ever teach law at Harvard."

I smiled. "I gotta say I'm blown away."

She flashed a prideful smile as she stared into my eyes. She was so close I could taste the spearmint on her breath. After a long moment of gazing into my eyes Re-Re cleared her throat and gestured for me to have a seat. She came around and sat on the edge of her desk.

A moment later she was telling me about how her morning had been full of non-stop calls and conferences.

"But enough about me." Her eyes were careful in their intense close examination of me. "I'm delighted that you came by."

"I talked to a couple of mutual friends." I sat cross-legged, resting my hand on my right ankle. "I was pleasantly surprised by what I found out."

She grinned at me. "Pleasantly surprised? That sounds promising."

"I have some good news for you."

"Let me guess." She looked at me with suppressed eagerness, "I am the newly appointed executive head and attorney of the South First Commission?"

I nodded. "Do you accept?"

"Absolutely." She smiled again. "I'm honored and humbled by the faith you placed in me."

"I have a signing bonus for you." I reached inside my jacket and took out an envelope stuffed with cash. I handed it to her and told her, "With great power comes great responsibility."

"Sir I will protect and do what's best for you." She looked inside the envelope and gazed fondly at me. "Wow! My morale is high for the coming task, and I look forward to doing you this honor."

I gave her a simple nod. "You understand that the potential consequences of your failure to live up to your end of this bargain is the loss of your life."

Her face relaxed. "I assure you of my utmost loyalty and devotion."

I let my gaze drift over her. "You have all of my confidence."

Her cell phone vibrated on the desk, and she glanced at the number. She told me that it was an important call from the mayor that she had to take and excused herself. She slipped from the desk and strolled nonchalantly across the office to the windows that overlooked the southern tip of the Downtown Mall.

I stared unable to take my eyes off her. I watched her ass for a moment, the skirt pulled tight across it. She didn't have a big ass nor a small one. But it's just right. Modest and apple shaped.

Lust washed through me instinctive and strong. *Ugh*! I shuddered away from the thought. I closed my eyes for a moment willing myself to control my desires. I was here on business. Pleasure was not an option. The two don't mix at all and should always be kept completely separated.

It was impossible to ignore her sumptuous derriere. She turned sharply from the window as if she had felt my gaze on her ass. She saw me looking with admiration at her body.

After she finished the call, she came toward me. She stepped in front of me and looked at me.

"You were looking at my ass, weren't you?" She accused with a soft chuckle.

I did not answer. Just sat there watching her. It was incredibly quiet. I swear I could hear the beating of her heart, fast and steady. She was waiting for me to say something. She licked her lips, and a subtle change came into her face, it seemed almost bestial. She took off her suit jacket and tossed it aside. Slowly she unbuttoned her blouse and reached in her bra and exposed her breast. She smiled and stared at me, her teeth catching her lower lip, nibbling it for a moment.

I stared at her with wonder, my eyes resting on her breast. She had pretty tits, one of my weaknesses. They were full with an upturned curve, their aureoles wide and dark as milk chocolate. Her nipples were so elongated they seemed to point at me. They were breast any woman in the world would trade their soul for.

She eased into the wedge of my legs and gently rubbed her breast over my face. I inhaled a sweet and sensuous smell. I should have moved away from her, but I didn't.

I could hear desire burning under the casual tone of her voice when she said, "Now that you've hired me, everything that I have, that I am, is at your disposal."

I smiled. "Boss status has it's privileges hunh?"

"Absolutely."

I took a deep breath, meeting the lust in her green eyes. "Fix your clothes so we can talk business."

Her eyes looked deep into mine. She was waiting for me to say I was joking. But I wasn't and I looked steadily at her until she lowered her eyes. A kind of disappointment flashed across her face. A lonely look. She looked momentarily defeated.

I almost breathed a sigh of relief when she stepped back

from me, pushing her breast back into her bra. She stood before me, hands at her side, motionless. Her blouse was open, her lavender lace clad breast on display.

A slight sigh escaped her lips. "My blowjobs are a journey. You might be surprised where it takes you."

I took a deep breath. "Give it up counselor."

She licked her lips before she said, "Giving up isn't who I am."

My gaze traveled slowly from her face down to her breast and up to her face once more. I glanced around the room frantically looking to divert my thoughts toward a different path. I might forget all logic and fuck her, thus eliminating all possibilities of us having a profitable business relationship. It proved far more difficult than I had imagined. I looked into her eyes and lost my train of thought.

She simply smiled, as if to assure me that she would not be denied. It was obvious that she was used to getting her way.

Slowly she sank to her knees. I reached to help her to her feet, but her hand caught mine and stopped me. Then she reached and unzipped my slacks. I stared at her, speechless. I could not think of a single thing to say to her. I felt a pulse of excitement. Every instinct in my body told me to get up and leave. But I couldn't. I ached for her.

She reached in and pulled out my hardness and gently moved her fingers over it with a feather-light touch. I touched her face, lying my hands on her cheek. She exhaled at my touch and looked up me. The hungry possessive look in her eyes plainly said that she wanted to fuck.

I relaxed.

She took the fullness of all I had to offer, her eyes never leaving my face. I gave a grunt of pleasure. As her mouth leisurely moved up and down, she looked up at me with those big soulful eyes. I sat there transfixed. Scared the hell outta me when she made me bust off in record time.

She swallowed it all then placed my limpness back into my pants and zipped me up. Then she stood and laughed at the look on my face. Lust gave way to regret. Regret that made me cringe.

After a long moment I said, "You're a very talented young lady."

She smiled. "You just received my version of a signing bonus."

"I'm not a man easily impressed, but Ms. Braxton I must admit I'm impressed by the entire package that is you."

She said, "There's an art to being Rebekah Braxton."

I checked my watch. It was noon. I let out a quiet whistle and said, "Lunch time, you hungry?"

As she buttoned her blouse, she told me, "I know a nice little Chinese restaurant uptown in Preston Plaza. We will take the firms limo. Lunch is on me."

Chapter Eleven
SHEIK

If you know the enemy and know yourself, you need not fear the result of a hundred battles. If you know yourself but not the enemy, for every victory gained you will also suffer a defeat. If you know neither the enemy nor yourself, you will succumb in every battle.
—Sun Tzu

Re-Re and I migrated uptown to a modest Chinese restaurant. Sitting outside on the tiny patio enjoying the breeze we were grubbing while observing the lunch hour bustle of the small shopping center.

Finishing off her sweet and sour pork she asked, "On paper, what's your primary source of income?"

"A coffee/banana import business based in Brazil. Sun Life Inc." I told her, "I also have a shit load of investment properties that I snatched up at bargain prices."

"And where is the bulk of your cash?"

"Sparco stole a lot of money from me." I exhaled a deep breath. "I never found out what he did with it."

She spoke a sympathetic. "You took a substantial loss."

"Yeah. But it's a lesson well-earned."

"Set your plans back?"

"Majorly." I sipped my beer.

"Where is the remainder of your money?"

"Gotta lot stashed. The rest is tied up in a few small businesses in the city. Bonds, mutual funds, stocks, real estate, offshore accounts. The bulk of it in the Cayman Islands."

"The International Bank of Zurich is better than the Grand Caymans."

"How?"

"They have experts who can manufacture impeccable trails of money laundered enterprises." She smiled. "I have close ties with them."

"Fill me in."

"Later." She sipped her beer. "The wisest way to hide and launder dirty money is through offshore dummy corporations."

"I'm aware of that,"

She told me, "Tomorrow I'll make a few calls and set up a few for us."

We toasted to a profitable future.

Re-Re regarded me curiously as if she searched for the secrets of my soul. "Your multi-layered street swagger is extremely attractive. An aphrodisiac."

I chuckled. "You're good."

She laughed gently. "What are you talking about?"

"Your top-notch game."

Smiling she said, "I was speaking the truth."

I smiled at her.

Toying with the pearls around her neck she flashed a bright smile. "Your dick taste as sweet as chocolate cake."

"You switch gears quick, don't you?"

"I believe in speaking my mind."

"Honesty. That is what I always want from you."

"I assure you that honesty is all you'll ever get from me."

I smiled at her.

She licked her lips seductively, "You're every woman's fantasy."

I told her, "That was a one-time episode that happened at your office. I don't fuck my employees."

She laughed.

I said, "When you mix business and pleasure it begets confusion."

"You're a party pooper." She playfully pouted.

I chuckled. "You almost had me." I sipped my beer. "You're good at what you do."

"I'm the best at everything."

"A black widow."

She laughed. "Never been called that before."

"It befits you."

"Maybe." She shrugged. "I hate to lose."

"Those who hate to lose, win most of the time. Even if they must cheat."

"That's me. Exude gentleness and politeness but I will bite your fucking head off if the situation calls for it." She said, "There is something undeniable satisfying about conquering and capitalizing, winning in a system designed to oppress people of color. I love the battle. Love to win. Love the euphoria I experience at the apex of victory."

I said, "Sounds like we're gonna have a very fruitful relationship."

She nodded while gazing at me curiously. "You've been constantly texting and trying to reach someone on your phone. Important business?"

I chuckled and slipped my phone into my pocket. "Lil' young broad got my nose wide open."

"Love?"

"Nah. I just met her."

She laughed. "Good sex?"

"Nah. I ain't never been with her."

"Wow, this young lady must be incredibly special. All the women I've heard that you have, and this one has you so distracted."

"Distracted?"

"Yes sir." She smiled. "I've counted exactly sixteen times that you've attempted to call her since we left my office."

"Observant."

"That's what I get paid for."

We conversed for a little while, partaking in quite a few

laughs. She had a good sense of humor. She joked about her sex life. Had a bunch of comedic freaky stories. She was bisexual. Loved pussy. Loved young college age white girls. She confessed that she was secretly having an affair with her stepfather, who just so happened to be as pastor. Said that she hated her mother and wished she were dead. Told me that her mother was an undercover alcoholic that had physically abused her and her younger sister most of their lives. Her sister was her best friend. She said that she had always been a little jealous of her sister because of her extraordinary beauty and saintly ways.

Suddenly Re-Re whispered, her focus on something behind me. "Sheik, I think we have company."

I turned to see what had seized her attention. Leaning on the brick wall of the building was a mean-mugged thug his hand casually under his white T-shirt, his piercing eyes on me. Instinctively my hand eased to the holstered pistol concealed by my suit jacket My eyes simultaneously surveyed my surroundings, searching for more danger.

It did not take long to see that I was boxed in, without even a hint of escape. The shopping center was loaded with over a dozen guys, watching, waiting, wanting something that I had. I just hoped that it was not my life. Nonchalantly, they blended in with the terrain, with the stirring lunch hour crowd their camouflage.

Re-Re's head continually swiveled, her eyes wide "Sheik they're everywhere."

My heart pounded as I thought about what was about to go down.

Re-Re whispered, "Who are they?"

"I suppose a ghost of the past."

A red Range Rover with dark tinted windows and massive chrome rims cruised through the parking lot and parked in a vacant spot a few yards away from us. A moment later a tall, slender woman with smooth skin the color of dark chocolate and a beautiful face stepped from the rear of the Range Rover. She was in a blood-red skirt suit with matching heels, her long thin dreadlocks pinned-up in a beehive. Rose gold and diamonds decorated her body.

I exhaled a breath of relief. If she was present, I knew that death wasn't imminent. My hand released the grip of my gun, and I took a sip of my beer.

It was Rita Johnson, Goldie's' oldest daughter, the official queen of the J.F.M.

Rita stood there for a moment like she was meditating. I could see myself reflected in her oversized mirrored designer shades. Her cellphone chimed and she answered.

Re-Re asked, "Do you know her?"

I nodded, "Yeah. She's an old acquaintance."

"Former lover?"

"Something like that."

My gaze followed Rita as she walked towards me, the click of her heels on the pavement loud and crisp, like the tick of a grandfather clock. She strutted like she was on a runway, her long legs resurrecting memories of our many erotic romps. Those secret sweaty sessions that only her and I knew about had been many moons ago. Back when she was young and naïve. Way before the days of her ascension to the top spot of her family. Back in the old days before she had re-invented herself into a no-nonsense boss of organized crime. A time before life had made her ruthless.

I knew exactly why she was here. She wanted answers. I knew that there would come a point when I would have to deal with the problem head on. I could not avoid it forever. It was precisely the kind of bullshit that I did not need nor want in my life. But again, Crook had forced me into a potentially explosive situation.

I turned toward Re-Re. "Maybe you should leave."

With her gaze fixed on Rita, Re-Re lips barely moved. "No, I'm part of the team now." She flashed a quick smile and glanced at me. "I'm in good hands." She held on to an unexpected poise. "I'm S.F.C. now."

Rita took a seat, across the table from me. Strain was written all over her soft, sweet face.

I politely greeted "Good afternoon, Rita. It's been a while. To what do I owe the pleasure?"

She took off her glasses and stared at me for a long time. Finally, she said, "I am trying to figure out what gives you the audacity to show your face uptown?"

"The last time I checked, this was America. The home of the free."

Rita said, "You're not welcome uptown."

"I see." My eyes quickly scanned my surroundings. "What's up with all the goons?"

"You can't be trusted, and I need your undivided attention."

I chuckled, "And you expect my undivided attention with this type of bullshit around me."

"Lack of civility," Re-Re spoke in a matter-of-fact tone. "Primitive thinking."

Rita spoke dismissively, "Sheik keep your lil' bitch in her place before I have one of my guys put her in a place where she will never overstep her boundaries again."

Re-Re responded with an edge of sarcasm, "Ewwww I am petrified." She rolled her eyes.

Rita spit in Re-Re's face as if it was the most natural thing to do. And without fuss Re-Re laughed then took a napkin and wiped her face.

I told Rita. "That wasn't lady-like."

She snapped, "Nigga stop playing games. I should have your ass killed right now. You bitch ass nigga."

I held on to my best poker face. "I'm feeling slightly disrespected."

She regarded me with hatred. "You make me sick to my stomach."

"I thought we were friends."

"Fuck you, Sheik!" She snarled, "Where in the hell is my dad?"

I asked, "How would I know the whereabouts of your father?"

Her voice was low, her tone flat. "Because you were the last person to see him before he disappeared."

Of course, I lied and said that I knew nothing of Goldie's disappearance, but I could tell that she was not buying it. I told her that he never made it to our scheduled meeting.

Rita wore a stubborn expression. Her eyes narrowed. "You killed my dad."

"You're embracing those views pretty enthusiastically,"

With a hint of accusation, she spat. "Muthafucka you're hiding something......"

I held up a hand before she could continue. "You're implying that I have knowledge of your father's disappearance. And you're dead wrong."

She looked more frustrated than angry. "Is it money that you want? Are you holding him for ransom?"

"Stop being foolish."

She growled. "Man-up you son-of-a-bitch!"

"You're being extremely confrontational."

"Nigga you ain't seen confrontational yet," she said quickly. "I'm not the same pushover that you used to fuck and dog-out. I can make your life miserable before I bury you."

"So, this is really about you harboring ill-feelings from years ago."

"It's about you being a coward." She pointed her finger at me. "You were a coward then and you're a coward now."

I made no comment. I could not ever remember feeling so stressed.

She furiously blasted me about how I was less than a man and hid behind Crook who was more of a man than I would ever be. She told me that I deserved death for making her abort two of her kids. Her father was everything to her and she warned that if she did not receive any answers from me that she would put a price on my head.

I smelled alcohol on her breath.

The best defense is a strong offense. I said, "Yo, it's clear that you have some personal issues that you need to confront on your own time. But if you threaten my life again, I will put a slug in your face before any of your lil crew can blink." I told her, "I have a reverence for peace. The raw drama of my life is enough to drive the strongest of men insane and I don't need you placing your problems on my plate."

Rita's speech was slow as she dished out threats. She called my bluff knowing good and well that I wouldn't risk my freedom by committing a murder in broad daylight.

Sitting completely still, I absorbed her words. I let her talk without reacting. Patience was the key.

Silence fell between us.

Rita looked at me with wounded eyes. "There is a troubling fact that I cannot ignore. My father is going to see you and is never heard from again. And he was coming to extort you. I know you oh-so-well. You are an arrogant bastard." She spoke with sarcasm, "Nobody pushes around Big Sheik. You dealt with him the same way that you deal with everything that comes against you."

I said, 'Unexpected occurrences happen all the time. On his way to me he must have run into something else."

"That's not satisfactory."

"I'm exercising a great deal of patience towards you and this situation, but…."

She cut me off. "Give me one reason why I shouldn't have you killed right now."

"Either way it doesn't matter to me." I told her, "But for the record, I'm not resistant to discussing your dilemma but I'm not gonna sit here and continue to be disrespected."

She shook her head slowly. "I can't believe that I once loved you."

I stayed silent.

She said, "Sheik, he's my father."

"I'm powerless over this situation."

"The streets are talking. Everyone is pointing the finger at you."

"We're ultimately influenced by what we see and hear." I sipped my beer. "But when did you become someone easily influenced."

"Stop playing with my intelligence."

"Stop slandering my name."

"I need closure. It's torture not knowing."

"I honestly don't know."

"My brothers want you dead."

"Then tell your brothers to come and do it."

"I'm the only thing keeping you alive."

"You give yourself too much credit."

She shook her head. "Your arrogance is gonna kill you." She said, "I'm thoroughly investigating my father's disappearance and if I find out that you're responsible I promise you'll die a slow death."

"It's crazy how everything could go down the tubes with just one mistake, one misjudgment."

"Sheik, I am giving you the benefit of the doubt. I know that you are not that stupid to make such a foolish move." Her eyes narrowed. "It was that dyke bitch Crook. She is stupid enough to make that mistake."

"If you think there's foul play with your father's disappearance then I suggest that you look inside your own unit. Life has taught me to be inclined that no one is trustworthy."

She shifted. "My crew is all family. Blood. Relatives. Same DNA nigga. So don't give me that garbage."

I took a sip of my drink and told her, "If you need my help in any way feel free to reach out to me. Contrary to how you feel about me I still care about your well-being."

She asked in an angry tone, "Bitch nigga do I look stupid?"

Despite my continual show of politeness and respect, inside my anger simmered. Gazing deep into her eyes I held back my anger. "Respect me, Rita."

"You ain't worthy of respect." Her face held a grim expression. "And you gotta couple of days to come up with some info about my dad."

"And, if I don't?"

"Then you're a dead man."

I warned her that I would not submit to her bullshit demands.

She spoke flatly. "Proceed with caution." Then she stood.

I said, "These are a can of worms that don't need to be opened."

She smirked at me. "Fuck you chump." She picked up my beer and gulped it down. "If I don't hear from you, I'll take it as a sign of disrespect." And with that she turned to leave, followed by her small army of goons.

I took a deep breath and told Re-Re, "Under such hostile conditions it's gonna be almost impossible to maneuver around and conduct my business."

Her tone was confident, her voice smooth. "Don't worry boss let me handle all of that. You need to focus on that bitch."

"Yeah."

"And you just do what you do best."

"What's that?"

"Be a boss!"

Chapter Twelve
WILLOW

Supreme excellence consists in breaking the enemy's resistance without fighting. —*Sun Tzu*

"Re-Re is going to kill me," I said as I glanced at all the shopping bags I toted. "I've charged over ten thousand dollars to her credit cards."

Mya laughed. "That's something extremely small in comparison to her whopping bank account."

"Yeah, I guess you're right."

"You know I'm right." She giggled and teased in a mocking tone "And she does not care. You are her spoiled precious princess."

"Stop it."

We laughed.

Mya was cool and fun to be around. We had been acquainted for about a week. She was the 16-year-old daughter of one of my sister's wealthy clients in New York City. Under Re-Re's supervision, Mya's father had sent her down to Charlottesville for a two-week tour of UVA. The school was on her shortlist of prospective universities. Re-Re had asked me to hang-out with her and show her around while she was in town.

It was Saturday evening, and we were strolling the crowded Fashion Square Mall. Like me, she was carrying all kinds of shopping bags, spending her dads' money.

We had taken a break from our shopping spree to grab a bite to eat at Chick-fil-A. The restaurant was packed but we managed to find a table in the rear corner near the restrooms.

I sipped my lemonade. "I know a good spa on Barracks Road that we can visit when we leave here."

"Get pampered a little?"

"Stress has me tense. I need a good massage."

"And I could use an avocado facial."

"You're always worried about that pretty face of yours."

We exchanged smiles.

Mya was beautiful and everywhere we went everyone always let her know it. She resembled the model Naomi Campbell in her younger years So much it was scary.

I took a bite of my chicken sandwich and almost choked when I saw Sheik step into the restaurant. I thought my mind was playing tricks on me. I had to take a second look to see if it was really him. Yep, it was him. It felt as if the oxygen in the room had left.

Hooked on Sheik's arm was an extremely beautiful woman with long flowing hair. She looked to be a mixture of Asian and African American descent. She had the body of a super model, her crimson dress intimately hugging her graceful curves.

They shared smiles and laughs, a unique familiarity living between them. Strangely, I drew jealous.

They ordered and ended up in a booth in the front. A minute or so passed before they were joined by an attractive chocolate-skinned sister who also had super-model looks. Donned in a royal blue mini-skirt and White blouse she kissed them both on the lips with a quick peck and slid in the booth.

I studied both women critically. They were intriguing and mysterious, naturally sex, both beaming with sensuality and confidence. The sight of them made me angry.

Turning my attention to Mya as she talked my ear off

about fashion, I forced myself not to watch Sheik. But I could not get him out of my head. The curiosity had been eating at me, refusing to go away. I wished that I were anywhere but in the same room with him.

I found myself watching him, my gaze settled on his face. I wanted to look away, but I couldn't manage it.

In the company of those two goddesses, he was relaxed like he is the Zen master of calmness. I grew angry, hatred choking my heart.

As if he felt the heat of my gaze, he suddenly looked at me. Our eyes locked in an intense stare down. My heart skipped a beat. He simply watched me, his expression nonchalant. I looked away, diligently avoiding his gaze. Time passed with incredible slowness.

Sheik nodded at me, and I didn't respond. My eyes refused to leave his face. He shrugged apologetically with an atoning smile.

He mouthed the words *I'm sorry*. I looked away refusing to entertain a counterfeit apology.

Maya and I finished our meal then gathered our bags. I dreaded the fact that I had to walk past Sheiks table. I could not stand seeing him with not one but two women who made me look homey in comparison. At least their constant giggles portrayed the fact that they were bimbos.

I gathered the courage to make the journey.

As we walked to the exit Maya asked, "Willow are you okay?"

I cleared my throat. "Yes. Why do you ask?"

She laughed and nodded towards the table where we had sat. "You left your purse."

"Shucks." I forced a chuckle. "My mind is somewhere else."

Hurrying back to the table my legs felt rubbery. My heart was racing, my palms growing damp.

As soon as I grabbed my purse, I spun around to find Sheik standing a few feet away staring at me with a boyish smile.

Forcing myself to think straight I asked, "What do you

want?"

"You."

Why did he have to be standing in front of me smelling so fresh looking so good in his Timberland's, blue jeans, desert tan V-neck sweater and Yankees baseball cap.

Sheik smiled at me. "I owe you an apology."

"An apology?"

"Yeah. I apologize for my lack of composure."

"Lack of composure?" Frowning I said, "I can't believe you're actually minimizing what you did to me."

"I'm not minimizing anything."

His nonchalance made me angry, and I took a step to leave but Sheik grabbed my arm and held me in place.

He asked, "Why haven't you returned any of my calls?"

I yanked my arm out of his grip. "I've moved on, now please get away from me."

"Moved on, what does that mean?"

"It means that I don't want anything to do with you."

He looked longingly into my eyes. I glanced at Maya she was standing near the exit watching me with inquisitive eyes. I signaled for her to give me a moment.

Sheik exhaled hard. "I thought that we had established a friendship."

"Friends don't violate trust."

"You have the right to be angry, but I'm extending a hand of peace."

I hissed resentfully, "You tried to rape me. Count it a blessing that I did not report it."

"Rape?"

I snapped, "Yes, Rape."

He laughed. "You have a twisted imagination. It was an attempted seduction."

"Is that what they call rape these days?"

"Come on Willow, it was poor judgement."

"It was a terrifying experience."

He frowned and his gaze intensified. "Get rid of the victim mentality. You were enjoying it."

I gasped. "You have some nerve!"

"I credit myself with being a pretty decent guy, and deep down you know that I am."

"You're a man with a depraved mind."

He responded calmly. "You don't believe that."

"You've proved it"

"You need to stop playing and embrace your role as my future wife."

I drew in a long breath. "What do you want from me?

"I want the opportunity to experience the comfort of your soul."

"No." I spoke flatly. "You want what all men want. Sex."

He shrugged. "Maybe you're right. But what if you're wrong and miss the opportunity to experience true love?"

I glanced at the two beautiful women sitting at his table.

He told me, "I'm the only one alive that can make you happy."

"Your overconfidence reeks of desperation."

"Come here." He reached for me.

"No, I don't want you around me." I took a step back.

"Resentment is like drinking poison then waiting for the other person to die."

"I have no resentment."

Rubbing his chin he said, "Tell the truth and shame the devil."

"I always speak truthfully."

"Liar.

"You're being immature."

"And you look tired and defeated."

"I'm an extremely busy person."

He said, "Busy nurturing a bunch of dead relationships."

"My relationships are none of your business."

He licked his lips. "When you needed a counselor, all of you was my business."

"Stress wrecked my judgement."

He rubbed his neck, "I wanna be your friend."

My tone was ice-cold. "You do not need me as your friend. You already Have two friends over there waiting on you."

He chuckled, "Jealousy."

"Never." I whined feebly, "You can have any woman you want. Why won't you just let me be?"

He brushed a lock of my hair from my face. "Because being around you is like a deep tissue massage for my soul."

"You're a man with a well practiced game of persuasion."

"Nah I simply recognize excellence where others ignore it. I know your value."

"So does the devil."

He exhaled a deep breath. "The brief time we spent together revealed a deep well of affection inside of me that I didn't know was there." He paused a moment then said, "In an extremely personal way the misery in your eyes feels like mine. We are destined to be together."

"You sound like a stalker."

"I'm a realist."

"We had one date."

"One date that was more meaningful than every date combined that I ever been on. We connected."

His persistence was soothing my resistance, but I continued to fight his overwhelming charm.

I told him. "I was vulnerable, and you took advantage of it."

"I think we both took advantage of each other." I looked at him, but I did not say anything.

After a moment of silence I said, "Look I have to go. God bless you and I wish you well."

Without another word I picked up my bags and left him standing there.

As we walked up the mall Mya said, "Slow down, you act like the devil is chasing you."

"He is."

"Who was the handsome guy you were talking to?"

"The devil."

"The devil sure is gorgeous."

"If you don't want the fruits of sin, then stay out of the devil's garden."

"A man that fine is worth the risk."

"You sound stupid."

"Damn Willow I was just joking."

"I'm sorry for snapping. It's stress."

As soon as we stepped out into the cool night, I stopped, closed my eyes, and took a deep breath of fresh air. So much confusion was in my heart draining my joy, eroding my peace.

I glanced behind me checking to see if Sheik had followed me.

Maya asked in a concerned tone. "Are you sure you're, okay?"

I nodded.

She placed her bags on the ground and asked, "Then why are you crying?"

I shrugged. She pulled me into her arms and embraced me. I dropped the bags on the ground and hugged her.

A few moments later we were strolling to my car. I glanced back at the exit of the mall. Thought I would see Sheik running behind me. Sort of hoped that he would.

I am a firm believer that God answers all prayers and sometimes the answer to the prayer is a no.

Chapter Thirteen
SHEIK

A friend loveth at all times, and a brother is born for
adversity.
—King Solomon

Crook said, "I'm on my way outta the door right now nigga, so stop calling my phone."

"You are gonna be late for your own funeral."

"Shit! I hope that I am."

Yawning, I told her, "Hurry up." Then I ended the call and turned the A.C. on high.

I was sitting in my Range Rover, parked in front of Crook's apartment building. I was waiting for Crook so we could hit the breakfast buffet at Woodgrill Buffet, her favorite restaurant.

Today was her 33rd birthday. It had been a long-time tradition for us to eat breakfast at Woodgrill Buffet, go shopping, and then catch a movie. This was exactly how she liked to honor the day that she came into the world.

Many times, over the years, I had offered her several grand gifts, like taking trips to somewhere out of the country or throwing her a mega birthday bash but she had always declined. She liked it simple and private. Always said that her birthday wasn't a big deal.

I had been waiting for almost fifteen minutes and was growing impatient. But when she finally stepped outta her apartment, I found that the wait was well worth it. I had to do a double take to make sure that it was really her.

My jaw dropped.

Crook was wearing a knee-high, powder-blue sundress that melted around her sensual curves like a second skin. Her trademark cornrows were retired, replaced by a classy do, her long hair cascading past her shoulder's. A pair of metallic-toned sandals with a small heel complemented her diamond jewelry.

Standing on the stoop of her building she stood there for a moment as if she were scared to take a step. She slipped on her sunshades and glanced up the block, then her gaze rested on my Range Rover. Nervously fiddling with the small pendant of her necklace her attention went to a group of guys standing on the corner.

I rolled down the passenger side window and yelled, "Yo, come on!"

Full of curses she just stood there hesitating, casting shy glances to see if she was being watched. For the first time in her life, she wanted to look like a lady.

As she took her first step off the stoop, a brief look splashed across her face. One I had never seen before. Timid, shy, vulnerable. This powerful woman, who has gangsters shivering in their Timberlands was reduced to a little girl. In a rushed and forced slowness she did her best to saunter to the Range. It was at that moment, a brief forever that I could see her heart exposed. Could she really feel this way? Was there more to her than even I knew?

As soon as she hopped in an alluring fragrance of sweetness engulfed me. Dumbfounded, I checked her out from head to toe. Pedicure, manicure, shaved legs, her lips glistening with a silver-toned lipstick.

"Happy Birthday." Smiling, I asked, 'What's up with the new look?"

"Trying something new for today." She spoke flatly, "Let's go."

Pulling off I glanced at her. "Are you okay?"

"Yeah. I am cool."

"You look good." I cleared my throat. "Sexy."

"Whatever." She sucked her teeth and turned on the music. Settled on Floe-try's, "*Flo'ology*." Staring outta the window she sat there, still as a pond listening to the smooth grooves. Her mind was obviously somewhere else. As I watched her my concern was strong, but my lust was stronger.

I could not keep my eyes off her.

After we ate breakfast, we went to the mall and spent a few hours shopping. Crook was not her usually up-beat self. She had not eaten much and picked over her food the entire time. And we had not talked about much of anything. Concerned, I had pried trying to see what was bothering her, but she had continually brushed me off. Kept our conversation specifically on a business level. Kept avoiding eye contact with me as if she were hiding something.

As Crook and I left the mall, I gotta a call from Brittany, one of my female friends, inviting me to a cook-out at her crib. Said that it was gonna be a bunch of her family and friends celebrating her promotion at work. I asked Crook if she wanted to go to the cook-out and she told me that she did not care one way or the other. So, with hopes of brightening Crook's Day, I hit Interstate-64 and began driving the fifteen minutes that it took to get to Zion Crossroads.

Brittany's an Alicia Keys look alike that earns a good living as a Systems Coordinator at a local community college. She is a bright and high-spirited broad that loves to fuck and has the gift of making me feel like a king. I'd met her a few months ago downtown at an African Art Show, at the McGuffey Art Center. I was searching for an original ivory sculpture, and she offered to help me find one. Conservation led to flirting which led to a couple of drinks at the bar, which led to my house and the rest is history.

Brittany owned a fly little one level rancher on a couple of acres in Fluvanna County. Her country abode was hedged by a forest of tall trees and her nearest neighbor was about a quarter of a mile away. She lived a private life, most of her downtime spent landscaping and gardening, along with throwing her famed cookouts.

Crook and I pulled into the long graveled driveway at a little after four o'clock. Vehicles and people were everywhere, smiles on everyone's faces.

Red plastic cups and beer bottles occupied their hands. Frankie Beverly and Maze blared from the speakers. The aroma of delicious food was thick in the air.

As soon as Brittany saw us step into the backyard, she hurried over to me. Excited, she almost tackled me when she ran into my arms. Squealed how happy she was that I had came. She ecstatically expressed how much she loved Crook's fresh look. To Crook's displeasure Brittany kept showering her with compliments. It wasn't until Crook growled to her an ultimatum of leaving her alone or "get fucked up" that she let it go. Frightened poor Brittany to death.

Brittany insisted that I meet her friends and family, and I did not resist when she held my hand and dragged me around the yard. She introduced me to everyone as her boyfriend. Caught me off guard with that. She bragged about my success and said that I was probably the wealthiest Black man in the city. I even met her parents who inquired about when was I going to marry their daughter.

By the time I met all her folks, I was dizzy. I had been hit with a million and one questions, but I took it all in stride. It all amused me.

Crook had disappeared and while Brittany momentarily took care of her many guests, I slipped away searching for my best friend. I found her on the far end of the property, sitting on a cast iron bench in a clearing of a grove of trees where a small pond sat. She was sipping a beer staring blankly at the still waters. The diamond encrusted floral earrings she had been wearing were sitting on the bench beside her.

I picked up her earrings and took a seat beside her. "You've been quiet and reserved all day. What's wrong?"

Crook drew in a slow breath. "I gotta lotta shit on my

mind."

"Wanna talk about it?"

She murmured something about having to get home soon.

I was silent, gazing at her, amazed at her beauty. All day, I had secretly been smitten over the transformation. Seeing her dressed like a woman stirred up unexplained feelings.

I leaned over and whispered in her ear, "Yo…...I just want you to know that…. uh……I think that you look pretty today."

Her manner was all business. "What are we gonna do about this JFM situation?"

"Did you just hear what I said?"

She ignored my question. "What the fuck are we gonna do about these niggas?"

I exhaled a frustrated breath and stared at the pond. "We're gonna leave the situation alone."

"It's not gonna go away."

I handed her the earrings, picked up a rock, stood, and pitched it, watching it skip across the pond.

I asked, "Why are you worried about that on your birthday? You should be relaxing and enjoying the day. Every birthday should be cherished. It's another year that you are above ground. Alotta dudes ain't make it."

"That's not my concern."

"What exactly is your concern?"

"Me, myself and I."

"You're tripping." I hurled another rock at the pond. "You're entangled in too many petty problems in the streets for you to be truly concerned about yourself."

She spit on the ground beside my feet. "Punk as nigga."

I could not take another moment of her shitty attitude. I snapped. "All day I have been catering to you and your schizophrenic ass, tryna make your birthday pleasant. I've tolerated your slick talking and disrespect long enough. Speak your mind and stop acting like a bitch. If you gotta beef with me then put it on the table so we can deal with it."

"Don't play gangsta with me. My trigger finger is itchy."

"Is that a threat you simple minded muthafucka?"

Standing directly in front of her, I pushed my index finger into her forehead. I wanted to punch some sense into her.

Her expression went vulnerable. "I hate you." Then she stood, pushed me out of her way and marched away, heading down a path that led down to a creek.

Standing there I watched her disappear through the woods. My anger was in hurricane mode, and I took a few minutes to gather myself.

Everyone up in the yard had begun dancing the electric slide led by Brittany. I glanced at the path and exhaled a breath then strolled in the direction where my best friend had vanished.

Crook had slipped off her shoes and was sitting on an old wooden dock. Her feet were in the creek.

I walked up behind her and stood there. "You're going to ruin your dress sitting on that filthy dock."

"Fuck this dress. I don't even know why I put it on, or why I even fixed my hair." She laughed but there was no happiness there. "Lipstick, perfume and fucking makeup, I done went crazy."

"You did it for me."

She did not respond to my accusation. Instead, she said, "The only solution for this JFM situation is to begin killing them off."

"A move like that would be too high-risk."

"I'm not in the mood to play games with these chumps."

"The key to dealing with these dudes is you manage them by letting them think they got the upper hand." I plucked a ladybug from her hair. "Never expose your hand without seeing theirs first. We're gonna maintain that we know nothing of their father's disappearance."

"I hate being on defense, I want this over."

"I wish I had a quick resolution to this problem, but I don't, so exercise patience. Problems test your strength. This ordeal is gonna make us stronger and wiser."

She sighed. "Look what I got us into. I made a big mistake, didn't I?"

"What counts is how you handle yourself after the

mistake."

She stood and slipped her sandals back on. I brushed off the dirt and debris that had collected on her backside. With every swipe of my hand the silk fabric of her dress smoothly slid across her phat ass, forcing sensual thoughts to run through my head. My desires displanted my sanity when I eased behind her, merging our bodies.

Crook groaned. I chuckled when she pushed her ass into me and reached a hand back and gently touched my cheek.

I yawned.

Suddenly the mood switched, and she walked away mumbling curses under her breath.

I shouted, "What is it now?"

She abruptly stopped and turned on her heels. Her lips were tight. She exhaled violently, "How are you gonna yawn during one of our special moments?"

Slowly walking towards her, I replied, "I have been busy for like two weeks straight. No rest. I'm suffering from sleep deprivation."

She yelled at me, "You are spreading yourself too thin. You need to concentrate on what matters."

We were toe-to-toe.

I said, "The last time I checked, I was the one steering this ship."

"You're slacking. You're slipping. You're blind and can't even see."

"My vision is what got us where we are."

Frowning she said, "If your vision were so sharp you would have remembered that we had a meeting in D.C. with Fats. But where were you?"

I snuffed, "Damn." I admitted dispiritedly. "I forgot."

"I called you a million times. You never answered." There was something desperate in her expression. "I was worried about you. And you ain't even check in for three days. With all this shit going on, I thought that you were dead. Then, you pop up yesterday like everything is supposed to be all right."

I spoke regretfully, "Kenya and I drove down to Virginia Beach for the weekend."

Her jaw tightened. "It has always been about you and your hoes. Never about what really matters."

"Is that where all of this attitude stems from?"

"You just don't get it do you?"

"Actually, I don't. Why don't you enlighten me?"

Sarcasm spats from her mouth. "You're the genius. Figure it out."

"For once, can we have a conversation without the contempt and the bickering?"

Her tone was cold. "For once, can you respect me and my feelings?"

I scoffed at her. "Oh, okay this is about your jealously?"

She shook her head. "Nah nigga. It's about my issues…...our issues. It's about my heart. You fucking with all these bitches ain't settling with me. I can't take it no more."

We stared uncomfortably at each other.

I spoke somberly. "I don't want you to have unreasonable expectations of what I can offer you in terms of a relationship."

Her eyes revealed nothing.

I told her, "False expectations rob you of your joy, your peace."

She winced like she has been stung by a bee. "I don't have peace or joy if it ain't with you. I don't wanna live if it ain't with you."

She looked away. Probably wishing she had not uttered those words. We both were silent for quite a while.

She took a deep breath and spoke softly, but urgently, "I have to get this shit off my chest." She asked directly, "Do you love me?"

"Of course I do."

"No!" She exclaimed. "Do you really love me? Like…....you know…....like…....like, wanna be with me love?"

"Crook." I paused to gather my thoughts. "You are my best friend and of course I love you. You're my other self. But us being a couple is not gonna happen. It would not even feel right."

She snapped, "It feel right to me."

"All of this because we fuck every now and then?" I asked, "What happened to the hard I-don't-give-a-fuck Crook?"

With sadness in her eyes she replied, "She fell in love."

I grimaced and told Crook. "You gotta protect this business we built rather than your selfish personal interest."

Shaking her head slowly she said, "I ain't nothing more than a cheap thrill to you ain't I? You put me in the same category with all the rest of them hoes that you got on call, don't cha?"

"You know that's not true."

"When we make love, you express what I really am to you. It's so obvious."

"You're receiving the wrong signals."

"I'm not stupid, when you kiss me…...touch me…...hold me…...fuck me…….eat me…...you cherish me like I'm your all."

I admitted, "Okay I'm gonna keep it real. I've been concerned about a lot concerning us."

"I made myself look like a damn fool for you."

"But you're beautiful."

She blushed. "Am I really?" Her hand traced the scar on her face. "Do you really mean it?"

I spoke truthfully, "Sexy and gorgeous."

Her lips parted as if she wanted a kiss.

"Hey, you guys are missing all of the fun!" Brittany shouted cheerfully as she hurried down the path. "We are doing the *Soul Train* line."

Crook turned to me and whispered "Do not make any plans tonight. I wanna finish this conversation. I'm staying with you tonight."

I nodded.

Brittany came to me and wrapped her arms around me. We shared a quick kiss.

Crook looked away, disgust broadcasted on her face.

Brittany asked, "Why did you disappear?"

I lied. "I was showing Crook all of the property."

Brittany beamed. "Yeah, isn't it wonderful?"

I asked, "So, what's up?"

146

Brittany replied. "We are going to party all night. Everybody is waiting for the sun to go down, so it will cool down a little bit."

I glanced at my watch. "Well, I'm gonna run Crook home and I should be back later."

Brittany grew disappointed. "Shucks. Crook, my cousin Kiana wanted to meet you. She is into girls too, and she thinks you are beautiful."

Crook spoke flatly, "Not interested. I got something special waiting for me when I get home." She glanced at me.

With a teasing tone in her voice Brittany asked, "Well, well, well, who is the special little lady?"

Crook threw back her head and cracked up with laughter. "If you only knew." Then she walked away heading up the path.

Holding Brittany close to me we shared a deep kiss.

She purred, "Please tell me that you're spending the night with me."

"We'll see." I yawned. "Let me get her home then I'll call you."

She whispered in my ear, "Do you want a blow job before you go?"

I chuckled. "I'll take a raincheck."

"Oakey dokey."

I patted her ass. "Lets' go before Crook throws a tantrum."

"We definitely don't need that."

"Nah, we don't need that."

Chapter Fourteen
SHEIK

Pride goeth before destruction, and an haughty spirit before a fall.
—King Solomon

It was a muggy Monday morning, and I was grabbing grocery bags from the back seat of my Range Rover, while thinking about Re-Re.

She had called me fifteen minutes ago and said that she had something extremely urgent to discuss with me. The pressing tone in her voice had consumed me with curiosity.

Right when I shut the door and turned to walk towards my building, Re-Re's brand new candy apple red Porsche 911 GT3 zoomed into the parking lot. She almost hit an elderly white lady walking her dog as she beelined to the parking space beside mine.

My all-purpose pit bull in the legal world climbed out the Porsche looking like a wealthy power broker, sporting a business suit the same color as her car. Her hair was in a sophisticated bun, and she had a briefcase in her hand.

"It's a fucking sauna out here." She growled at me. "This is fucking crazy for October."

She flashed a smile as her eyes grazed over the full length of my body. "Don't you look unusually shabby this morning."

I had on sneakers, gym shorts and a white t-shirt.

"I just threw something on." I yawned. "Quick grocery run."

"I didn't know that kings did their own grocery shopping."

We shared a laugh as we headed to the building.

In the elevator ride up she ranted on about how she was sick and tired of the hot weather.

In the kitchen I had began putting up the groceries when Re-Re sashayed in and settled on a stool at the center island. She had slipped outta her shoes and jacket.

I asked, "What was so important that you had to rush over here so early in the morning."

"We have a potentially disastrous predicament in front of us."

My eyes were glued to her perky tits that looked as if they were about to bust through her white buttoned-down blouse.

She said, "Here I am with some weighty info and you're hungry for my breast."

"Okay I'm listening." I smiled. "Way to stay focused." I teased, "You better stay focused, or I will ship your ass outta here. You are expendable."

She laughed. "Is that so?" She asked, "How has my job performance been thus far?"

"Mediocre." I chuckled.

With a smile she exclaimed, "Mediocre! More like stellar. In the month that, I have officially been your consigliere I have made moves that would have taken you, at least a year without me." She winked. "I have made several sound investments and business moves. I've connected you to some immensely powerful people."

I teased. "You've fucked all of them too didn't you. Every single one."

She gasped and laughed. "What a tasteless remark."

She followed me into the living room where I plopped down on the couch and turned the television on. She took a seat beside me, folding her legs underneath her.

I asked, "What's up?"

She spoke in a defeated voice. "I have bad news."

"Spit it out."

"I have a friend who is the personal assistant to the Deputy Director of the DEA here in this district."

I raised a brow. "That sounds interesting."

She cleared her throat. "The DEA is investigating you."

I shrugged. "That ain't nothing new."

"This is different." Her voice inflected a serious tone. "Tom Lawson, the DEA director suspects that you are fucking his wife. He's launched and informal under the radar investigation, solely motivated by humiliation. He is furious to find out that his wife is having an adulterous relationship with a notorious drug lord."

My heart rate accelerated and suddenly I did not feel so good.

She said, "He's become obsessed with getting you."

I asked, "How did he find out?"

"He followed her one night when you two met up at the Doubletree Hotel."

"Shit." I asked, "And you're sure about this?"

"Positive."

She told me, "His personal assistant, Julia Duncan is a lover of mine. I trust her."

I stayed silent and meditated on her words. I have always been a general that adjusted my tactics to whatever situation I was confronted with, but this was different. A DEA big wig with a personal vendetta was colossal. It was like being attacked by a hungry shark as I swam in the middle of the ocean. Chances for survival was slim.

Re-Re expelled a deep breath. "He's digging into your income records, financial info, tax records, everything."

"Do I have anything to worry about on that end."

"No. All of that is in order. Thanks to your attorney prior to me your financial history is immaculate. I only made better what was already excellent."

"Okay advisor, earn your paycheck and advise me."

"Well for the time being, stay away from narcotics. I know that is your livelihood, but I recommend that you avoid handling any of it. You are being closely watched. He has you under surveillance."

She sat up, opened her briefcase, grabbed a manila envelope, and handed it to me. She said, "And I certainly would stay away from this guy's wife."

The envelope was full of surveillance photographs of me hanging out in various places throughout the city. The only ones that alarmed me were the ones of me on South First. The entire hierarchy of my organization were together in quite a few photos, all of us with wide smiles. That proved association. If the pressure ever came with a federal conspiracy, it would be impossible to deny that we knew each other.

I had to admit, the agents taking the photos were good because I had never had a hint of their surveillance, and a lot of the photos were in broad daylight. I decided at that very moment to distance myself from all the fellas. They were the ones that handled the coke, not me. I had no reason to be around any of them. That was Crooks job.

There were a few photos of me and dude's wife together. Nothing that suggested that we were intimately involved. There were shots of us standing outside of a movie theater downtown, but that's it.

Re-Re had eased up beside me, her breast pushing up against my shoulder. Her gaze was fixed on the photo of Liz. She spoke gently. "She's very pretty." She took one of the photos from my hand and inspected it closely. She said, "She looks like she could've been a model in her early years."

"Letting my dick lead the way has gotten me some very unwanted attention." I released a breath of frustration and dropped the photos on the coffee table. "Director of the DEA. He got a lot of pull in Washington. If he chooses to play dirty, he can fuck up my life." I sat back on the couch and ran a hand over my head.

Re-Re assured me, "This is only a minor obstacle. You are too smooth to get snagged by this peckerwood." She smiled. "Your budding legitimate empire is an immaculately ordered entity that absolutely cannot be connected to your cocaine business. They can bring the best IRS auditors in the agency, and it would be a waste of time"

I nodded in agreement because I knew that she was right. I was sure of it. Covering all angles was her greatest strength. Ever since she had taken full control of my business affairs, she had proven that she was the best. A master of her craft, she had been the missing link.

A priceless asset like Re-Re was a rare find. Especially, one who was as cunning, immoral, and corrupt as her. She played the game dirty and had the rare ability of bringing out the wickedness of people who usually prided themselves on their moral and decent conscience. So-called good wholesome, members of society, got the criminal spirit pulled outta them by Re-Re. Then she manipulated them to her benefit which was my benefit. Judges, prosecutors, police officers, and city council members had been seduced by her deceitful mind and then exploited to further and support my agenda.

Re-Re looked me in the eye. "This is the first time that I've seen you intimidated by someone."

"I'm not intimidated." I exhaled a deep breath. "Just thinking about what I'm up against."

"Relax." She smiled, moving her had to my crotch. "You are a king. Untouchable. We will simply adapt to existing circumstances."

I stood and walked over to the window and gazed out at the city. "Last man standing is the winner."

"And you will be the winner. You are a revolutionary that is destined to fade into the world of legitimate big business."

I turned and looked at her sitting on the couch, her eyes bright with admiration. I held a genuine fondness for her.

I told her, "Gotta take the bitter with the sweet, right?"

"Separate yourself from your crew." She said, "Disappear for awhile and live off the grid."

"Yeah, I was thinking the same thing." I walked over to

her and gently ran the back of my fingers over her check. "Good job counselor."

"Anything for my king." She asked with an affectionate smile, "Of all the women in the world what possessed you to stick your dick in the Director of The DEA's wife?"

I released a soft laugh. "I didn't know who her husband was until afterwards." I spoke seriously, "But fuck that cracker. I'll murder that chump."

"That is a little too extreme. You will have the CIA after your ass and absolutely nobody beats the CIA. Just ask Saddam Hussein and Osama Bin Laden."

We shared a laugh.

I plopped down on the couch beside her. "One of my mottos is nothing should ever catch me by surprise. Always expect the unexpected. But I swear I ain't expect this one."

"Confucius once said that the flame that burns twice as bright, last half as long." She flashed a smile, "Reduce the radiance of your flame. Go into vacation mode. Let me and Crook run your empire. She'll handle the sweat and toil portion, and I'll guide her in an appropriate manner, that ultimately reflects your style and wisdom."

I scratched my head. "That'll take a lot of trust on my part."

She gently touched my cheek and smiled. "Take some time off and chase that little girl that you told me about."

I shook my head to clear it. "Seems like that is a dead end. Shorty girl refuses to see me. Won't even return my calls." I spoke with a weak attempt at a smile. "I've taken everything from dreams to lives, and for the sake of my sanity, I can't get her pussy."

"You are the cities premier playboy, a heartbreaker." She smiled. "Maybe she's heard about you."

I spoke dryly. "Yeah, whatever." I admitted. "Feeling helpless is some miserable shit."

"We will come out of this situation unscathed and on top."

I chuckled. "You should be a motivational speaker."

Smiling broadly, she said, "I am good, aren't I?"

We both laughed.

Re-Re said, "I have a few more friends in the DEA office. One of them is a covert DEA operative. I will make a few calls and cash in a few favors that I am owed. Maybe I can dig some dirt up on this guy."

I told her. "You cannot rely on the thankfulness of favors you have bestowed on others in the days gone by. People catch amnesia as quick as you can catch a cold. You gotta make motherfuckers appreciative for blessings that you will grant them in times to come."

She nodded with a smile.

I said, "Help them understand that it will be in their best interest to promote yours."

"Yes, sir." She giggled. "You are a genius."

"Yeah, whatever." I stood and stretched. A yawn escaped my mouth. "I need a nap."

She gave me a devilish grin. "No, you need some of this good pussy to help ease your stress."

"Yeah, you might be right."

"I'm going to call and cancel my appointments for the rest of the day."

I yawned. "I'll be upstairs."

"Give me a second and I'll be up."

I headed upstairs to the bedroom and collapsed on the bed, trying to collect my thoughts and calm my nerves. I cleared my anxiety a little bit by smoking a blunt. I was certain that I had to take a big step back from everything that was my life. It would be foolish to consider doing anything contrary than what Re-Re had suggested.

As I lay there in the bed listening to the radio Willow was heavy in my thoughts refusing to release her hold on me. It had been a month since our last communication. Every time that I called her, I always got the voicemail. I always left a lengthy message begging her to at least talk to me. Everyday I felt increasingly like a sucker. I don't know what she had did to me that had me so strung out on her, but I could not get her out of my system. Like an addict I was fiendin' for a hit of Willow.

I picked up the phone and called Willow, but she did not answer. Tired of leaving messages on her voicemail I hung up and tossed the phone aside.

A few moments later Re-Re strolled into the bedroom with a martini in her hand. She sat the glass on the nightstand and stripped down to her panties, leaving her clothes neatly draped on the black leather swan chair. Then she climbed on bed beside me and let her hair down.

She relaxed against me and planted a few kisses on my chest.

Re-Re said, "This DEA situation is not as serious as it seems. If you precisely follow my instructions, it will blow over after a while. You must be patient though."

"Yeah, I know." I held her close and tight, appreciating her company. I was stressed but I knew that with Re-Re at the reins of my affairs the chances of me coming out on top were great.

She said, "You are my priority, and you have to trust me to maneuver our ship through this storm."

"I do."

"Really."

"Of course."

I kissed her and she told me that she was gonna spend the entire day with me, spend the night. Said that she had cleared her schedule.

I told her, "Yeah, that's cool."

"Sounds like a plan."

"Tomorrow, look into buying some property in the county. Maybe our first construction venture could be building a sub-division."

"Northern or southern Albemarle County?"

"Northern, going towards the airport."

Her tone was sensual. "Your wish is my command,"

I kissed her forehead. "I suppose that you're cooking me dinner tonight."

"Let's cook out on the grill, relax by the pool and talk money."

"Steaks, potato salad, and corn on the cob."

A sly grin washed over her face, "I can feed you some of this good pussy too. I bet you that would satisfy your hunger."

At that moment we kissed passionately and from that point forward we wrapped ourselves in a blur of sensations, our bodies becoming one.

After our lust apexed we lay there, our sweaty bodies cuddling. We went a long time without speaking. Finally, she kissed my cheek and said, "Your dick is too good." She laughed "Toooooo goooooood."

We both laughed.

She sat up and got outta bed. She stood beside the bed and looked at me with adoration. She was so sexy, her beautiful body without a flaw.

I said, "I have that thing to do Saturday."

She shook her head. "Considering our present dilemma with the DEA, I suggest that you let me handle that thing while you stay as far away from it as possible."

"That's a whole lotta coke. And dude might not deal with you because he doesn't know you."

"Either he deals with me, or he misses out on the sweetest deal he's going to get this side of the Mississippi River."

I smiled. "You do have a point."

"Trust me."

I lied, "I do."

We kissed deeply for a long time then she giggled and went into the bathroom. A moment later I heard the shower running. I was tempted to join her, but I had a lot on my mind. Too much was on my mind. I needed a vacation.

Instead of using either of my cell phones I picked up the satellite phone and called Willow. A few moments later I was surprised to hear Willow soft voice answer, "Hello."

"Willow how are you doing?"

"Sheik?"

"Yeah."

She exhaled a deep breath. "Sheik, I have to go."

"Why are you avoiding me?"

She was silent for a long moment. "Look Sheik, we aren't compatible and have nothing in common. I think…"

I cut her off. "About that episode at your house, I apologize for placing you in such a compromising situation."

"It's more than that."

"So, tell me what it is."

She said, "Look I really don't have time right now."

"Willow."

She cut me off. "Our lives are traveling in two separate directions. I love Jesus and you don't. *The Bible* clearly states in second Corinthians chapter six verse fourteen 'Be not unequally yoked together with unbelievers for what fellowship have righteousness with unrighteousness and what communion have light with darkness."

Re-Re walked into the bedroom with a towel wrapped around her. She came over and climbed on the bed, flipping through the channels on the television. She simultaneously caressed my chest.

Willow said, "We have no future."

I spoke a frustrated. "Tell me that you don't have feelings for me."

"Sheik..."

"Tell me."

Silence.

I asked, "Can we at least have dinner tonight and talk about this face-to-face."

"No, I have to attend a banquet."

I asked, "What time does it begin?"

"At six. My father is the honorary speaker."

"Where is it being held? I wanna come."

She spoke quickly. "No."

"You're killing me with this bullshit."

She spoke firmly. "I'm back with Lamont. We decided to work things out. So, I would appreciate if you would stop calling. I don't want to be rude to you, but please leave me alone. Thank you and God bless."

She hung up.

A deep frustrated exhale rolled from my lips. "Shit!"

Re-Re's voice for soothing. "Boss, forget her. Lay back and relax. I'll take care of you."

Then she crawled over and place her mouth on my manhood and eased all my stress.

As I came in her mouth I hissed, "Ain't this a bitch."

Chapter Fifteen
WILLOW

One change always leaves the way open for the establishment of others.
— Niccolo Machiavelli

Lamont had just backhand slapped me so hard that I forgot where I was. Dizzy and disoriented, I sat on the concrete walkway, crying, rubbing my sore cheek.

He kicked my leg extremely hard, sending a deep pain through my thigh and my soul. I was scared for my life.

Lamont's eyes burned with rage, his chest rising and falling, the sound of his breath like the grumble of thunder. Hatred blanketed his face.

His big athletic frame was tense, fist balled up tight, teeth clenched, ready to distribute a severe beat down to me and anybody who wanted to interfere. He reeked of alcohol and marijuana.

Lamont roared. "This is what you deserve you ungrateful bitch!"

I screamed for someone to help me, my eyes darting back and forth over the many faces that were gawking at me. No one came to my aid.

Hopeless, I sat on the walkway of the frat house, distressed and horrified. It seemed as if the party had stopped, and everybody had poured out of the frat house and was standing on the porch observing the humiliating spectacle of me getting thrashed.

Lamont kept cursing at me, calling me demeaning names, pushing me down every time I tried to stand. My plea for mercy were ignored.

All of this because I'd popped up at a party at his frat house and caught him in an upstairs bedroom having a rump in the sack with two white girls. I should've been the one angry. Not him.

For the last couple of weeks, we'd been inseparable, doing everything together. I'd thought that we had made great leaps and bounds over the hurdles that had formerly afflicted us.

Clad in his boxers and sneakers, LaMont stood in the hot and humid night perspiring excessively.

He growled through clenched teeth. "I took you back after you dated someone else and you come here, to my party, making a scene in front of everyone, because I'm having a little fun." He grabbed my hair and dragged me across the yard.

A few guys from the football team tried to restrain him, but he swung a few wild punches at them. The cowards cowered and left me alone to fend for self.

LaMont had went completely insane. He grabbed me by my arm and flung me across the yard like a rag doll, sending me crashing into the tall hedges that bordered the yard.

My life flashed before my eyes. If I remained there, I'd surely die. I was convinced of that.

Jumping to my feet, I ran for my life. Heading towards the Rugby Road Ridge, I stumbled and fell but got right back up. I ran hard, with one shoe on. Sprinting as if the devil himself was on my heels. I ran until I couldn't run any longer. Ran until my dinner was laying on the concrete in front of me.

Until my chest felt like a raging fire. Until my legs refused to move, and my feet ached beyond compare.

I'd ran the entire length of Rugby Road and ended up sitting on the steps of the Rotunda. It took quite a while to regain a semblance of composure. Finally, when my breathing returned to normal, I took my cell phone from my pocket and called the one person that I knew could help me.

As soon as Sheik answered the phone, and I heard his voice I began crying. Fighting through my tears I told him where I was and that I needed him badly. Without hesitation he told me that he was on his way. I sat there, waiting, wanting something that I couldn't identify. All I knew was that I needed to feel safe and secure.

One of my shoes were gone. My khaki capris were now stained brown and green, a little bit of blood smudged here and there. My blouse was now without a single button, and I had to hold it closed with my hands. I could only imagine what my face and hair looked like.

I felt so alone, so lonely. Staring at the chipped nails of my feet I cried my heart out. Kept asking the Lord why he had placed me in such a horrible situation. Bitter, I cursed Lamont. Couldn't understand how he had transformed into such a monster. I have never seen him that way and didn't know that he could be so cruel. I suspected that the white powder around his nostrils has something to do with it. That and the alcohol.

There was a feeling that I was trying to get rid of, a feeling that frighten me to the core of my being. I tried to pray it out of me, but it refused to flee from my mind, my soul, my spirit. Rage, consumed me, and for the first time in my life I cursed God. At that moment in time, I hated the Lord, and I hated that I hated Him. I wondered why I'd grown so malicious. I couldn't understand why I was mad at God.

The tears wouldn't stop running.

A motorcycle speeded up the red-bricked walkway leading to the Rotunda and stopped in front of me. Sheik hopped off the bike came straight to me and held me while I cried in his arms. He held me for quite a while. Kept asking me what had happened. When I didn't reply he didn't push on. He simply embraced me in his arms and kissed me on the top of my head. Patiently, he waited until I was cried out until I could speak.

His voice was gentle. "What happened?"

I told him everything, not leaving out a single detail.

He asked calmly, "Where is dude right now?"

I replied, "Probably still at the party."

He asked me where my car was, and I told him that a friend had dropped me off. Sheik made a phone call to his friend Crook. I listened as he gave her the situation. After he finished his call, he held me in his lap and whispered soothing words of comfort to me. Kept repeating that everything was going to be fine. The tone of his smooth voice relaxed me. Deep in my heart I knew that everything would be okay. It had been almost a month since I last talked to him, and I found it moving how he had come to my aid without hesitation.

Suddenly, I felt horrible that I had ostracized him so coldly. I'd shunned him simply because of my weaknesses and insecurities. All he wanted to do was express his affection for me by touching me in an intimate way. I've been so selfish refusing to see his point of view, and I really like Sheik. I cared about him so much. I felt another bout of tears coming

The roar of motorcycles made me lift my face from Sheik's chest. Three sporty motorcycles zoomed up and parked beside Sheik's bike. When the riders hopped off the bikes and pulled off their helmets, I was shocked to see an all-female trio.

Sheik spoke gently, "Wait here." Then he walked over to the triad of women. They watched him closely as he talked to them. The tall pretty Latina kept cutting her eyes at me, her glare intimidating.

My attention went to the other two females. Curiosity was bubbling in me, wondering who they were.

The dark-skinned girl's skin was like a starless midnight sky. Her short hair was faded into a neat mohawk, her face cute but rugged. She was masculine and overweight, borderline obese and tall like Sheik. She had on wheat-colored Timberlands, baggy black jeans, and a black hoodie. Her eyes were sneaky, menacing, and frightened me. I saw no life in them. She seemed soulless.

The third girl was more feminine. She seemed almost prissy. Her light-skin was radiant. She had long hair pulled into a tight ponytail. Big doe eyes with a curvy body, skintight jeans, and a V-neck T-shirt under a grey hoodie. When she reached up to scratch her scalp, I caught a glimpse of two guns tucked in a shoulder holster.

The Latina woman snapped. "Nigga you trippin! All of that for that off-brand, wanna-be-white bitch!" She looked over at me and spit on the ground. Her eyes told me that she wanted to hurt me severely. Dressed in all black she looked like the Grim Reaper.

Sheik turned to me and called my name. As I hurried over to him the women climbed on their bikes. I walked into Sheik's arms, snuggling close to his hard body. He told me to tell them where the frat house was located. I gave them the directions.

All of them nodded and said that they knew where it was.

Sheik handed me a helmet and told me to hop on his motorcycle and I did. The engines of the bikes roared as they revved them up. Suddenly, I was hit with a wave of anxiety. The fear of the unknown made me have regrets for calling Sheik. I feared for LaMont's life. Feared that he was about to be killed. Feared that my conscience would forever be seared with the regrets of what was about to happen. Wrath was about to be administered, and no one had to tell me. I knew it. Felt it in my gut.

Sheik shouted, "Hold on!" Then the bike took off at breakneck speed, going so fast I feared the worse.

Racing up Rugby Road the bikes dipped in and out of traffic, breaking all types of laws. Death defying weaves, inches away from smacking poles and vehicles. Had my bladder ready to involuntarily release. In no time at all we were pulling into the yard of the frat house.

When I pulled off the helmet, I saw that the party was in

full swing, Hip-hop booming hard. A few people were loitering on the porch and when they saw us they laughed.

Sheik yelled, "Tell LaMont Carrington to bring his bitch-ass outside!"

A couple of guys ran inside, ready to see a good dose of action. It sickened me to see people so addicted to seeing violence.

Sheik got off the bike and so did I. He slipped off his T-shirt and casually handed me his gun. The heavy weapon was warm, and I was filled with dread as I stared at it. This was my first time holding a gun. I dropped it in the helmet and held it close to my chest.

Sheik was calm standing in the middle of the yard. He had an expression of absolute concentration. The girls had spread out, each of them standing in a different corner of the yard. Their hoods were on, their eyes focused on the house.

Standing there I was frozen with panic and uneasy about what was about to happen. I felt nauseous. My mind was telling me to tell Sheik that it had all been a misunderstanding, a mistake, and that we could walk away without incident. But the aches and pains caused by the cruel beat down rejected all rational thoughts. Instead, I desired to see Lamont get his just due.

Lamont came out of the front door, shirtless and raging, his loud voice, shouting curses. His threats pounded in my head like a bass drum. It seemed as if the entire UVA football team was behind him. Mean scowls and threatening words rolled from their lips. They all were ready for war. Massive warriors of the gridiron, ready to get it on in the streets.

Lamont had Sheik by at least twenty pounds. Standing on the porch, Lamont yelled at Sheik, "Are you the son of a bitch looking for me? Hunh motherfucker! Are you looking for me!"

My body grew rigid. Sheik was restrained and composed when he said, "Ain't no need for all that noise playboy. Come on down and dance with me. Let's get this shit popping."

The team went to rush Sheik led by Lamont but halted quickly when two gunshots rang out in the night. The three girls all held two guns in their hands pointed at the group of athletes.

The Latino girls snapped. "If I see a motherfucker flinch, I will empty both guns into the crowd. If you think I'm playing, then try your hand." Then she shot at Lamont's feet? The shot was so close that the splinters of wood from the porch landed on his sneakers. She shouted, "Now Mr. Star quarterback, step into the yard. My big Homie wanna see you."

Like a scolded child Lamont slowly stepped down the stairs, his eyes darting back-and-forth to all the guns on him. The crowd was quiet, stunned.

Moving as swift as a gazelle, Sheik attacked him. They wrestled hard. Lamont was stronger and he grabbed Sheik and overpowered him. Slammed Sheik hard on the ground, but Sheik was more agile than Lamont, more elusive, moving as slick as a snake dipped in oil. His punches were like a hurricane, connecting all over Lamont's body. Sheik reminded me of one of those UFC fighters that my Uncle Luke loved to watch on pay-per-view. He was good. Made everything seem effortless.

Lamont tried to conquer the chiseled warrior, but Sheik was too experienced. Sheik became a predator. Lamont was his prey. With every blow Sheik hit Lamont with the crowd, gasped and cringed. I did too.

The Latino girl shouted, "Finish that chump before the police get here!"

Sheik obliged and did just that. Three mighty blows cracked Lamont's face so hard that it sounded like thunder. Lamont fell like a chopped down tree. Knocked out, his head hit the ground with a loud thud.

Sheik wasn't finished. He viciously stomped Lamont's head into his face was disfigured beyond recognition. If I had not ran over and pulled Sheik away, I was sure he'd kill LaMont, if he hadn't already.

Sheik pointed to the motorcycle and shouted to me, "Get your ass on the bike!"

As insane as it sounds, I was utterly turned on by his

aggressiveness. I ran over and hopped on the bike.

What Sheik did next excited a heat deep down in the part of me that made me a woman. He dragged LaMont over to the concrete walkway and placed LaMont's right hand on the edge of the walkway. Then Sheik stomped LaMont's hand repeatedly, shattering bones with every stomp. That was LaMont's throwing hand. The golden hand that was to take him to the NFL.

Sheik left LaMont's fingers mangled and deformed. His career was over.

When Sheik finished, he looked at the stunned crowd and shouted, "Fuck UVA Football!"

As police sirens got closer, we sped away on the motorcycle. As we rode away, I held Sheik and thought about what he'd just did for me. I'd been a spectator to a ferocious violence that had left me horror-stricken yet intoxicated with infatuation. An unreasonable passion connected me to the man in front of me. Squeezing his torso, I felt so in tune with him, as if we had become one in body and soul. My hero had saved me. Protected me. Defended my honor. He did that for me after I'd been so mean to him.

The speed of the bike was an aphrodisiac. Our closeness arousing. I was itching in a place where it shouldn't be. A secret place that was sacred.

Sheik sat on my couch talking on his cell phone. His words were heated and forceful, an argument about me and what had just transpired. I instinctively knew that it was the Latina girl. He defended me, shouting, cursing. Dished out threat after threat.

Standing in the kitchen I eavesdropped. I was touched by his defense of me and my issues. He really cared about me. I waited until he was finished with the call before I walked in. I found Sheik slowly pacing the floor with distress on his face.

I went to him and hugged him. "Thank you."

"For what?"

"For helping me."

"Ain't nothing worse than a child molester, a rapist, or a woman beater. Every one of them is a coward. Dude should've never put his hands on you."

"I really appreciate what you did for me."

He sighed. "I gotta go."

I spoke quickly, desperately, "No, please don't leave me."

He gave me a skeptical look. "I don't need this game-playing-bullshit of yours."

"No games, I want you here….we….we need to talk."

He was silent for a long moment, his gaze serious. "I thought that all you needed was an on-call bodyguard."

I exhaled a deep breath. "No." I paused, gathering my thoughts. "Sheik, I was confused. I apologize for treating you so frigid, but I wasn't thinking clearly."

"And now you are?"

"Yes."

He smirked, "Dude must've knocked some sense into you huh?"

I pushed away from him and stood there with my feelings hurt. "That was so wrong. Please stop being mean to me." My eyes grew moist. "I don't deserve this."

"You deserve the truth."

"And what is the truth?"

"The truth is that you're a scared, spoiled little brat that hides behind religion."

"That's not true."

"Look in the mirror. Have the courage to see what's inside you."

"The spirit of God resides in me."

"That's not what I see at all."

"I beg your pardon."

"You're a fucking hypocrite. You preach love and kindness but shun it. You preach turn the other cheek, but tonight you took part in an eye for an eye. You came in your little panties when I fucked your boyfriend up. You think I ain't notice that did you? It was all on your face like a post fuck sweat."

"Get out of my house!"

"You ain't gotta kick me out. I was on my way out."

"I never want to see you again."

He laughed as he walked away. "Until that nigga fuck you up again."

I screamed, "Fuck you!" And as soon as those words left my mouth, I clasped my hands on my mouth. Couldn't believe that I'd just uttered such profane words. I had no idea where that came from.

Sheik laughed as he walked out. He said, "Check your loyalties." Then he left me alone to deal with myself.

Depressed I bathed, soaking my wounds and aches. I cried a lot, wondering why God was taking me through so much tribulation. What had I done to deserve such trials.

As I lay in bed I kept replaying the fight in my head. Sheik had been so valiant. He was like this Superman that had no equal. The guns, the drama, the gangster girls, everything had been so exciting and adventurous. As I thought about it all I experienced an adrenaline rush. I was so turned on by it all. Erotic thoughts scampered through my head, and I imagined Sheiks face between my thighs. My hero, the man of my dreams, a man that I want with all my heart.

I picked up my cell phone and called Sheik. He answered on the first ring.

Before he uttered a single word I apologized.

His voice was gentle. "I apologize too."

"Sheik. I'm confused about a lot of things in my life. You are the primary source of my confusion."

"I mean you no harm."

"I know." I released a sigh. "But I'm so scared of you."

"Scared of me?"

I admitted. "I'm frightened by how weak I get when I'm around you. I don't trust myself in your presence."

"Do you trust me?"

"Yes."

"Then you should know that I would never place you in a situation that would bring you misery or distress."

"But what you want from me I can't give you."

"We want the same thing." He told me, "We both want to experience this budding love in its fullest potential and that includes becoming one through the act of making love."

"Sheik I……"

He cut me off. "I've never felt this strongly about any woman."

Processing my emotions I remained silent.

He said, "Ever since we've been dealing with each other a lot has changed within me."

"What do you mean?"

"You've made me wanna be a better person. Made me wanna be more of a man that appreciates the many blessings of my life."

"I'm touched."

"And when you walked away from our friendship it made me feel betrayed."

I suggested, "Maybe we could start over."

"Yeah, I'd like that."

"Me too." I smiled. "I'm glad that we talked."

"Friendships are about communication. Dialogue is healthy."

"I get the point."

He asked, "How do you feel?"

"I'm sore all over. Bruised." I sighed. "I thank the Lord that LaMont didn't break any of my bones."

"Dude got what he deserved."

"I agree." I asked, "Do you feel any remorse?"

"Nah." He asked, 'What about you?"

"As cruel as it sounds. No."

He commented, "I wish I could hold you in my arms until you fall asleep."

"That would be wonderful." I asked, "Would it be too much to request that?"

"Just give me the word."

"My sister is staying with her boyfriend tonight. Please come and hold me."

"I'm on my way."

"I'll be waiting."

"Not for long. Open the door."

"Where are you?"

"Sitting in my car across the street from your house."

"What?" I got out of bed and hurried to the front door, I opened it and smiled when I saw Sheik across the street climbing out of his BMW.

He waved.

I asked, "How long have you been there?"

"After I left you, I took the motorcycle home, got into the car, and came back. I was gonna sit outside all night and make sure you were safe."

I ended the phone call and opened the storm door for him to enter. I immediately went into his arms and enjoyed the closeness.

I whispered, "I love you."

He nodded, kissed me then told me, "Go pack some of your things, you're gonna stay at my house tonight."

Without hesitation I scurried away to do as he had requested. My mind was made up; he was my man, and I'd never leave him. I loved him.

Chapter Sixteen
SHEIK

Men are driven by two principal impulses, either by love or by fear.
—Niccolo Machiavelli

My cell phone vibrating on the bed beside me startled me awake. Sunlight blazed bright through the windows as a cool breeze swept through the open doors of the balcony. Stretching I released a long yawn and glanced at the clock on the wall – 9:27 a.m. The clashing noises of the city poured into the room mingling with gospel music coming from downstairs.

The phone vibrated again.

I lazily grabbed the phone, yawned, glanced at the number, then answered with a groggy. "Yeah, what's up Re-Re?" I yawned again.

"Boss-man, did I catch you at a bad time?"

"Yeah. I've only had a couple of hours of sleep." I yawned.

"What's up?"

"After church, I'm going to stop by and drop some documents off for your signature."

"The insurance papers for the housing development?"

"Yes." She told me, "I'm going to meet with the contractor tomorrow morning."

"A'ight, cool." I yawned.

She cleared her throat and was silent for a moment before she said, "I was wondering if we could have a quick romp in the sack."

"I got company."

"Kick her out."

I chuckled and yawned. "Nah, she's my future wife."

She whined. "Boss-man I'm stressed. Need your dick to pound my tension away."

"Stressed about what?"

"Family problems. Some drama with my sister."

"Wanna talk about it?"

"No, I want to get fucked."

"Not gonna happen."

"Not even a quickie in the car?"

I laughed, "You're unbelievable."

She said, "I'll stop by after church.

"A'ight."

We hung up.

Reluctantly, I got up, my head and muscles aching, remnants of last night's battle. I went out on the balcony and smoked a blunt while gathering my thoughts. Inhaling the aroma of the city, I gazed out at the smog filled skies.

I took a shower then slipped on a pair of shorts and headed downstairs. I found Willow in the living room, curled up on the couch, reading the *Bible*, the radio tuned to 92.7 KISS FM playing Sunday morning gospel. She was dressed in a pair of lavender silk pajamas bottoms and a white T-shirt adorned with the words, "I Have Faith." Her hair was in a tight ponytail. She looked so innocent, so pure.

"Hey there lil' momma."

She looked up, smiled at me, then got up and came to me,

giving me an unexpected hug. She held me like she loved me. Kissed my lips quickly and told me, "I made breakfast for you. It's wrapped up in the microwave."

"Thank you." I asked, "How was the bed in the guest room? did you sleep well?"

She shrugged. "Didn't sleep much," she responded, returning to her seat on the couch.

I sat on the couch beside her and released a yawn. "I didn't get much rest either."

She spoke apologetically, "I hope I'm not intruding."

"Don't be silly." I told her, "You can stay as long as you need to." I asked, "How do you feel?"

"My body is sore and I am full of restless energy."

I gently ran the back of my fingers over her bruised cheek. She asked, "I look terrible, don't I?"

"Impossible."

"You're too kind."

"It's called honesty."

She shifted her body as if she was suddenly uncomfortable. "My heart is in a dark place."

I pulled her to me and held her close, comforting her. She rested her head on my shoulder.

She confided. "I'm feeling mountains of guilt."

"You didn't do anything wrong."

"Initially I felt joyous and triumphant. But like my dad says, in the end revenge seldom satisfies."

"You don't have the right to feel bad after what he did to you."

"It should not have gone that far. I was distraught and wasn't thinking rationally."

"He got what he deserved. Actually, he got it a little too light."

"That's cruel."

"Life is cruel. Get used to it."

She sighed then a faint smile creased her lips as she gently patted my stomach. "Go eat. You must be hungry."

I went into the kitchen and heated up my plate of food. She had made blueberry pancakes, a veggie omelette, turkey bacon and fried apples.

When I returned to the living room Willows nose was back in the *Bible* as she hummed along to the gospel music. Sitting beside her I got my grub on and didn't interrupt her *Bible* reading.

Occasionally I'd glance at her. Her brows were drawn in concentration. No matter how many times I looked at her I never quite got used to her mesmerizing beauty.

When I'd finished my meal she asked, "How was it?"

"Delicious." I sat the empty plate on the coffee table.

She told me that she had called her family early this morning and gave them the full story of what had happened, minus my name. She'd told them that a stranger had came to her rescue. Told them that she'd left town with her friend Selena and would be staying in Washington D.C. with her for a couple of days. Her entire family was worried. Especially her big sister. Willow had assured them that she was okay and simply needed some time away to clear her head. She told me that the incident had been all over the news networks and ESPN's Sports Center. A city detective wanted to talk to her, but her sister was handling that for her.

She asked, "Am I deluding myself?" There was a long pause. "Is staying here in my best interest?"

"What is your heart telling you?"

"My every instinct tells me that I'm in a safe place."

"Follow your heart."

She nodded while gazing into my eyes then said, "Those women last night…. they were thugs…...gangsters. I saw death in their eyes, especially the Latina girl." She asked, "What type of man has friends like that?"

"A smart one." I chuckled.

She simply stared at me, confusion in her eyes.

I told her, "We all have been acquainted since childhood. They look out for me. The one that you think is Latina is my best friend, Crook."

She was silent for a few moments then asked, "Why did you come to my aid so quickly? Especially after the contemptible way I treated you?"

"Because I consider you a friend, I felt obliged to help you in your time of need."

"It was valiant."

"I want to accommodate you in any way that you need. I'm interested in your sorrows, joys, and whatever other emotion that you go through. I want to learn to make them my own, because I want to be there for you."

She smiled. "I need nothing more in my life than to have you as my friend."

"You've had my friendship all along."

Her voice was low, her tone flat. "Satan teaches doubt then denial." She paused then said, "I doubted your sincerity. I thought that you had ulterior motives."

"My only motive is to experience the fullness of who you are?"

She nodded, smiled, kissed my cheek then left me sitting there and strolled across the living room. She exited the French door that led out to the balcony. I followed her. Found her standing at the railing staring out at the city. I eased up behind her, gently molding my body to hers, enveloping her in my arms. I rested my chin on her head.

She said, "This view is breathtaking."

"It can be yours every day."

"Tempting." She said, "You're full of surprises."

"Is that a good thing?"

She shrugged, "It's exciting."

"I can be boring. You're gonna see that side of me today."

"Boring is cool. I'm convinced that anything is cool when it comes to you."

I told her that my attorney would be stopping by later so that I could sign some paperwork. Willow teased me about my priestly devotion to my business, even on Sundays.

I drew in a short breath. "What'cha thinking about?"

"Still struggling to wrap my mind around everything that occurred last night."

"Forget all of that bullshit."

"Easier said than done."

"You're embarking on a new improved life. Stay focused

on that and only that."

"I assume that you're talking about a new life with you."

"Of course, I am." I told her, "You gotta let go of your past to make way for your bright future."

She was silent.

I hugged her warmly. "Despite the heartache you gotta keep striving, gotta keep moving forward."

She was silent for a long moment then said, "Deep down I knew that LaMont and I were a done deal, but I didn't want to admit it. But last night was enough to convince me and send me packing forever."

"Sometimes we hold on to the things that we know are no good for us."

"My dad always says that the truth hurts but it sets you free."

Nibbling her earlobe I said, "You are free indeed."

Giggling and squirming she said, "Thanks for everything."

"We will make it through this together. Calling me last night was the single most significant act of your life thus far."

"I'm glad that I called," she spoke tenderly. "I'm going to allow the warmth of your concern and affection to anchor me for a while."

"You can stay as long as you want."

She said, "I'm going to be the talk of the country. Known as the girl that destroyed the career of the forerunner for the Heisman Trophy."

"So, what."

"I don't want to be the object of anyone's scrutiny."

"Time passes and memories fade."

"Everyone will blame me for what happened."

"They blamed Jesus for being a troublemaker."

I said, "And he was the savior of the world."

We both laughed.

We headed inside and went into the kitchen, both of us craving something sweet. So, I pulled a cheesecake out of the fridge and cut us two big slices. Topped off our little treat with a scoop of strawberry ice cream.

Sitting at the kitchen table we fed our cravings while

discussing the dynamics of good relationships. Talked about love and pain and how they went hand in hand.

When I heard the front door open and close, I cringed because there was only one person who had a key to my house. Crook.

Crook yelled, "Yo Sheik you home?"

A moment later Crook was standing in the doorway of the kitchen. She looked at me then at Willow.

Crook didn't waste a moment claiming her territory. She snapped, "What the fuck is she doing here?"

Ignoring her rudeness I formally introduced them. Willow as my special friend. Crook as my best friend.

Willow stood and walked over to Crook extending a hand. She spoke a perky, "Thank you for your help last night."

Crook eyed Willow from head to toe. With an expression of disgust Crook refused the handshake, smirked, and growled, "Bitch get the fuck out of my face!"

Then Crook bumped Willow with her shoulder, almost knocking her down as she walked past her, heading to the refrigerator.

Obviously rattled, Willow rushed over to me and climbed onto my lap, snuggling close, like a frightened little child.

Crook rummaged through the fridge making a lot of noise, her anger apparent as she mumbled under her breath.

I spoke calmly. "Chill out with that attitude before you break something."

Crook gave me a hard look. "Nigga don't talk to me like that in front of that strange bitch!"

I kept my cool. "Crook respect my company."

Crook rolled her eyes, sucked her teeth, and went about searching for something in the fridge as she murmured curses.

Willow whispered, "Maybe I should leave."

I said, "Nah. This is my home and you're my guest. She doesn't live here, and I suggest she check her manners."

Crook held a beer in her hand and slammed the door to the fridge, then came over to the table and sat across from me. She stared at me with hatred in her eyes.

I asked Crook, "What's up with the early morning visit?"

"I need to talk to you in private."

"Can it wait?"

She considered for a moment before responding, "Nigga, if it could wait then I wouldn't be here." She snapped at Willow. "Bitch you keep staring at me like you got something to say."

Willow was trembling, her voice frail. "I was simply admiring your beauty."

Crook growled. "High-siddity-bitch talk like a white girl."

Willow gasped. "I beg your pardon."

Crook snorted. "You beg my what! Bitch I'll fuck you up!" She stood, her fist balled up ready for battle.

Crooks' behavior pissed me off. I shook my head. "Excuse me, Willow." I eased her from my lap and stood. Glaring at Crook I barked, "On the roof right now!"

Crook stormed away, huffing and puffing, her curses loud and leading the way.

Once we made it to the roof I asked, "What's our fucking problem?"

She shouted defiantly. "You're my muthafuckin' problem!"

Struggling to fight the anger consuming me I said, "You need to grow up."

She kicked the plastic chair into the pool and glowered at me like I was her worst enemy. Like she wanted death to take me away.

She yelled, "You're a bitch! Without me you would probably be a homo sucking a niggas dick for a dollar! You spineless-chicken hearted bitch! I should take you outta your misery right now." Then she threw a jab that I easily weaved.

She came back with a three-punch combination. Two I bobbed and weaved. The third caught me square on the chin.

I was stunned speechless.

She furiously blasted me. "No more games! I ain't gonna take this shit no muthafuckin more! You ain't fuckin nobody else but me from this point on! Now go tell that bitch to get out!"

Rubbing my chin, I watched her in disbelief as she

bounced around with her hands up ready to box.

"Crook you better get back in your position and stay there."

"Make me nigga!" She pulled her gun from her waistline. "Make me nigga!" She held the gun close to her leg, her angry eyes on me. "Nigga, I'll murk you right now!"

There was a suffocating tension between us.

I growled. "Put that shit up before I shove it up your ass."

"Nigga we just spent a muthafuckin' week on a yacht making love like we were a couple and you diss me for this strange bitch." She shouted, "Fuck you and that bitch! You bitch ass nigga!"

I gave her face a fierce backhand slap that sent her stumbling back a few steps. Then before she could recuperate and gain her bearings I pounced on her. Gripping her neck with two hands I choked her, then hurled her sending her tumbling over a couple of chaises.

She hit the ground hard. Choking through violent coughs she slowly stood, wobbling a little bit, gradually regaining her composure. Then she screamed at top of her lungs while simultaneously raising the gun to the sky squeezing off seventeen shots.

I snarled, "Get the fuck out of my face before I throw your stupid ass over the ledge of this roof!"

Crying she screamed that she hated me then ran away and disappeared down the stairwell. My thoughts were so chaotic that I was unable to concentrate. I took a few minutes to calm down then I went down to check on Willow.

Chapter Seventeen
SHEIK

Minds are of three kinds: one is capable of thinking for itself; another is able to understand the thinking of others; and a third can neither think for itself nor understand the thinking of others. The first is of the highest excellence, the second is excellent, and the third is worthless
—Niccolo Machiavelli

Willow and I relaxed on the bed in my bedroom as I channel surfed. The curtains were closed, and the room was dark, a single candle glowing on the nightstand. We found the movie, *Love and Basketball,* and without a word we cuddled and watched the movie.

About an hour into the movie the urgent chiming of the doorbell made both of us cringe. Annoyed I checked my phone to see who was at the door. It was Re-Re. I told Willow that I'd be back in a few moments after I handled some business with my attorney.

When I opened the front door Re-Re breezed inside with the grace of a fashion model. She was wearing a fuchsia dress that left nothing for the imagination. Rocking pearls on her limbs her hair was in an elegant updo. She'd topped off everything with a floral print silk scarf around her neck. Briefcase in tow she smiled at me.

"Consigliere, good morning." I returned her smile. "You're looking fabulous."

She gave me a kiss and moaned. "Damn I miss you so much."

We strolled into the living room.

Re-Re whispered, "Where's your friend?"

"She's upstairs."

"Cock blocking bitch."

I laughed and took a seat on the arm of the couch. "Jealous."

She smiled and winked. "I'm not stingy. You and I know who that dick really belongs to."

I laughed. She smiled at me.

Re-Re opened the briefcase and handed me a thick stack of paperwork. She said, "Look those over today and I'll pick them up in the morning."

I asked, "Does everything look all right?"

"Yes." She stressed, "Everything is up to par."

"Good."

Re-Re came over and stood in the wedge of my legs. She kissed me and whispered in my ear, "I don't have any panties on. Bend me over the couch for a quickie. I'll be quick. I promise."

I chuckled. "You're crazy."

She put her mouth close to my ear and whispered. "Let me suck it."

Her words gave me a sudden hardness. I patted her ass. "Chill out." Then I stood.

Re-Re's eyes suddenly widened in shock as she stepped away from me. She spoke a breathless, "Willow? What the fuck?"

I turned and saw Willow standing in the middle of the living room with a look of complete shock on her face. With her mouth wide open Willow stared at Re-Re.

Re-Re darted over to Willow and placed her hand on her shoulders. Both spoke at the same time. "What are you doing here?"

Then they both looked at me and called my name simultaneously, "Sheik!"

Confused I stared at them wondering what was going on. Then like a lightning bolt smashing into my forehead realization hit me. They resemble each other so much it was crazy. It was a stunning revelation that caught me completely by surprise. They were sisters.

A degree of panic sizzled the air.

Re-Re regarded me suspiciously. "Why is my baby sister here? What in the hell is going on?" She held Willow close under the protection of her arm as if she was in danger.

Re-Re tore into her sister with questions. It was beginning to feel as if she was being cross-examined by a prosecutor. I was really surprised when Willow left her sister's interrogation, strolled over, and hugged me.

Willow told Re-Re, "He's my special friend."

I controlled my shock with great effort.

Re-Re began blasting me, her temper flaring, accusing me of taking advantage of Willow, manipulating her innocence.

I held up a hand before she could continue. "Hold up. Respect me in my home. If you shut the fuck up, you will have the opportunity to hear what's going on."

Re-Re's expression didn't change.

Willow frowned thoughtfully. "I should be asking, how do you know each other?"

Suddenly Re-Re looked more jealous than angry.

I said, "She's, my attorney. Handles all my business interests and negotiations. Oversees all my commercial enterprises."

Re-Re stared at me, mad as a hornet. Her hands were on her hips. I assured her that I had no idea that they were sisters. I told her that they're different last names made the oversight even more plausible.

Willow took control of the moment and gave Re-Re our full history from the instant we met in the park and to the very second, we stood there in the living room. She didn't leave out a single detail.

Re-Re stood there, speechless, glaring at us.

I said, "Counselor this is the first time I've seen you at a loss of words."

I was certain that Re-Re would reveal the intimacies of our relationship.

After a few moments Re-Re exhaled a deep breath and told me, "Look, this is totally crazy, but thanks for being concerned and supportive of my sister's well-being."

Re-Re was sending a signal that everything was cool. My immediate reaction was relief.

Willow seemed comforted that her sister had blessed us with her approval. Her wide smile could have illuminated the entire universe when she kissed my cheek.

Re-Re walked over to the couch and sat down. We sat around having general conversation. Re-Re had a load of questions about me and Willows *special friendship*. Willow boasted of how special I was and how much that she thought I was a gift from God.

Re-Re kept telling Willow to recall the fight and each time it seemed as if Willow grew more boastful and excited. As we all talked, I noticed the way Re-Re watched me with a suspicious eye. Re-Re hung out for about an hour then she stood to leave. Said that she had something important to take care of.

Re-Re kissed and hugged Willow.

Re-Re told her that she would call her in a couple of hours. Told her baby sister that she loved her and for her to stay in the house and relax.

Then Re-Re asked me to accompany her down to her car. On the elevator ride down, she told me not to take advantage of her sister. She said that Willow was frail and easy to manipulate because she'd been sheltered all her life. She made me promise that I wouldn't hurt her.

Standing beside her BMW Re-Re looked deeply into my eyes.

She smiled. "You fucked LaMont up."

"He deserved it."

"I know that better than anyone."

I glanced down at my bedroom slipper clad feet. "I really like your sister."

Her face held a strange look. "She's a virgin."

"I know."

"Be her friend. She needs a friend." She sighed. "She's a good girl. Sacrifices a lot for others. She doesn't have any real friends, except me. People use her. They take her kindness for a weakness."

After a moment of silence I said, "Why are you so receptive of me and Willows relationship?"

She shrugged and took a deep breath. "You make her happy. It's so evident that she cares about you. I just want to see her happy." She flashed a grin. "And maybe if she gets some good dick, it'll help her see that there's much more to life than the Bible."

I nodded with a grin.

She gave me a smile. "I don't mind sharing your big dick with my baby girl."

I said, "Let me get back to the house."

She smiled. "You owe me."

"What are you talking about?"

"If I would have told her to leave, she would have left with no question."

"Whats your point?"

"Tonight, when she's sleeping, give me a call. I want some dick."

I chuckled. "That's cool."

"Excellent," she spoke excitedly.

As she climbed into her car, she raised the back of her dress flashing her bare ass.

I laughed and thought to myself how I loved my life

Chapter Eighteen
SHEIK

---

*The more sand has escaped from the hourglass of our life,
the clearer we should see through it.*
—Niccolo Machiavelli

When I got back to the house, I found Willow standing near the hallway that led back to my office. Her attention was on the painting on the wall.

I walked beside her and asked, "What are you doing?"

She pointed. "That's a Vermeer print of *Girl Reading a Letter at an Open Window.*"

I glanced at the painting then looked at Willow. "Nah that ain't no print. That's the original. Well at least it better be. I paid a lot for that. It damn well better be authentic."

Her jaw dropped. "An original Vermeer? No way. Do you know how expensive it would be?"

I laughed and stared at the painting. "Damn right I know. I paid for it."

She asked, "Where did you purchase it?"

"At an auction last month in London at the National Gallery. Your sister has a friend there and she advised me to invest in some art. She advised that I purchase artwork to diversify my portfolio. Own some culture that was priceless."

She nodded, her gaze transfixed on the painting. Just above a whisper she said, "That cannot be a Vermeer." With her arms folded across her breast she walked over to the painting standing directly in front of it, thoroughly inspecting it. After a couple of minutes, she looked at me with a wide grin of approval and whispered, "Oh my God! It is the original. Do you have an idea of what you have here?"

I laughed. "You're whispering like it's top secret."

"Come here baby."

I went to her.

She said, "Let me help you understand the voice of this masterpiece."

"So, you're an art expert?"

"I took an art class my first year. Fell in love with the language of art."

I slipped an arm around her waist and listened as she told me that the young white lady was reading a love letter and that she was dealing with a lot of inner tension as she concentrated on the words. The window was open because it represented the woman's desire to extend herself beyond her home life, longing for contact with the world outside of her bland existence. She craves to be free from her isolation. She wants adventure. The letter is the start of a love affair. The overturned bowl of apples and peaches is a representation of Eves fall. It's a symbol of an extramarital relationship. The fruit reminds us of Eves ultimate transgression.

I raised a brow. "And you got all of that from that painting?"

"Yes, that's what Vermeer intended. All great works of art tell a story and has a figurative meaning for the observer." She asked, "What do you see?"

I shrugged. "A white chick standing at an open window getting some fresh air because it stinks in the house. Maybe somebody farted or she's cooking chitlins. She's mad because she's reading the phone bill, and somebody has run the bill up making long distance calls. She's sick and tired of having to keep cleaning up after the kids and now one of them has knocked over the bowl of fruit. She's beefing with her man. He's tight with the money. She wants a new dress."

Willow cracked up laughing. "You are so crazy."

Smiling I asked, "What's wrong with what I said?"

In between laughs she replied. "Vermeer painted this in the seventeenth century, phones weren't invented yet. The painting symbolizes secret yearnings." Her voice was low and sensual when she said, "It's a secret yearning. A concealed desire that she wants to experience the forbidden. All the elements represent a growing appetite, a passion, to break free from her bland life and experience the unrestricted passion that awaits her outside the window."

Willow licked her lips. "She can see it and smell it in the air, but she's scared. Mmm, so scared."

We headed upstairs and, in my bedroom, we got in bed, spooned, simply relaxing. The TV was off. Drapes closed. Candles burning. Slow jams playing low and soft.

We chatted for the next hour and had an enjoyable conversation about life. We had been silent for a long time, listening to music, enjoying the peace of our friendship.

Willow stirred a little and said, "I feel it on my butt."

"What are you talking about?"

"Your penis is hard. I can feel it."

I smiled a little. "I'm horny."

She giggled. "Well, you need to get that under control."

"Ain't nothing but one way to do that."

She didn't reply. I didn't utter a word. For a few minutes we both were silent.

When she finally spoke, her voice was low and sensual. "I have yearnings, cravings." She hesitated a moment then said, "I want to do things with you, but I'm scared to cross that line. I fear being like Eve and fall into ruin."

"Don't be scared."

"Why shouldn't I?"

"Because I won't hurt you. I want the best for you. Want

to cherish you"

"But what about my morals, my principles, my dedication to the Lord."

I kissed her cheek. "You're changing, growing, evolving. It's a natural process. The fulfillment of our desires."

She turned her body around so that we could be face to face. We shared a few gentle kisses. An intense sexual energy was brewing. She wanted me as badly as I wanted her. It was all in her eyes.

With a teasing expression she asked quietly, "Do you think that I really want it?"

"The eyes don't lie."

She licked her lips. Her voice was husky. "You make me feel sexy, like I'm someone else, like I'm the sexiest woman on earth. You make me wanna sin."

I see chaos in her eyes, then suddenly a flood of desire drowned her confusion making her look like a starving nympho. There wasn't a trace of the good and pure Christian girl in her at that moment. She had become someone else.

She whispered. "If you just eat it, I would still be a virgin. Am I wrong for wanting that? For wanting you to lick my vagina? Am I wrong for wanting that?"

An adrenaline rush went through me, and I took a slow breath to calm me.

I asked, "Is that what you really want?"

My hands went to her ass, and I squeezed it. I loved the way it feels in my grip. I eased my tongue inside her mouth. Kissed her passionately. I slipped my hands into the back of her pajamas, and I grabbed her bare ass. Held it with a firm grip. Baby smooth skin.

She responded by giggling and easing out of my clutches, playfully backing away.

She eased off the bed.

Strolling the room, she wore a mischievous grin as she examined the furnishings and paintings. When she reached the wall mirror, she stared at her reflection for a moment, then kept it moving, continuing her journey around the room.

My gaze followed her, amused by her playful demeanor.

She was giving me flirty glances as she quietly hummed along to the song *All of Me* by John Legend that was coming from the surround sound speakers.

She stopped at the fireplace and looked at the framed photograph of me and Muhammad Ali sitting on the mantle. Then she moved to the bureau. I had a few pieces of jewelry haphazardly tossed over the surface and a thick wad of cash. Willow picked up one of my black diamond chains and playfully put it on her neck. Then her eyes rolled over me from head-to-toe, a sensual expression on her face.

She waved her hand through the air and said, "You have everything that a man can ask for."

I sat up. "Except you."

Grinning she asked, "What does that mean?"

"I won't be complete until your mine."

She spoke in a warm inviting voice. "You've learned to transform obstacles into opportunities. I'm sure you'll figure something out."

That made me laugh. "I've always gone the extra mile to accomplish my goals."

"I'll tell you one thing, confidence is everything."

I laughed and she giggled.

"Sheik the look in your eyes is disturbing."

"Oh yeah?"

"It reeks of carnality."

"Carnality is good." I told her, "Come here."

Without hesitation she got on the bed and crawled over to me, easing into my arms. She kissed me tenderly.

She gave me a wanting look and confessed. "I've had oral sex before."

I raised a brow. "Gave or received?"

"Always received."

"Interesting."

"Does that shock you?"

"Yes, it does." I kissed her lips.

"I've had moments of weakness. I'm not proud of it." She added. "But never penetration."

I kissed her neck, her shoulder, her arm.

She told me, "Lamont wanted to have oral sex with me, but I wouldn't allow it. He used to suck my toes all the time. Used to massage my privates through my clothes with the palm of his hand."

I scooted down until my face was in her crotch area. I could feel her heat, smell her sweet aroma through her pajamas. I snuggled my face into the meeting of her legs and planted a few kisses there. When I went to tug her pajama bottom down, she stopped me, grabbed my wrist, and pulled me back up.

She asked that I respect her. Told me that those moments of weakness when she let someone suck her pussy was years ago. She'd been manipulated in her weakest moment by someone she trusted and loved. I was patient, didn't push it.

We kissed some more for a long time.

Chapter Nineteen
WILLOW

---

*One who deceives will always find those who allow
themselves to be deceived.*
—Niccolo Machiavelli

Sheik stirred beside me, but he didn't wake up. Sleeping soundly, a slight snore rolled from his lips. His head was nestled in his folded arms. Resting on my side I was giving careful study to the man that I had so quickly fallen in love with. I'd been in a trance for the last hour watching him sleep.

Sheik was like the perfect statue carved out of rich milk chocolate. He was God's masterpiece. My hand was on the small of his back and occasionally I planted a few kisses on his cheek simply because I could. I wonder what is going on in his head. My hope is that he is dreaming about me. The love songs I'd been listening to had placed me in a romantic mood. I was brimming with love.

My voyeurism of his boxer clad body had me jaded with lust. Wanting to kiss him all over I giggled as I thought to myself how I must be crazy allowing my thoughts to marinate on such indecent things.

But to tell the truth and shame the devil I had a devouring need for Sheik. So many days of my life I'd fantasized about meeting a man like him. But for fear of rebuke, I never openly shared those leanings with anyone. What kind of a Christian lady desires a wealthy handsome Playboy as a mate? Yet deep down in the hidden recesses of my being I had always been curious to see what it would be like to be smitten by a charismatic heartthrob who is the object of the fantasies of scores of beautiful women. A man respected by all. A man who has fused sophistication and street swagger into an unapologetic *fuck you* of the system. A man who plays by his own rules. A man who has no fears and is courageous enough to defend my honor. I found all that in Sheik.

The Lord is my witness, I crave Sheik with an agonizing intensity that frightened me. It was like I was possessed by a demon. His simple touch sent my spirit into a frenzy. The weakness he created in me was unparalleled. And I know that eventually it would open a door that would lead to me sinning.

Sheik startled me when he grumbled, "What time is it?"

I smiled and kissed his forehead. "It's almost six. Go back to sleep. You need your rest."

He yawned. "Come here. Let me hold you."

"Sure."

He repositioned himself, now lying on his back. I relaxed against him, resting my head on his shoulder. He wrapped his arms around me and held me close. I felt so safe and protected. Like I was the most special woman alive. A few moments later he was snoring. I listened and using the steady rhythm of his breathing I traveled to the land of nod.

When I woke up, I was surprised to find myself alone in bed. I was lying on my belly enveloped by a mountain of cloud soft pillows. I raised my head my eyes searching for my boyfriend. I spotted him sitting in the opening of the French doors of the balcony, relaxing on a humongous beanbag while eating ice cream out of a bowl. His attention was fixed on the world outside the room.

A cool breeze was sweeping through the room bringing the fragrance of an imminent thunderstorm. Slow jams were still playing, and the candles were still burning.

I sat up and stretched.

Sheik looked over at me as he shoved a spoonful of ice cream into his mouth. "What's up?"

With a grin I spoke a perky, "Hey there sexy."

He smiled. "Did you sleep all right?"

"Yes." I asked, "How long have you been up?"

He shrugged. "About an hour." He told me, "Your sister came by. She said that she will call you in the morning."

I glanced at the clock on the nightstand. It was almost 9:00 p.m.

I commented, "I smell rain in the air."

"Thunderstorm is coming." He asked, "You hungry?"

"Yes." I slid from the bed and went into the bathroom. Rinsed and gargle with mouthwash. Then I washed my face.

Staring at my reflection in the full-length mirror on the bathroom wall, I thought to myself how for the first time in my entire life I felt sexy.

I went through several poses imitating the sexy sirens from the rap videos. It was a secret to most, but I've always had self-esteem issues. I've been that way since I was a little girl. Except for this moment in time.

Grinning, I enjoyed the vision that was in front of me. I was beautiful and luscious. I love my big fat booty, my big hips and big C cup breasts. Sheik had whispered to me that I was *the most exquisite creature on the earth, heaven manifested* he said that my *sex appeal made him intoxicated with lust*. Lamont had never told me things like that.

When I left the bedroom, I went directly to Sheik and curled up on his lap. He fed me ice cream and we shared small talk and spirited laughs. Sheik held me like I was his greatest love, and I clung to him like if I let go, I'll die.

Together we are silent gazing out at the night sky. The clouds were drenching the city with rain.

I commented, "The world is coming to an end."

"What are you talking about?"

"Its mid-autumn and it feels like summer."

"Global warming."

"It's crazy."

We sat in silence for a few moments. While I rest my head on his chest he toyed with strands of my hair.

He asked, "Do you wanna eat out or in?"

"Whatever you want to do."

"I'd rather eat here."

"Okay."

"Chinese or pizza?"

"You decide for us. I want you to lead me."

My words sounded desperate and as soon as they had escape me, I found myself wishing I could take them back.

He said, "Okay pizza it is." He asked, "Domino's or College Inn?"

I felt honored that he didn't take my suggestion and continued to include me in the decisions, even though I did mean what I said. He can lead me anywhere. If he would have said let's eat a raccoon for dinner I would have smiled and said yes dear.

I told him, "College Inn."

While he went to make the call for the pizza I stepped out onto the tiny terrace. The rain had slowed to a drizzle, and I stood at the ornately carved marble rail and ran my fingers over the smooth stone.

The city was clashing, alive and vibrant.

Gazing at the sparkling lights I listened to the many clashing sounds of the metropolis and enjoyed it. The euphoria I experienced was magical. I felt omnipotent. Powerful. Standing high above the city in a luxurious abode, a palace in the sky. This is the fairy tale that all little girls dream about. The life of a princess.

When the pizza arrived, we cuddled on the couch in the living room while watching television. Sheik turned me on to an old school movie called *Love Jones,* with Nia Long and Larenz Tate.

When a love making scene occurred between the main characters, I felt Sheik's manhood rise and I glanced at the bulge in his boxers. I even shifted my body a little bit so that I could get a better look. He saw me trying to sneak a peek

193

and smiled at me. I quickly averted my eyes, my embarrassment making my face flush with heat.

I grew angry when he laughed and teased me, calling me a closet freak. My anger quickly subsided when he stuck his tongue in my mouth and kissed me.

I spoke softly, "In my heart I knew that that one day I would find true love."

He didn't reply. And no words were required. His face said it all. He loved me too.

Curious I asked, "The women of your past, what were they like?"

"What do you mean?"

"Have the women of your past been similar? Are you attracted to women with certain characteristics?"

"I never really paid too much attention to it."

"What's the most professional?"

He smiled. "Are you sure that you want to dip into those waters?"

"If I couldn't handle it then I wouldn't ask."

He exhaled a deep breath. "Most professional hunh? Well, I've dated models, a couple of R&B stars, doctors, lawyers…"

I spoke a jealous, "Okay stop it. I don't want to know."

Sheik laughed and nibbled my ear.

He had been with women that I couldn't begin to compare with. It was like holding a candle next to the sun. Suddenly I didn't feel so sexy. I felt inadequate.

He planted a few kisses on my cheek. "What's wrong?"

I playfully pouted. "Nothing."

He made me warm inside when he whispered in my ear that I was his sweet thing and that he would never look at another woman. I believed him and I hoped that I could hold his attention well enough that the ghost of his past couldn't swoop in and take him away from me.

We kissed and caressed each other. Sheik knew exactly how to make me feel like a woman. It was wonderful being in a real man's arms.

With a grin I told him, "I appreciate these tender

moments."

"Expect this all the time."

"Promise?"

"I promise."

We both were silent for a while, our hearts speaking a unique language of love. I was searching for words to describe the elevation of my soul. I closed my eyes thanking the Lord for sending me such a wonderful man. Had to pinch myself to make sure that it wasn't a dream. Honesty is the best policy, and I pushed out the poison that was in my heart so that it couldn't fester and grow.

I spoke a defeated, "Baby, sometimes I have murky feelings of doubt about us and your motives." Peering deep into his eyes I said, "I don't like those feelings."

"I suppose that's natural when you invested your all into a chump that repeatedly betrayed you."

"How do I rid myself of such destructive feelings?"

"Trust me and trust your heart." He kissed my cheek. "I apologize for what he took you through. For the sake of healing, I apologize on his behalf. As a Black man I want you to understand that you don't have to hold on to the pain that he has caused you. I want you to learn to let it go and move on."

"Thank you." I kissed his lips with a few gentle pecks. "I'm glad that you didn't take my remarks as a personal assault on your character.

"The only things that I ever take personal in life is if you mess with me my woman, my money, or play with my intelligence."

I giggled. "Well baby this woman is definitely yours and you don't have to worry about her ever going astray or even desiring another man."

He smiled. "You better not even look at another nigga."

"The way that you thrashed Lamont I don't think that will ever be a problem."

We laughed.

I said, "We all search to become who our mates want us to be. Being in love is like being a second-class citizen, living under the umbrella of another with hopes of pleasing him."

"Is that a good thing or a bad thing?"

"It could be good if our mate desires positive and virtuous qualities. However, if they desire indecent and immoral attributes then it it can be quite devastating."

He said, "I think if they're both striving for greatness together, focused on the oneness of love, then it's beneficial for the relationship on all levels. Together they are strong, invincible, and apart they are sick. I'm strong when I'm around you and you make me wanna be better than I was in the past."

With a grin I said, "That was so kind."

"It's the truth. We all want validation, so we'll know that the investment is worth it."

"Yes," I said.

I sat there thinking about how I desperately needed validation because the result of that is trust and I wanted to trust Sheik. I needed to trust him until he proved otherwise. I couldn't allow my past issues with Lamont to hinder my joy when it came to Sheik. If I did, then I'm doomed for failure.

Attempting to evaluate what I truly felt about Sheik I grew confused. There's a raging debate within my soul. Is this a fascination that I felt? A fascinating love is what I want it to be. Love is what I think it to be. My biggest fear is that he will break my heart. One thing that I was certain of was that I absolutely loved to be around him.

Sheik got up and went upstairs. A few moments later he returned with a Montecristo 1935 Anniversary Edicion Doble Diamante cigar and a sandwich bag full of marijuana.

As he sat on the couch, I sat directly beside him while gently rubbing his back. I was being nosey, watching him carefully roll a blunt.

I asked, "You smoke a lot of marijuana, don't you?"

Licking the blunt closed he replied, "I suppose I get high more than the average." He spoke with a smile. "Now be a good girl and grab me a beer from out of the fridge."

Without hesitation I sprinted into the kitchen and returned with two beers.

Sheik said, "I only wanted one."

Grinning I said, "One of them is for me."

He lit the blunt and asked, "When did you start drinking?"

"Today." I told him, "I want to bond with you."

"What does drinking a beer have to do with bonding?"

I shrugged. "Its time for compromise."

He laughed and said, "Hold up."

He grabbed the beers and headed into the kitchen. A few moments later he came back without the beers. Instead, he was toting a bottle of cranberry juice, lime juice, a cocktail shaker, lime wheels, a small bowl of ice, and a couple of glasses.

As he sat down beside me, he said, "Grab that bottle of Beluga Lalique Epicure Vodka from the bar."

I went over to the bar and searched the dozens of bottles until I found what he'd requested. I handed him the bottle then plopped down on the couch beside him and watched him attentively as he transformed into a bootleg mixologist.

When he'd finished mixing our drinks, he poured us both a glass. I'd watched enough *Sex in the City* reruns to know that he had made Carrie's favorite drink, a Cosmopolitan.

He handed me the drink and smiled at me. "Enjoy."

Giggling I took a sip of my drink. "Tasty."

He chuckled. "Your first drink should be something sophisticated. Not a beer."

We toasted to love.

Curious I asked, "Why do you smoke weed?"

"It calms me. It gives me peace. It helps me evaluate my thoughts." He took a long drag of weed. "Makes the world a more pleasant place."

"My sister says the same thing." I told him, "She says that it elevates her mind to heights she couldn't achieve without it."

Blowing out a cloud of smoke he said, "Exactly."

I reached for the blunt and spoke shyly, "Mind if I try?"

He handed me the blunt and for a moment I stared at it in my hands. I found it hard to believe that I was about to do drugs. Sheik coached me along with every step and I smoked marijuana for the first time. Deeply inhaling the peculiar tasting smoke, I coughed violently but kept at it until I could inhale without coughing.

As I smoked, a strange kind of calm came over me that was as gentle as a summer evening breeze. Everything felt so serene around me. Everything became so wonderfully glorious. I was floating amongst the stars. I began smiling and couldn't stop it. Giggling and could not stop it.

It was the best I've ever felt in my entire life.

We sat around and finished the blunt. Downed a few drinks. We were joking around talking stuff to each other, both of us laughing hard. I laughed until my stomach hurt, and tears rolled down my cheeks. We had so much fun joking about life. One time the laughs were rolling so hard that I accidentally and embarrassingly released a loud fart. Instead of being mortified for releasing gas in front of Sheik, something I never did in front of LaMont, I found it hilarious.

We both were laughing tears.

As I caught my breath I told him, "I'm a little dizzy."

He chuckled. "That's because you're high."

"Oh yeah, you're right, I am high?"

We both cracked up with laughter.

In between laughs I shouted, "Yeah I'm high!" I farted again. "Ewwww baby I'm gassy!"

More laughter.

His cell phone vibrated, and he answered it in between his laughs. He suddenly grew serious and began talking business. It was obvious that he was talking to Crook.

My gaze scanned over his body and momentarily stopped at the slit of his boxers. It was slightly open, exposing a generous portion of his penis. Quickly I looked away embarrassed by the indecency that I had just witnessed.

My attention went to the television, yet the vision of his penis was branded in my mind. My arousal was unwelcome. I was ashamed and I said a silent prayer begging the Lord to remove those lustful thoughts. I repeatedly rebuked the devil in the name of Jesus. With all of that calling out to the Lord for strength, no help arrived, and my intoxicated mind kept whispering for me to take a look.

I found myself cutting my eyes at his penis. With concealed curiosity I scolded myself. *Girl you ought to be ashamed of yourself.*

Sheik laughed while staring at me.

I asked, "What's so funny?"

"You."

"Me?"

He laughed. "You keep sneaking peeks at my dick."

I gasped and blushed. "I am not."

He spoke softly, "Calm down. It's no big deal. Nothing to get upset about."

I took a deep breath and shook my head willing myself to relax. My voice was gentle and full of regret. "I apologize for reacting in such a harsh manner."

His warm smile put me at ease. "Just keep it real with me like I do with you. Don't fear honesty."

He kissed my cheek and pulled me close to him. His tone was soothing. "Now go ahead and look at it. It's completely natural, nothing to be ashamed of."

Gazing into his eyes, I pleaded, "Don't make me do this." I had a feeling of anticipation growing in me.

"Willow it's only a dick. God made it. It's perfectly natural to be curious. It doesn't make you a slut or a sinner. It makes you human, a woman." Then he whispered, "Look at it." He watched me with a sense of expectation.

I found myself drawn to his crotch area and I yielded to the impulse to touch him, slipping my hand into his boxes. Hesitantly I grabbed his penis and delicately squeezed it.

I giggled because it felt rubbery like thick latex.

Sheik laughed.

A raging fire was deep inside of me.

He coached me on. "Go ahead and pull it out. Feel it."

I replied, "Noooo, I can't."

Sheik said, "Let me help you."

He shocked me when he quickly slipped out of his boxes and tossed them aside. Stark-naked he sat there gazing warmly into my eyes.

He spoke just above a whisper, "Touch it again. Come on, it's okay. It ain't gonna bite you. It's yours and you should be familiar with it."

Searching for words I stammered, "But Sheik my principles. I can't."

"It ain't sex. You're simply exploring who I am physically. This is God's masterwork. It ain't no different than enjoying art. Appreciate it. Look at how beautiful it is like you did with that painting. Tell me the story behind this piece of art."

Sheik was far too tempting.

Smiling, my eyes traveled to his secret place, and I observed it through the eyes of a frightened little girl. It was huge. I wasn't an expert on penises, but I had seen quite a few porno films, that my sister loved to watch. And I don't remember any of the penises from those films being anywhere as big as Sheiks.

Sheik said, "Touch it. Do that for me."

Sheik could talk a rat into eating rat poison. He's very persuasive. Smooth as can be. He could probably talk Satan into repenting and convince him to come back to God for divine service.

My heart began to thump in anticipation as my gaze remained fixed on his penis. Curiosity made me reach over and hold it in my hand.

He spoke calmly, "Enjoy it. Tell me what you see and what you feel." He spread his legs open and relaxed back on the soft cushions of the couch.

Fascinated by his penis I couldn't pry my eyes away. My throat was dry, and I licked my lips. Cleared my throat. My face was flushed with heat.

Engrossed by the moment I fondled his penis, analyzing the thing that drove women to act like savage beasts. In my hand was the thing that drove women insane, making them stab their boyfriends, throw bleach in their eyes, destroy their cars, shoot them, murder them. At the jail I have ministered to countless female inmates who had committed crimes of passion that didn't have a thing to do with love. It had been the power of the penis which had drove them all to madness.

As I held his penis, I felt a sudden empowerment as it became clear that I was in possession of a woman's weakness.

I gasped and stared at his penis when I felt it growing in my hand.

Sheik chuckled.

Smiling I gently smacked his arm. "That's not funny. It scared me."

Quickly his penis grew to over five times its size. I was amazed. I was stunned as it transformed into a thick rigid pole that I could barely hold in my hand. It was an intimidating sight. As if it would hurt if it struck me in the head with a hard blow.

His voice was low. "What do you think?"

I shrugged. "I don't feel comfortable discussing your penis with you."

"It's natural."

"Maybe it is but I'm not acquainted with such openness."

"I want us to have the ability to discuss anything without fear of judgment or rejection."

My hand was still gripping the hulking wand.

I said, "It's so big."

He laughed and I cracked a smile. Studying it with a curious intent I asked, "How does a woman take something so massive inside of her is totally baffling."

He chuckled.

I asked, "You're aroused, aren't you? That's why it's so hard and swollen."

"I'm always aroused when I'm around you."

Sheik had evoked a mixture of emotions in me. Some I liked. Others I feared.

"Block out everything and focus on it." His voice was so soothing. "Grow familiar with it. Act like I'm not here. Block out everything and focus on it. Let your creative mind place you in a realm of artistic observation." He kissed my cheek and said, "This is yours forever. Get used to it."

His hand went to my shoulder and very gently he guided me towards the floor. I didn't resist. I slid off the couch and kneeling in front of him I eased in between his thighs. I couldn't pull my eyes away from his penis. My lust compelled me to examine the mysterious wand of taboo at eye level. All apprehension was gone, replaced by intrigue.

He spoke softly, "That's right, get familiar with it."

Everything that made him a man was directly in front of my face. The organs that separated our genders was on full display, inches away from my face. His odor was potent, a mixture of soap and musk. I inhaled it, enjoying the unfamiliar aroma.

I whispered to him, "When I'm around you I don't have a will of my own." I studied his face deliberately gauging his reaction to my words.

He simply smiled and nodded. "Good." Then he said, "Kiss it. Kiss it baby."

I laughed. "Are you crazy?"

His face was serious. "Do I look crazy?"

Gazing into his eyes I saw that he was completely serious. With a raging arousal I regarded him curiously. Thoughts of tasting him flooded my mind.

I cleared my throat and did as he had requested. I planted a few kisses on the tip of it. I thought I would feel guilty or embarrassed but surprisingly I experienced neither. It turned me on.

Gently stroking my head, he smiled warmly. "You make me happy when you do as I ask."

I felt my heart flutter. I wanted to make him happier, so I kissed it repeatedly, my excitement growing with every peck.

He joked. "He likes you."

I looked longingly into Sheiks eyes and whispered, "I like him too."

There was a burning desire in his eyes.

"Take your hand and move it up and down. Pump it at an even pace."

I did as he wanted.

He hissed. "Good. Yes, squeeze it. Harder. A little faster. Yep. Keep that tempo. That's exactly right."

I asked, "How long should I do this?"

He smiled. "Believe me. You'll know when to stop."

As I stroked him, I studied his face. His hot-blooded facial expression turned me on in ways that were foreign yet welcomed. A sensual rush shot through me, commanding my hand to pump harder, faster.

There was an intense electricity surging between us. A fire raged within me, my heart thumping violently.

He hissed with pleasure and groaned in some type of primal sound when I licked a circle over the tip. I'd did it because it just seemed like the right thing to do.

Shame has left. I'm a courageous pioneer on a journey to a city named erotica. Sheik had surrendered to my touch and my lapping tongue, and I controlled his pleasure. This made me feel immensely powerful.

The pulsing hardness in my hand is the key to controlling him. I see it in his vulnerable face as my stroking, licking, and lapping continued. Focused on the task at hand I smiled when he groaned, and the shaft twitched and swelled considerably. Then his penis shot out a stream of white creamy liquid, erupting like a geyser. He released a great deal of his life force, a little of it squirting in my face, landing on my chin and the corner of my lip. A few sprinkles were on my breast, my cheek.

Sheik laughed and I giggled.

Amazed by what I'd just experienced I stared at the slowly shrinking penis in my hand, as semen oozed down my fingers like lava from a volcano.

He asked, "Are you okay?"

"Yes." Suddenly I felt shame. I didn't have an idea of where the swift feeling of guilt came from, but it hit me hard like a tidal wave, flooding my senses.

Without a word I stood, went upstairs to Sheik's bedroom, and got in the shower. As I stood under the hot water, I experienced a sense of failure, as if I was worthless. I had let down the Lord. I couldn't understand why I did something so foolish. I prayed earnestly and begged the Lord to not chastise me severely.

When I heard the bedroom door open, I froze. Sheik walked to the shower, and I could see his nude silhouette outside of the foggy glass wall.

He asked, "You, okay?"

"Yes." I spoke truthfully, "I feel like I let the Lord down by what I just did."

"Don't feel bad. It was nothing vulgar. It was simply an experience that you took part in to help you understand me." He laughed. "You're still a virgin, don't worry."

I smiled. His words made me feel a lot better. I told him, "Thanks."

He asked, "Do you mind if I join you? Mind if I come in?"

I debated in silence for a few moments if that was a good idea. It would be a major leap to shower with a man.

Sheik said, "It's okay baby. You go ahead and I'll get in when you finish."

"No!" I exhaled a deep breath. "Please come in. But...but...please remember to respect me."

He opened the door and stepped inside. My back was to him, embarrassed to show him my frontal nudity.

Sheik turned on all four shower heads and asked, "You sure you're, okay?"

"Yes." I glanced back at him, my eyes skimming over the full length of his body, lingering at the part of him that made him a man.

As he soaped up his rag he said, "You have the sexiest body that I've ever seen." His gaze was fixed on my ass. He said, "Turn around let me see you."

Reluctantly I turned around until I was facing him.

He smiled seemingly impressed by what he saw. He spoke in a tender tone. "Wash me." He handed me the washcloth.

Without hesitation I did as he'd requested. I washed his entire body from head to toe and left him in the shower alone.

By the time he finished his shower I had dried my hair, pulled it into a ponytail, moisturized my body, and slipped on one of Sheiks big T-shirts. I said my prayers and was relaxing in his soft bed while I listened to slow jams.

Sheik came into the bedroom a few minutes later and put on some deodorant. As he stood at the bureau, he stared at me for a long moment then said, "Are you still high?"

"A little." I told him, "I feel very mellow."

"Do you want to smoke this with me?" He asked as he picked up a blunt from the nightstand.

Without hesitation I replied, "Yes."

He lit the blunt then came over and sat on the bed. I asked, "Aren't you going to put on some underwear."

He chuckled. "Nah. Is that a problem?"

I shrugged. "No. I'm cool with that." I sat up and fluffed a few pillows behind my back.

My attention was fixed on his penis.

We sat there and got high, and I loved it. Loved the way the marijuana gave me the ultimate peace. I wonder if heaven felt this splendid. This magnificent. This wonderful.

I was playing with Sheik's penis when he said, "Let me give you what I know you want."

I didn't respond and got out of bed. I walked out onto the balcony. My high was so awesome that it felt like I was floating. My thoughts were on how I was strongly inclined to take Sheik up on his offer and give him what he most desired.

My smile wouldn't leave my face as I stood at the railing gazing out at the city. A light rain escaped the heavens soaking the T-shirt I wore. I didn't have to look behind me to know that Sheik was standing in the doorway behind me, watching me.

Without looking back I said, "I feel so good."

"Why?"

"I'm high and I absolutely love it." I turned and faced him. "I'm rediscovering love with you."

"To rediscover you would had to have had before."

"I did. Still do. I love Lamont. I can't deny that truth. Love is not something I can just turn off. But with you it's different. I'm in love with you. I mean really, really, really, in love with you."

He smiled. "You're getting soaked."

I teased. "Stop being a wimp and come out and get soaked too."

He stepped out onto the balcony, his semi-hard penis leading the way.

Standing beside me he leaned on the railing and said, "Take that shirt off."

I did.

He smiled. "Panties too."

I took off my panties and draped them over his shoulder.

He chuckled and held my panties to his nose and sniffed them. He said, "You're getting very loose aint'cha?"

I giggled. "Isn't this what you want." I pointed to my feminine cleft.

He glanced at the apex of my thighs and smiled.

As my eyes searched his face, I thought about how much I loved him. My desire had grown out of control, and I wanted to experience what he had to offer.

I leaned over and whispered in his ear. "Eat me." I giggled. "Do it out here in the rain." I walked over to one of the chaise lounges and relaxed on it, spreading my legs.

Something had come over me that I couldn't explain. I felt possessed by some dark, primal force. It had turned me into a promiscuous woman of easy virtue.

Sheik watched me closely with a smooth grin on his face. "Be careful what you ask for."

The air between us was charged with electricity. The way that he was looking at me made me feel extremely sexy.

I laughed lightly and closed my eyes. Let the soft drops of cool rain massage my nude body. Everything felt so right, so perfect, the exhilaration overwhelming.

When I finally opened my eyes, I saw that Sheik was sitting on the small table directly beside me. His penis was hard pointing towards the crying sky.

I study him intently.

He said, "I want to make love to you."

The thought of submitting to his desires overtook me. Even though I wanted him to perform oral sex on me I couldn't quite grasp the boldness of giving up my virginity. I don't think any amount of marijuana in the world could persuade me to do that. I held a primitive fear of indulging in the secret desires of my body.

I cautioned myself to stay strong. I sat up.

He asked, "Are you okay?"

"No." I stood and raked my fingers through my wet hair. "This is crazy. I need to put some clothes on." Heading inside I halted when he called my name.

His voice was commanding. "Come here."

I couldn't find the strength to stay away, and I walked over and stood in front of him.

"You're not a little girl." He whispered to me, "It's time to prove that."

"I'm scared." I whispered, "Scared of what comes with it."

"Let me take away all your fears." He kissed me passionately.

I gently ran my hand over his hard penis. Being close to him robbed me of all reason. I relished the thought of partaking in the forbidden and had a strong, strange compulsion to to be deflowered. I imagine making love to him.

Standing there I began stroking his hardness. I spoke truthfully. "I want to yield to the demands of my body."

He planted tender kisses on my collarbone. "I'll do anything to have you."

I clung to my feeling of passion, wanting to explore the depths of what he could offer me.

His hands went to my buttocks, and he gripped them. I struggled against the lust that swiftly encompassed my entire being. But as I gazed into his eyes, I was reminded of the fact that I was in love with him.

He asked, "Don't you want someone as special as me to have such a precious gift."

I shrugged with indifference.

If I had any sense at all I would flee from his presence and never see him again. But I was senseless, and I would remain there with him because I really wanted to do it with him.

His hand tenderly traced the curve of my butt. My body seemed incapable of resistance when he took my breast in his mouth. The sensations were overwhelming.

Forecasting the impending sin of me losing my virginity I prayed, *Lord help me.*

Teasingly slow he ran his tongue over my breast, my nipples, sucked them like they were his favorite treat. A wave of longing swept over me as I wondered fearfully if this would be the night.

His phone chimed inside.

"You're...mmm...Sh.... Sheik...your dick is ringing...I mean...your phone is ringing." I moaned. "Mmmmm, inside...inside your phone is ringing."

"Fuck that phone." He managed to say as he feasted on my breast.

The rain began falling harder. A flash of lightning and a roar of thunder rippled through the sky when Sheik dropped to his knees and began dining on my womanhood.

"Lord have mercy! My God!" I screamed out as my hand palmed his head pushing his face into the inferno between my thighs. My breathing quickened. My knees got weak and I stumbled but Sheik had me in his clutches, lifting me high in the air. I wrapped my legs around his head, my thighs a vice grip on his face as he held me in place.

In a rush of ecstasy, I screamed. I wonder if anyone could hear me or see me so high in the sky. My arms were outstretched like the wings of an impious bird. The rain was coming down hard, smacking me, stinging my flesh. Consumed by the heat of passion I held on for dear life grinding my vagina into his face, my hips savage and wild.

The lights of the city seemed brighter, the sounds louder. Lightning and thunder. More lightning. More thunder.

I screamed.

Sheik slammed me hard on the chaise. His face remained buried in my feminine mound.

Lightning.

Thunder.

Inhibition deserted me when I screamed, "I want it in me! Put it in me!"

Inflaming my hot-blooded passions he licked, sucked, and nibbled my vagina as if he was starving. Tenderly French-kissed my anus. Made me feel new sensations when the tip of his tongue began going in and out of my tightest hole, my puckered cove. He took me to the extreme. Spasms rocked me to the core. Moaning his name Nirvana rippled throughout my body. My insides were ablaze, in a rapture. I trembled uncontrollably.

He slid up my body until we were face to face. Hungrily we kissed. The fragrance of my most private place engulfing my nostrils. I tasted my honey.

Gasping for air I attempted to stop him from having his way, but his determination was too great. Pinned to the chaise my squirms to get free were futile. His penetration forced a reaction from me that frightened me to the core. I began screaming and punching and clawing and biting and jerking and thrusting my body, trying to get free.

Lightning and thunder assaulted my senses.

It didn't faze him. His face held a focus that made me shiver. I felt a sharp jab of excruciating pain and I began crying. The rain washed away my tears. The thunder drowned out my constant screams of how much I hated Sheik.

With my back arched I screamed out in agony. "You're killing me!"

He ignored me filling the hollow inside of me and with an agonizing slow rhythm he moved in and out of me. My nails dug deep into the flesh of his back. My jaw was clenched tight, the pain unbearable. It felt like my flesh was ripping. His hardness filled me, stretching me.

I looked fixedly into his face. I observed a confident and satisfied smile pierce his lips. He had conquered. I hated him so much.

He spoke a calming and relaxing, "Everything is going to be all right."

"Please Sheik!" I cried. "Please!"

At some point his slow groove transformed into violent thrusting. Quick short strokes. My legs were on his shoulders as he pounded me like a jackhammer. The sound of his flesh smacking mine filled the night, mingling with the unique melody of nature at work.

I'd never experienced such heated sensations before.

He grunted. "Am I hurting you?"

I grunted back. "You're not hurting me. It...it...it...it...it feels so good, so good! Please do it harder! Fuck me, Sheik! Fuck him out of my heart! Fuck me hard!"

I was genuinely surprised that I uttered those words. His pounding became fierce and vicious as if he was trying to hammer me through the chaise. With each stroke it caused a sharp pain that was delightful, creating magical sensations that I'd never experienced before.

I convulsed in ecstatic spasms that kept coming and coming. I couldn't remember much more of what happened after that except that it was full of bewitching sensations with Sheik sexing me in a variety of twisting positions. I do remember intense, mind-blowing orgasms rolling through me when he sexed me doggie-style while his finger slipped into my anus and he finger-sexed it simultaneously.

When it was all over and done with, I sat curled up on the chaise, my knees pulled to my chin. Rain came down in torrents, drenching me, washing away the sweat of sin that was thick on my skin. A strange soreness between my legs made me cringe. I felt a distinct tightening in my groin.

A flash of lightning lit up the world, bringing the illusion of daylight for a few fleeting moments. I knew that it was the Lord shining his light on my sins for the angels of heavens to see. The piercing screams of thunder that followed were their chorus of wails. It was their disappointment for the fallen Willow. Monumental and mournful tears from heaven, full of sorrow, bathed me, cooling off my red-hot body.

"Willow come inside."

I raised my head and saw Sheik standing in the doorway. His nude frame was dark and lovely, a flawless masterpiece, Satan in the flesh.

He reached for me, and I gave him my hand and let him guide me into his arms. He's so strong, so much of a man. He scooped me into his arms and held me like I was a newborn baby. Then he walked me into the house. Took me into the bathroom where a bubble bath in the hot tub awaited us. It was a romantic setting. The lights were out, candles were everywhere, with slow jams playing.

Immersed in the hot water I snuggled close to him as we shared a blunt. Neither of us spoke a word.

As we got high my thoughts were floating in an abyss of confusion. In a whirlpool of emotions, I sat there trying to make sense of who I was and what I'd become. Deep down I know I should feel guilty, and truth be told I wanted to feel guilty, but the reality of the matter was that I felt liberated. Maybe it was the marijuana that had me indifferent to the huge sin that I had just committed or maybe it was all meant to happen to show me that I needed to live for myself a little more. Enjoy life on my own terms. Whatever it was I knew one thing for sure, I like getting high and absolutely loved sex.

Tonight, I fell profoundly in love with Sheik.

My attention went to Sheik's face. I couldn't believe that I had taken part in the actual art of sex. Staring at his handsome face I felt something magnetic tugging at my soul.

I had no idea that such a wonderful man would eventually cause me such immeasurable pain. The Lord said that the only sex that is lawful is that which is between a husband and wife. When we go against that there are severe repercussions. No matter how much we love the Lord, He still chastises us when we go against His will for our lives.

In chapter twelve of the book of Hebrews, in *The Bible,* it tells me that the Lord will punish me severely. And eventually He does, in ways that I would have never imagined.

The power of the penis!

The strength of Satan!

The weak will wither away. The strong will be blessed.

Lord, please have mercy!

Please!

Chapter Twenty
SHEIK

---

*A man who is used to acting in one way never changes; he must come to
ruin when the times, in changing, no longer are
in harmony with his ways.*
—Niccolo Machiavelli

After spending the entire day shopping with Jada, a little
buddy of mine from Uptown, we headed to my sports bar in
Belmont to have dinner with Crook and to watch a few
college football games.

Jada was a real cool chick, fun to hang out with, but was
just ghetto as they came. A real live hood rat. I met her a few
months ago downtown at the drive through window at the
McDonald's on Ridge and McIntire. She was working there
and had fucked up my order. We ended up arguing and her
crazy ass cussed me out and threatened to cut me with a box
cutter. A broad with that type of sass and heart was somebody
I needed to know. The rest is history.

Jada is a four-foot-eleven tiny chick with killer curves, light
skin, and an irresistibly gorgeous smile. She had a fuck-the-
world attitude and some Grade A Prime Choice pussy. Today
she was rocking a beige mini dress that left nothing for the
imagination. Her long brown hair had honey-blonde

highlights perfectly matching her crocodile Balenziaga crisscross platforms.

As we approached the front door of the sports bar Jada said, "It's hot as a muthufucka out here." She giggled while fanning her face with her hand. "It's fuckin November and it feels like summertime."

I said, "Global warming."

She spoke with a naughty smile. "Sweat got this pussy all salty with flavor for you when you lick it later."

"Is that all that you think about?"

"Damn nigga you are acting all different. What's gotten into you? I thought you loved the taste of my pussy."

Right when I grabbed the handle of the front door of the bar to open it Jada quickly lifted the hem of her dress revealing that she won't wearing panties. Crazy bitch had her pubic hair trimmed in the shape of an S. She laughed and pulled her dress back down.

"All for you nigga and nobody else," she said with a giggle.

I chuckled. "And anybody else who will buy you some Prada."

She frowned. "Nigga are you on your period or something?"

I warned. "Watch your mouth."

"Nigga, we ain't seen each other in over five months and you acting like you got a fuckin attitude!"

"Jada I gotta lot on my mind." I exhaled a deep breath.

"Well Mister Sheik how about when we go inside, and we head to your office so that I can give you a quick blow job because I want the happy nigga back that always knew how to make me feel like I'm floating." She rolled her eyes. "Not this red nosed clown nigga on his muthafuckin period."

I snapped. "Bitch I'll take every bit of that fifteen grand worth of clothes off your broke ass right now and send your ungrateful ass back to that muthafuckin roach infested shack that you live in with your slut-ass mother and crackhead sister."

She snapped back, "Nigga you ain't make me! So, what you bought all this shit! You can have it back right now muthafucka!"

I took a deep breath and said, "Yo, why can't you just chill out?"

She said, "Maybe I could chill if I wasn't dealing with a two-faced nigga like you!

"Two-faced?"

She spoke angrily, "Yeah two-faced! The last time we were together you take me to Hawaii, and we have a ball and then we get back and you don't call for over five months! Son of a bitch don't even return my calls and then you pop up, take me shopping, and spend a little money on me like everything is cool. With a stank ass attitude to go along with it. All day you've been acting like a little bitch!"

I reached over and plucked her forehead as hard as I could. "Didn't I tell you to chill out."

She went hysterical, screaming and cussing, threatening to cut me. It all sounded good, but she won't stupid. She had enough sense to run her mouth while simultaneously moving out of arms reach. Massaging the tension in my temples with my index fingers I watched as she let off a little steam.

Crooks Infiniti cruising down Hinton Avenue caught my attention. Jada saw it also and quickly calmed down. Her anger was instantly replaced by uneasiness. Rubbing her forehead, she cleared her throat and watched Crook parked in the lot across the street.

Jada quickly apologized and spoke a feeble. "I deserved that shit, didn't I?"

Shaking my head I chuckled and guided her inside the bar.

As we headed into the lobby I felt a flutter of pride. I always experienced overwhelming pride when I entered my spot.

Sheiks Bar and Grill had undergone a remarkable transformation since renovations were completed last month. The timeworn tables and chairs had been replaced with lounge style oak leather seating. The interior now consisted of oak panelling, stately oak wood floors, a massive, illuminated resin bar top and custom-made pool tables.

All of it was the unique stylish design of yours truly. Yep, it was my creation. The once hood hangout had been transformed into a posh establishment that the working middle-class had claimed as theirs. A classy and contemporary place to meet over sports, alcohol, and delicious food.

"Good evening Mr. Andrews," Greeted Kimberly the gorgeous maitré de.

I returned her smile. "Hey sexy," I spoke in a hushed voice where only she could hear me. I watched her blush, and I smiled inwardly.

Through the sheer curtain shielding the bar I could see that it was packed to capacity. Without another word I escorted Jada through the bar, threading our way through the packed room. We went to my favorite booth in the rear of the room near the hallway that led back to my office. A few moments later Crook and her date entered the room.

Crook was dressed in all black. Jeans, wife-beater, sneakers, and a Vintage Vinegar Hill baseball cap cocked on her head.

Crook introduced her date as Tiffany and after all the formal introductions were finished, we ordered our food.

Jada was snuggled up close to me. Her nervous eyes were on Crook. And my eyes were on Tiffany. She was a copper-colored beauty. Tall and slender, her auburn hair in coils. The peach-colored dress clung to her modest curves. She had a dimpled smile, dreamy bedroom eyes with high cheekbones and a cute little button nose. Had an exotic look like she could be Ethiopian or from one of the northern countries of Africa. She had the type of looks that grabs your attention and made you just want to stare.

Crook flashed a smile. "Well, well, well, I haven't seen y'all together in quite a while."

I spoke with a weak attempt at a smile. "You of all people know I've been busy."

Crook smirked and leaned back in her seat draping her arm over Tiffanys shoulder.

Tiffany spoke with an easygoing smile. "Sheik I've heard a lot of great things about you."

I smiled. "Crook feeding you some bullshit I see."

We all laughed.

Crook winked at me.

Tiffany spoke with a shy smile. "She didn't warn me that you were so handsome."

I recognized her flirting with a slight nod.

When the waiter finally brought our food, we dug in, everyone obviously hungry.

Staring at Tiffany I asked, "You're from Harrisonburg, right?"

She spoke with a proud smile. "Yes, born and raised. I moved here about two months ago after I was offered the position as assistant Commonwealth attorney."

I raised a brow. "Commonwealth attorney. Wow, a woman fighting for justice. That's an occupation full of responsibility."

She replied. "I have a passion for the practice of allocating each his or her just do according to the laws of this wonderful country."

Crook was watching me closely, grinning knowingly. She gently ran a finger across Tiffany's cheek then kissed her lips with a gentle peck and told her to feed her some fries. I smiled when Tiffany affectionately began feeding Crook fries.

Tiffany smiled. "She thinks that I'm her slave."

Jada laughed and whispered in my ear. "That bitch is pussy whipped ain't she."

We both laughed.

The four of us sat around talking and grubbing and at some point, in time Jada took over the conversation. She had everybody laughing as she told funny stories about her dysfunctional family.

My phone rang in the middle of a laugh. It was Re-Re. She spoke a pissed off, "How could you do that shit to my sister?"

"What the fuck are you talking about?"

"Don't play stupid!"

"I'm in the middle of something so this will have to wait."

She growled. "No, you've been purposely avoiding me all week. Not even returning my calls."

"I've been busy Re-Re."

"Selfish." She paused a moment then spoke an exasperated, "Sheik you promised that you wouldn't hurt her."

I stood, excused myself, then walked over to the bar and took a seat on a stool. I told Re-Re, "You need to mind your business. Re-Re this shit don't have nothing to do with you."

"My baby sister is my business."

"Re-Re I gotta go."

"Sheik, you took her virginity then dropped her like she's a bad habit." She growled, "Even after I told you that she was delicate. I told you she couldn't handle being hurt and you gave me your word. I trusted you."

I told her, "It ain't gonna work out between us."

She told me that Willow had went into a deep depression. She refused to eat and was staying confined to the house, bedridden, crying all the time. Willow had turned to drinking heavily.

I exhaled a deep breath. "I hope things get better with her. But Willow and her are a done deal."

"You cold-hearted muthafucka!"

"Watch your mouth and play your position. The only thing that I need from you is what I pay you to do."

"Twelve fucking days she's been trying to get in contact with you! Twelve days you inconsiderate motherfucker! You didn't even have the decency to drop her face to face. You handle the situation like a coward. You're going to reap what you sow!"

"Is that a threat?"

She spoke a venomous. "Take it how you want to take it! It's the law of the universe. Reciprocity, karma, the justice of life."

"Re-Re you're speaking words that's going to get you in a fucked-up place."

"Sheik, did you know that four days ago Willow tried to commit suicide by taking a bunch of pills."

"Not my business."

"Why are you acting like this? Why? Sheik just tell me why the coldness?"

Jada had walked over and eased in between my legs, hugging me, resting her head on my chest. Jada asked, "Baby-daddy is everything okay? You look like you need your dick sucked."

"Shut the fuck up!" I grimaced and shook my head, pointing towards the booth, signaling for her to leave me.

Jada didn't budge. She sucked her teeth and remained right there.

Re-Re snapped, "Who the fuck is that?"

Jada heard Re-Re and yelled into the phone, "I'm his future baby mama bitch! Who the fuck are you?"

Re-Re shouted back. "I'll have you murdered! Bitch, do you know who I am?"

Jada yelled. "Come bring it bitch! Bring the drama bitch! I'm at Sheiks sports bar!"

I ended the call and cussed Jada out for her recklessness. Well, that started a big argument. She kept shouting at me how I'd disrespected her by talking to another chick while I was out with her. Trying to talk some sense to an eighteen-year-old hood rat is like trying to tell a rock to jump.

I walked away from Jada. I had to cool down.

After my blood pressure had returned to normal, I went back and chilled with Crook, Tiffany, and Jada and watched the Virginia versus Virginia Tech football game. Sipping beers, everyone was relaxed and enjoying the evening. Everyone except me. My body was present, but my mind was elsewhere.

Willow was heavy in my thoughts. She had hung around the penthouse for about a week as I fucked her relentlessly. Then I drove her home and completely cut her off. Since then, she's been calling me all day, every day, but I refused to take her calls. She'd left countless messages. Initially the messages were sweet and tender words full of love. A few with her reciting poetry and singing love songs. But as the days rolled by and she didn't hear from me the messages went from love to words of anger to complete sadness. Last Monday she had popped up at the crib and for an hour straight she rang my doorbell screaming into the intercom that she was going to kill herself if I didn't let her in. Building security had to escort her from the property.

I seriously contemplated calling Willow, but I couldn't find the backbone to do it. It was cool that I had gotten the pussy because after all that's what I'd been working for all along. But now that I'd conquered, I had to move on. Yeah, I enjoyed her company but won't no need in acting like there was going to be a future with her, because there wasn't. My life is already too complicated. I definitely don't need the added stress of another nagging broad trying to force me to be her man.

A nigga did what he had to do to get what he wanted. Now it was time to move on. I can't front, being around Willow makes me feel good. When she was with me, I felt like the center of the universe. I can truly let down my guard and be myself, minus the stress of maintaining my image. She has a good heart, and I know what to expect from her because she's genuine, innocent, and pure. I found it hard to believe that people liked her really existed.

The cuddling and snuggling and those warm green eyes gazing at me had become an addiction. I loved everything about her. Her soft voice always speaking positive words of encouragement, always wanting the best for me. Her peaceful spirit and her unyielding optimism, her open mindedness and nonjudgmental attitude. Her love for life and people. Everything about her was perfect yet with all her virtue I was uncomfortable with the idea of ever seeing her again because I had broken my number one rule; Never Fall In Love.

Willow had gotten me good. Stole my heart and left me hating that I'd been so weak. I'd let her sneak into my soul. The life that I live has no place for such destructive emotions.

I looked at Jada who was laughing obnoxiously as she told Crook and Tiffany how she loved for me to fuck her in her ass. I shook my head and thought about how ironic it was that out of all the classy, exotic broads that I have on call I chose to spend the weekend with one that was the opposite of Willow.

I touched Jadas arm. "That's enough."

"Baby we all grown." Jada glanced at Tiffany and flashed

a grin. "Ain't that right Tiff?"

Crook laughed and Tiffany had a look of uncertainty on her pretty face. I assumed that this was her first time hanging around a certified Uptown, Grady Avenue hood rat. This was the most candid conversation she'd ever been in.

Crook's eyes were on me. She said, "What's wrong big fella? Scared that ol' girl going to put some shit out there that embarrasses you?"

Jada giggled. "With Sheiks big dick he ain't got nothing to be embarrassed about."

I said, "Chill out."

Tiffany glanced at everyone's face trying to figure out what was going on. I needed to get away from all these crazy motherfuckers for a little while. So, I stepped out back behind the bar and stood in the parking lot and smoked half a blunt to clear my head.

By the time I got back to the table I was relieved to find them talking about something other than me.

Jada asked Tiffany, "How long have you been into girls?"

Tiffany blushed and glanced at Crook then spoke with a shy smile. "I'm not into girls I'm into people's personalities, their inner self. Crook is the first girl I've ever dated."

Jada smiled. "Y'all make a good couple."

Tiffany giggled. "This is only our third date. We met in court. I was prosecuting her on a trespassing charge. She was found not guilty and, on the way, out of the courtroom she had the audacity to walk by me and squeeze my ass. Then she discreetly slipped me a piece of paper with her phone number on it. She whispered a few vulgar yet tender words in my ear that made me feel a certain way. Then she walked away. It took about a month before I worked up the nerve to call her."

Jada laughed. "Curiosity got your ass Tiffany."

Tiffany nodded with a smile and leaned over and kissed Crook.

Jada said, "I ain't into eating no pussy and I ain't into no bitch eating my pussy. I tried it once when I was sixteen and it ain't nothing that I like. I love big dicks and salty nuts. But if I ever decided to do the lesbo thing full time it would be with somebody sexy like Crook. She's a beautiful bitch that niggas fear and respect like God. Thinking about it got my pussy wet."

Everybody laughed except me.

A bunch of ruckus in the lobby caught everyone's attention. Arguing females, yelling, and screaming, then the clash of something being thrown. I heard my name being shouted. The voice sounded remarkably familiar.

Suddenly Willow appeared in the front of the bar. At first, I thought that my mind was playing tricks on me.

Crook uttered a surprise, "Hey big homie I know that's not who I think it is it."

It was Willow. She looked horrible. She had on a tiny pair of pink boy shorts with no panties, obvious because it looked like she had pissed on herself. The crotch area was soaked making the thin lace material transparent. She wore a white tank top with stains on it and a long pink silk robe. Her hair was wild, all over her head, and she was barefoot. She looked like she hadn't slept in days. Bags were under her bloodshot eyes.

Willow spotted me and began walking towards me with an urgent pace, bumping people as she passed them. She beelined to me like a hungry predator on its prey. When she reached the booth, I stood. She stood directly in front of me, toe to toe. She glared at me, her face painted with rage.

Her index finger was pointing in my face as she growled how much she hated me. Jada attempted to come to my aid and I was shocked beyond words when Willow quickly fucked her up. She thrashed Jada so quick and thorough that I found it hard to believe that this was gentle Willow.

Everybody in the bar's attention shifted from the TV screens to Willow.

Willows attention came back to me. Pushing and shoving me she screamed, "You're a cold-hearted piece of shit! I gave you my fucking heart and you treat me like a common whore! Do you think that you can just play with people's hearts you lowlife scumbag!"

Willow's words were slurred and her breath reeked of

alcohol. Her skin was moist with sweat. Her eyes shimmered with tears. She had a distinct odor coming from her that reminded me of the funky winos from the corner store that used to smell like garbage.

Crook was laughing hysterically. The scene had everybody's attention on us, their gawking eyes hungry for drama.

Standing there cool and composed I let her vent for a little while.

I pushed her fingers away from my face and in an even tone I said, "Calm down."

My words fell on deaf ears. She screamed, "You don't tell me to calm down, you no good piece of nothing! I hate you! I hate you! You manipulative son of a bitch! You played me!"

She spoke with a sarcastic, "Mr. Shakur Andrews, you're a big bad gangster aren't you! What are you going to do, shoot me like you shoot everyone else? Hunh? Kill me like you kill everybody else? Yeah, I've heard everything about you!"

I was on the verge of losing my temper. "Willow you're drunk. Shut up and go home."

She screamed, "You don't tell me what to do! Fuck you, Sheik! You don't own me! I'm not scared of you!" She quickly turned in a 360° circle and waved her hand. "You might own all of them, but not me! I'm not scared of you!"

The crowd laughed.

Crook spoke harshly, "Shorty, can't you see that you dropped? Move on before you get moved!"

Willow's attention went to Crook. "Shut the fuck up you crazy bitch! You fucking Neanderthal!"

Crook jumped to her feet. "Neanda-what! Bitch I'll smack the teeth outta your mouth! What the fuck is a muthafuckin Neandasoft…umm..Neandathot…"

Willow screamed, "It's Neanderthal you dumb cave bitch!"

Crook raised her hand to smack Willow, but I grabbed her wrist.

With her hands on her hips Willow told Crook. "Go ahead and hit me and I'll have you locked up before you can say the word bondsman! You brain sick demented lunatic!"

Willow's attention came back to me. "You know what, Sheik, I hope you die! I hate you!" Tears begin streaming down her cheeks as she kept repeating that she hated me.

I had enough. I turned and walked away heading to the restroom to check out Jada. Next thing I know Willow is attacking me from behind with a blitz of punches. Anger stripped me of all control. It was my reflex, a force of habit, but I reached for her neck, squeezing, seeking to choke some sense into her.

After I saw her face turn dark red, I hurled her across the room, sending her crashing into an occupied table. Willow lay sprawled out on the floor disbelief and shock covering her face as she struggled to regain her breath. Then suddenly she began bawling like a baby. A few people went to her trying to comfort her and help her.

I barked, "You stupid bitch! I told you to go home!"

In between sobs Willow sounded so pitiful when she said, "Why? Why Sheik? Please tell me why… why… me? I love you! I love you and you called me a bitch! Why? What did I do to deserve this? My God, you choked me! I thought you loved me! You told me that you loved me!"

My anger quickly transformed to shame. For the first time since my mom and sister died, I felt sad and genuinely heavy hearted.

Staring down at Willow laying there with her heart broke ripped me up inside. She really loved me, and I loved her too. Why had this happened the way that it did? I'm not supposed to be in love with a chick. I'm not supposed to love anyone. If history proves correct, I'm supposed to die in the street by hail of bullets from some up-and-coming gunslinger or get shot in the head by some type of revenge from a seed I sowed somewhere down the line. But love, no way. That bitch died long ago and was buried with my family. It's better to to be that way. It has to be that way. Love is a distraction, a weakness that betrays you and leaves you grabbing for air, unable to place your hands on anything solid.

How had I allowed this little church girl, the preacher's

daughter, to come into my life and steal my heart? Frustration flooded my senses, and a million thoughts ran rampant in my mind.

Willow looked so innocent. I wondered if she had seen this day coming when she was a young girl. There's no way that her father could have prophesied this moment in time.

I took a deep breath, and it took everything in my power to turn and walk away. She begged for me not to leave her, and it tore me up inside to keep walking. But I had to protect myself. I had to protect my heart.

When I got to the hallway that headed back to my office Jada followed me into the office and shut the door behind us. Jada was talking shit about how she was going to fuck Willow up the next time she saw her.

I sat down behind my desk and told Jada to shut up and she did. She went over to the black leather couch, pulled out a folded dollar bill with some coke in it and sniffed a little bit. Her eyes were glued to me. Silent I sat there feeling terrible inside trying to make sense of my life.

Suddenly the office door flung open, and I shook my head when I saw Willow stumbling in crying hysterically. Jada stood ready for battle her focus on Willow. I motioned for Jada to sit down and relax and without hesitation she did.

Willow hurried over to me. Pointing a finger into my forehead she screamed, "You are a liar! You're an unworthy compulsive liar! I can't believe that I trusted you!"

I didn't respond.

Willow continued. "You're a drug dealer. You're a gangster. You kill people and sell poison in the street. How could you be so deceitful?"

Suddenly she puked directly beside my feet. Ended up with vomit all on my shoes and pants leg. It smelled like a damn distillery. She wiped her mouth with the back of her hand and went straight back to yelling at me.

She said, "You take my virginity and my heart and throw it in the mud! You are garbage! You are a filthy drug dealing piece of garbage and I hate everything that you stand for!"

Silence lived between us as we both glared at each other

then she caught me completely off guard when she slapped me so hard that my head snapped back. I jumped to my feet, and she moved out of my reach.

Rubbing my face where she had smacked me, I spoke calmly, "Are you finished?"

Standing on the other side of the desk she stammered, "What…what…do you mean am I finished? What do you have to say about all of this? You're not going to deny it?"

"For what, it's the truth. Yeah, I'm a drug dealer. Yeah, I'm a gangster. You made your point. In fact, you made it very well."

She hadn't expected this reaction. It was written all over her face. She'd anticipated me throwing up a defense. She stood there staring at me. I sat down.

She asked, "Why didn't you lie?"

"I don't owe you an explanation about anything concerning me and I appreciate it if you would excuse yourself from my presence."

Willow began crying and screaming, grabbing items off my desk and hurling them at me. After a few moments she finished her tantrum then without a single word she stormed out of my office and slammed the door behind her.

Jada shook her head and exhaled a breath. "That dick of yours drives them crazy."

"Can you talk about anything besides sex, drugs, clothes or clubbing?"

"That's all I know."

"Then learn something else."

"I don't need to learn nothing else. I'm happy the way I am."

"What you need to do is learn how to fight. You got fucked up by a church girl who ain't never been in a fight."

She snarled, "Fuck you nigga! That bitch stole me. If she would have given me a fair one, I would have fucked her up."

"Go home. Get the fuck away from me and go home. Go somewhere and leave me alone."

"I thought that I was going to spend the weekend with you."

"Change of plans."

"Change of plans?" She pleaded, "Come on Sheik do not do this to me. I want to be with you."

I was about to cuss her out when I heard a whole lot of gunfire from automatic weapons coming from outside. Instinctively I reached for my gun. I ran outside.

I found Crook in front of the building crouched behind a car. She had her gun in her hand, her body shielding both Willow and Tiffany, both women hysterically screaming for help.

Crook saw me running towards her and yelled, "Yo I'm hit!"

I crouched beside her as my eyes searched for danger. The commotion of hundreds of people running around screaming and yelling made it hard to concentrate.

Squatting beside Crook, I lifted her off the girls and saw that her left arm was soaked in blood.

Crook quickly explained that her and Tiffany had stepped outside for a cigarette when an old brown Buick full of dudes had stopped at the intersection and screamed "JFM for life," then opened fire.

Helping Crook to her feet I said, "We gotta get you to the hospital."

Crook said, "I can make it." She handed me her gun and said, "Just leave before the cops show up. Take Tiff with you so that she won't get caught up in the middle of all this shit. She could lose her job."

Willow had taken off running down the block screaming for help. I called her name, but she kept running. Jada and Tiffany squeezed into the passenger side of the Ferrari, and I sped away. What in the hell was going on? I was certain that I would know soon enough.

Today had been a fucked-up day.

Chapter Twenty-One
WILLOW

*There is a way which seemeth right unto a man, but the
end thereof are the ways of death.*
—King Solomon

Re-Re had been texting someone for the last ten minutes while being rude to me by completely ignoring me. She had been uncharacteristically distracted all morning. Finally, she placed her phone on the table and took a sip of her smoothie.

She spoke quietly, "I feel like shit."

I sipped my smoothie. "A ten-mile run would do that to anyone. We ran it at an amazingly fast pace too. My legs are sore I need to stretch."

She cleared her throat. "It has nothing to do with jogging."

I was silent for a few moments while staring at Re-Re. I asked, "Well does it have something to do with why the doctor prescribed all those pills to you? Is there something going on with you that you are not telling me."

"How did you know about my pills?" She frowned thoughtfully. "Why are you going through my things?"

"I needed a pair of socks and went in your sock drawer to get them and saw all of those pill bottles."

With an accusatory tone she said, "You are always snooping through my shit! I am not going to warn you again, stay out of my things!"

Slowly shaking my head, I refused to feed into her poisonous spirit. She was looking for an argument and she was not going to get it from me.

We were uptown at a juice bar on University Avenue. The trendy establishment was packed with college students, most of them in study groups preparing for midterm exams. Hordes of laughter and soft chatter brewed with Top 40 Hits. Re-Re and I were perched on bar stools at one of those tall tables facing the humming traffic of the street.

"Baby-girl I apologize for snapping at you." Re-Re said, "I'm fucking stressed out."

"Give it to the Lord."

She spoke dryly, "Jesus can't help me with this one."

She was unsettled, doubt and sadness drowning her typically happy face.

I looked into her misty eyes and said, "I'm worried about you."

"I'm worried about me too."

I pleaded. "Please tell me what's going on with you."

I quoted Ecclesiastes 4:8-12 and she snapped.

"Fuck that Bible! Fuck Jesus! Fuck God! Fuck every damn thing!"

I gasped.

Re-Re had rebelled against God her entire life but she had never been so blatantly disrespectful towards Him. Something was definitely going on with her and it was scaring me.

I exhaled a deep breath, sipped my drink, and glanced at my reflection in the mirror on the wall. I looked a hot mess. We both did. Our jogging gear was soaked with perspiration. Our ponytails were frizzy and ragged. Our faces had ashy white lines of dry sweat.

Re-Re confided. "Baby-girl I am scared. I am horrified. The doctor did some blood tests and I…uh…I…."

She is badly shaken. She closed her eyes as if anguished. Over the years she had sometimes overreacted with sorrow to get attention but this time I sensed that this was serious.

I reached across the table and gently held her hand. "Big

sis, will you please tell me what's wrong."

Her eyes shimmered with tears as she sniffled. "Look at you. My little sister concerned about her big sister." She sniffled and told me. "I will be fine. Please don't worry."

I said, "That's easier said than done. I have never seen you so distressed."

"Hormones." Her face softened into a warm smile. "As you get older your periods become a psychological storm."

I asked skeptically. "Are you being honest?"

She sighed. "Yes dear. Stop worrying."

I knew my sister well enough to know that she was lying. She could fool everyone else, but she could not fool me. I knew her well enough to know that when she was ready to reveal what was truly going on with her, she would tell me. I tried to lighten the mood.

I said, "My fucking back is killing me."

I got the reaction I wanted when she laughed.

She said, "Little Miss holier-than-thou cursing like a damn sailor. God himself might personally come down and beat his good and faithful servant."

We both laughed.

I watched her as she pulled herself together.

She asked, "What's up with your profanity?"

"A bad habit that I picked up from a scumbag."

"Speaking of bad habits, for the last couple of weeks I've been smelling weed in the house." She sipped her drink. "I found an empty bottle of vodka in the kitchen's garbage Saturday morning."

I shifted, shrugged, and swallowed hard. I told her, "I'm coping."

"When did you start getting high?"

I spoke with a frustrated. "I'm coping with a very bad decision."

"A very bad decision that you just so happened to be in love with."

"That's nonsense."

She rolled her eyes. "Liar."

"I am not"

She asked, "You miss him, don't you?"

"Absolutely not." I told her, "It has been two weeks since that night I humiliated myself at the sports bar. Believe me I am over him."

"Your pride is causing you to starve your heart."

"The anger and hurt that I initially harbored has waned considerably."

She shook her head then gazed at me sympathetically. "I've stood outside of your bedroom countless nights and listened to you crying."

I did not say anything.

She said, "The only person that can make you stop crying is the one that made you cry."

"Stop it."

"It's the truth"

I hesitated for a moment then blurted out, "I hate him."

"You don't hate him."

I asked, "Is he putting you up to this? Are you on the clock promoting your boss's interest?"

"Of course not." She said, "I want you to be happy."

"I am happy."

"Happy people do not mope around the house all day and do not skip classes get drunk and high alone. Happy people do not listen to depressing love songs and cry themselves to sleep every night."

I didn't reply.

She stroked my arm and said, "He always ask about you."

"So, you are being manipulated by your boss?"

"No, I'm being manipulated by my love for my sister."

"Why would you want me to date someone like him?" I frowned. "He's nothing more than a lowlife thug who undertakes corrupt business for a living."

"Willow there's so much more to him and you know it."

I sipped my smoothie and glanced at my reflection in the mirror.

She said, "You need to call him."

"I will not." I said, "He's a thoughtless womanizing whore."

"And you love him."

"He's a cold-hearted hoodlum."

"And you love him."

I spoke an irritated. "Stop saying that."

"Its reasonable to concentrate on the possible benefits of pursuing a friendship with him."

"Benefits? You are unbelievable." I shook my head. "Benefits for you or for me."

"Quit implying that I have ulterior motives."

"So, stop promoting that loser as if he's the best thing for me."

She took the scrunchy from her ponytail freeing her long hair. Scratching her scalp she said, "Sheik is a man of esteem. A gentleman."

"Re-Re he is a drug dealer. A guy who is personally responsible for several gruesome murders."

"That's all rumor. Mere conjecture. He has never been convicted of anything even close to homicide."

My tone was ice cold. "Stop talking to me like I'm a jury that you're trying to convince."

"That's not the case at all."

I vented. "Did you know that Lamont has been missing for five days?"

"How could I not know? It's been on every network all day, everyday."

"I think that Sheik had something to do with Lamont's disappearance."

"That's absurd." She told me, "You need to get such a presumptive thought out of your head."

"That detective Rogers called me again."

"What did he want?"

"Asking questions about Lamont's disappearance."

"Why are they asking you about that?"

I shrugged. "I think that it has something to do with the night that Sheik and Lamont fought. He keeps asking me for Sheik's name."

"Don't tell them anything."

"I know."

"Next time he calls tell him to contact me if he has any questions."

I asked. "Do you think that Sheik did something to Lamont?"

"Absolutely not."

We debated for a few moments before I gave up on trying to convince her that Sheik was the personification of evil. A true and living demon.

Re-Re said, "He regularly donates substantially large amounts of money to various charities, and he takes care of a lot of people who are less fortunate."

"He's brainwashed you."

"Come on Willow." She said, "You know that I'm too strong willed to be brainwashed by anybody."

"If you're so convinced that he's the perfect man then why don't you date him."

"Maybe I will." With a dreamy smile she said, "He does have a charming slyness that......."

I shouted, "Stop it!" I snapped, "I am tired of hearing about him! It is so hard to get him out of my system! I want him out of my head, my soul, my body, but he is an addiction and my God......Lord. He is like the most powerful narcotic."

Re-Re smiled and exhaled a deep breath.

"Re-Re it's like he's worked a spell on me."

She asked, "If he was standing in front of you right now what would you say to him?"

I tried to answer but I couldn't.

Re-Re giggled and nodded towards the street.

My attention went outside. It was Sheik. My breath became unsteady. I swallowed and tried to gather my thoughts. His BMW was parked on the curb, and he was leaning on the passenger side watching me with a composed assurance.

Our gaze was like a beaming laser searing the air between us making the temperature shoot up 100°. He beamed with raw sex appeal. His eyes asserted that he came to take back what was rightfully his and me saying no was not an option. I saw it. Felt it. Knew it.

He was dapper in a black suit with a black shirt minus a tie. His hair had dozens of thick waves. The goatee was gone now replaced by a full beared shadowed and neatly trimmed.

Sheik winked at me and cracked a smile.

Deep down in my heart I wanted to run to him. My love for him is so deep that the last couple of weeks have been complete torture. I miss him so much. I think about him every second. My days have been full of daydreaming about him, my body simply going through the motions.

Love can be painful when it turns on you and bites you in the ass. It seems that love always does me like that. My last two pitches have been curveball strikes, and I was so tired of playing the game. Fatigued, my soul wanted out of the game. Call it early retirement. Being *alone* does not mean being *lonely*. I just hope the Lord heals me from this one. I pray that he pulls my love for Sheik out of my heart so that I can move on with my life without the burden of a broken heart.

When I looked beside me to scold my sister for conspiring with Sheik to set me up for this meeting I was confounded when I did not find her there. My eyes scanned the restaurant, and she was nowhere to be found.

When I looked out of the window, I spotted Re-Re jogging up the block, smiling. She waved and picked up her pace until she disappeared.

A few moments later Sheik was perched on the stool that my sister had abandoned. He scooted over until our body's touched. Electricity shot through me and made me shudder. His seductive cologne tickled my fancy making me think of the many favorable moments of our brief and fleeting past.

I am weak. Oh, so weak! I imagine that this is how a recovering alcoholic feels after being clean and sober for weeks then being shoved into a liquor store with the door locked behind him while he is stressed out and angry at life.

The warmth of Sheik's body cooked my skin. I was struggling with the urge to get up and run away. I looked at Sheik but didn't say anything. We shared an intense gaze for a moment, but I could not hold it because I am going to cry if I do so I looked away and stared out of the window at the bustling thoroughfare.

Neither of us uttered a word yet strangely there is a silent communication going on. I assume that this is the language of love. It feels quite different to be in his presence now knowing that he's a notorious kingpin. I see him in in a different light. I wonder if we argue will he smack the hell out of me or maybe call me a bitch and place that big gun that I know he's carrying in my face and pull the trigger. Isn't that how gangsters operate?

I suddenly grew angry because he's a gangster and I'm in love with him. I sipped my drink and stared at Sheik. He was staring at me with eyes that were unreadable. The silence was suffocating.

Sheik's phone vibrated and it startled me. When he answered it, I heard a female's voice. Sheik told her that he would call her later. Oh God, now I'm hurt, and my feelings are injured. I'm about to cry and I really need my sister.

My voice was weak and shaky. "Excuse me." I went to get up, but he grabbed my arm and gently tugged me back into my seat.

His voice is calm yet commanding. "Sit down."

I sat and asked, "Why are you here?"

"I made a devastating mistake and I'm here to make amends."

I frowned and turned away. "I don't have anything to say to you."

With a subtle plea he said, "Come on Willow, it's been long enough for you to be angry at me."

"I'm not only angry but I'm very disappointed in you."

"You have the right to be."

"Of course I do." I released an exasperated breath. "Sheik please leave me alone."

He was silent for a few moments and then spoke regretfully, "I've long had a reputation as a womanizer and I'm not proud of that. It grieves me. Willow, my love, my past life influenced me to make a very fucked up decision that I regret every second that I'm away from you."

I spoke a frigid, "Another dose of your deceit."

"How can I restore my credibility?"

"Restoration isn't an option."

He excelled a deep breath. "Willow, I live life without apology so please feel privileged to have me ask for forgiveness."

"That was such an arrogant remark."

"It's the truth."

We stared at each other for quite a while.

His tone was tender. "I can look into your eyes forever."

"Too bad that you forfeited that privilege."

"Temporarily suspended but not forfeited."

"Semantics." I told him, "They both mean the same thing."

He glanced around and cracked a low-spirited smile and said, "I've never confided in anyone."

"With secret like yours I understand why."

"Being mean doesn't benefit you."

His phone vibrated on the table, and he glanced at the number but didn't answer.

"I hope you don't mind," I said as I picked up his phone. He looked as if he did mine, but he conceded with a smile and a nod.

I answered. It was a female with a British accent. I told her that Sheik was busy and that she could leave a message. Her name was Summer, and she said that her plane would land tomorrow at 2:00 PM. She told me to tell Sheik to make sure that he sent the car to pick her up when she landed.

Handing Sheik the phone I shook my head and relayed the message. The resentment on my face must have been apparent because immediately he offered me an apology.

My voice was feeble. "It doesn't matter."

He placed his hand on mine. "It matters because I care about your feelings."

"Do you tell all your women the same thing?"

He said, "I challenge your perception of me. You're who I love. What I did to you was a mistake." His tone was vulnerable. "I've been in a downward spiral since our separation."

"I find that hard to believe."

"Why?"

"You don't look like you've been in a slump." My eyes quickly scanned his body. "It looks like you've been doing just fine."

"Can we talk without the contempt?"

"If I don't will you kill me?"

"Willow that's not cool at all." He was quiet for a moment then spoke softly. "Up until I met you, I didn't know how to live as an emotional creature and due to my hellish past, I've always avoided any hints of love."

I told him. "You know nothing of love."

"You might be right." He paused. "But what I do know is that I'm in love with you."

"If you loved me, you wouldn't have fucked me then dumped me. If you really loved me, you would have never treated me so cruel and unkind."

"People make mistakes."

"And I bet that all of your mistakes are at the expense of others."

He said, "You're making it seem like I'm the scum of the earth."

"You're close to it."

"Willow, baby you came into my life and stirred something deep down in my soul."

"And you expressed that to me by treating me like a common whore?"

"No. It was stupid." He paused a moment and said, "My childhood was fucked up. Emotionally and psychologically, it left me with the inability to trust people."

My words were dipped in sarcasm when I said, "Thanks for your testimony but I'm somewhat ill equipped to deal with a guy so experienced and seasoned."

He frowned and slammed his fists on the table. He growled, "Stop acting like a stupid immature bitch! That's not who you are! I'm being sincere."

I sat there staring at him. His eyes were on fire as he glared at me. We remained silent, our thoughts brewing. I watched his anger slowly fade. I wonder why it is so hard for me to forgive him.

I glanced at the ceiling. "Why me Lord?"

"Be an adult and speak your mind."

I looked at him for a long moment. "Why do you have to be who you are?"

"Why can't you accept me as I am?"

"Because you can be so much better."

"I want you to help me be better. That's why I'm here." He hesitated then said, "I love you." He held my hand and kissed it. For a moment I was under his spell, tipsy from his touch, his closeness.

I complained. "Why me?"

His eyes were full of sincerity. "Because I'm in love with you."

I lowered my head and whispered, "Men like you break hearts. You die young or get sent to jail for life."

"I'm from the streets but not defined by them."

"A man is defined by his choices, his actions, his deeds, and reactions."

"I agree." He nodded. "I often worry about the value of my heart. Sometimes I feel that I'm not worthy of a woman like you. Like you are too good, too genuine, and too pure."

I was silent.

He said, "I avoid hasty decisions especially with issues of my heart and my love. Willow being with you gives me a peace and joy that no one has ever given me. I have a readiness and inclination to love you wholeheartedly."

I said, "You left me hurt and bitter."

"I was stupid."

"Yes, you were stupid."

He chuckled. I smiled.

I told him that the incident at the bar was humiliating.

"If I could rewind time and do it different I would. But I can't and I regret it." He cleared his throat. Paused for a moment and said, "Not being able to see you and express my feelings for you has been tearing me apart." He exhaled deeply. "I want us to start over. I want a clean slate."

"I'm afraid. I don't want to be hurt again."

"Loyalty is an extinct quality of man." He told me, "And the world I live in is one of treachery where no one can be trusted. I allowed that reality to prejudice me against seeing you for what you really are, which is a pure being with no ulterior motives."

"Having such an extreme distrust of others must be a horrible way to live."

He nodded slowly. "That's why I'm in desperate need of your companionship. I need your spirit around me. When I'm around you I want to be a better man. Only you can help me be a better person."

I held out my hand and he gave me his.

He said, "Despite our setbacks I need you to help me be a better person. Please be a part of my life."

I whispered. "Right now, I don't know what I want."

"You once told me that you teach a ministry of repentance and reconciliation"

"Yes."

"And that repentance is seated in the heart, right?"

"What's your point?"

He replied, "My point is that I truly feel remorse for failing you. I regret my conduct, and I want to make a change for the better. Want to be what you need."

"Sheik it's important that you understand that I choose to live an exemplary life. You represent everything that I'm against."

He excelled a deep breath. "Of course, we're going to face relationship challenges, but we can make it. I just asked you to look at my situation with your heart rather than your eyes and ears."

I told him that I did not approve of what he did to make a living. If we were to pursue any type of relationship, he would have to abandon his livelihood.

His serene expression indicated that he was receptive and desired to accommodate me in any way.

He said, "I'm here to accommodate you."

I asked, "Have you ever thought about an exit strategy?"

"Yeah. I'm in the process of walking away from my past. It's going to take a little time. About a year."

We both grew silent staring into each other's eyes. The truth was that my heart belonged to him whether I wanted to admit it or not. He was my all, my everything, and we could work through this if we put our hearts and our souls into it and ask the Lord to give us the strength.

Paul of Tarsus, the author of most of the epistles of the New Testament of the *Bible* was a murderer and a persecutor of early Christians and the good Lord came to him on the road to Damascus and changed his heart. So too could be the case with Sheik. With God anything is possible. If he parted the Red Sea to let the Israelites pass, then He will also part Sheik's life and make a way for him to pass from damnation to eternal life.

Sheik called the waiter and order a brand muffin and a smoothie and while he ate, we shared small talk. I wanted to kiss him but refrained. We still hadn't officially gotten back together yet. We talked about the weather and how life had been treating us since the last time we saw each other. We kept it slow and easy.

After he finished his muffin, he slid his arm behind me and draped it on my shoulder.

He whispered in my ear. "Let's stop playing games." Then he kissed my cheek.

I said, "I don't want to play games."

"I'm here because I love you and I know that you love me. I've been miserable."

"Me too."

He kissed my cheek. "I apologize for hurting you and misleading you."

"I forgive you."

"Thank you."

We shared a few gentle kisses.

He asked, "What's on your mind?"

"I'm trying to make sense of what's going on."

"You're going to need my help for that."

"I know."

"Let's start with you and how you're feeling right now."

"I'm glad that you're here. I'm extremely optimistic about our future because at least we're talking."

He kissed me passionately. Right there in the juice bar he kissed me with so much emotion, so much fervor, so much intensity.

When our lips parted I was dizzy. I licked my lips, smiled, gazed into his eyes and said, "How can you, this obviously marvelous man be who they say you are? I can't see it."

"So don't see it. Refuse it."

"That's not reality.

"It can be."

"That would be delusional."

"It's a matter of perception. Everyone does it. We see what we want to see and ignore the rest and make it nonexistent."

"Selective attention and perception is for the incompetent."

"Okay you're losing me with the psychological talk. Just come back to normal conversation." He smiled.

"Sheik, you lied to me about who you were and now I'm in love with you."

He stated seriously. "I didn't lie."

"Yes, you did."

"No, I didn't. You only heard what you wanted to hear. You saw what you wanted to see. Seems like you were the one suffering from selective attention and perception."

"What are you talking about?"

"Tell me what I lied about?"

"The investments, the businesses, the silent partner in the pharmaceutical company."

"None of those were lies. I can prove it all to you. I'll show you paperwork, business licenses, all legal documents. You can do research with the Chamber of Commerce."

"But...but...what about...."

He stated calmly. "I am what you think I am. The only misleading thing that I told you was that I owned a pharmaceutical company and the only reason that it was misleading was because you made it that way."

"Me?"

"Yeah, you chose to accept that I was speaking of legal pharmaceuticals. You never asked."

I nodded in agreement as I replayed our past conversations in my head. He was right.

He said, "I want you to understand me and who I am"

"How? Where? I mean where do I begin?"

"Come on let's go hang out."

"No." I glanced at my reflection in the mirror. "I'm yucky and I need to bathe." I paused for a moment or two staring deep into his eyes striving to read his motives, his heart. As much as I wanted to walk away from him I couldn't because I witnessed true love in his eyes.

I nodded with a smile. "Okay let's go."

Chapter Twenty-Two
WILLOW

Regard your soldiers as your children, and they will follow you into the deepest valleys; look upon them as your own beloved sons, and they will stand by you even unto death. If, however, you are indulgent, but unable to make your authority felt; kind-hearted, but unable to enforce your commands; and incapable, moreover, of quelling disorder: then your soldiers must be likened to spoilt children; they are useless for any practical purpose.
—Sun Tzu

Sheik and I became inseparable. A month had passed in a blur of laughter, concerts, clubbing, out of town trips, stimulating conversations, and awesome love making. I'll be the first to admit that I was deeply in love. Sheik made me feel good inside. He knew how to make me feel like a woman. Every second of my life was spent thinking about him and his unique love.

Absolutely never staying at home I had practically moved in with Sheik. Most of my things from home were scattered throughout the penthouse, markings of my new territory.

Sheik had blessed me with space in his humongous walk-in closet, setting aside half of it for my massive wardrobe and shoe collection. We lived together peacefully. I positively loved living with him. Loved waking up to him every morning. Loved catering to his every wish. Loved cooking breakfast and dinner for him. Loved when he lay sprawled and spent in the bed after one of our steamy love making sessions and he asks for my advice on certain issues pertaining to his business or a problem he had encountered. Sometimes we would sit up all night, talking about a major decision he had to make.

Sheik's life was interesting and there was never a dull moment. His life was like a 24-hour reality show on the life of a crime boss. I was so privileged. So, blessed.

It was two days before Christmas and Sheik was having a party at the penthouse for the dignitaries of the South First Commission. He had bought everyone gift bags stuffed with all kinds of expensive goodies. I was eager and excited to meet the elite personnel that ran Sheik's business. It would be my first time being in the presence of a bunch of real-life gangsters. Feeling a tad bit anxious I smoked a joint of some phenomenal weed and took a few shots of Grey Goose to ease my jitters.

Sheik took me shopping and bought me an exquisite form-hugging lavender Valentino dress, Christian Louboutin heels, and a collection of elegant Bulgari diamond jewelry. My hairdresser had hooked me up with a fabulous up-do and standing in the bedroom staring at my reflection in the mirrored wall, I had to admit I looked amazing.

Standing at the top of the staircase I finished my drink and listened to the happening's downstairs. I heard a lot of voices and hip-hop music thumping. Loud laughter and joyful screams filled the house. I was evolving, moving away from my former life of monotony into a thrilling adventure and I had dived in headfirst with no regrets.

A rush of excitement hit me at the sight of the crowded living room. It was a glamorous event, the vibe festive, every woman present remarkably beautiful draped in designer clothes and flashy jewelry. Most of the guys were dapper in high-end casual wear. A few were in fashionable urban gear. Their ages ranged from late teens to middle-aged.

A big dice game was under way over by the piano platform. Some people were playing spades while others were lounging around watching a movie on the large screen. A few were dancing, bumping and grinding. One girl who bore a strong resemblance to the actress Paula Patton was stark naked dancing on the piano. Her eyes were closed with a look of euphoria on her face as if she was in another world.

Weed smoke was thick in the air.

I cheerfully mingled my way around the room. Everyone seemed genuinely enthused to meet me. Compliments on my outfit and beauty came from everywhere and I knew that I was blushing, my smile broad and toothy. They were a provocatively enchanting people. Very charming. Nothing like what I imagined them to be.

My eyes searched the room for Sheik, but he was nowhere to be found. A couple of guys pointed to the rear of the house. Playfully calling Sheik's name I strolled towards the back rooms, opening doors checking for him.

I heard his laughter coming from his office. When I opened the door, I was hit by a thick weed cloud. Sheik was perched on his desk. As always, he was immaculately well groomed from head to toe. Slacks, a V-neck sweater, and a modest amount of jewelry.

Re-Re stood beside Sheik, her hands resting on his shoulder. Sheik flashed me the most brilliant of smiles and gave me a steady stream of compliments.

Re-Re flashed a stale look as if I'd interrupted something. She mumbled something under her breath, glanced at Sheik and gave me a weak smile.

She said, "Hey baby-girl don't you look pretty tonight."

She was very drunk. I could see it all in her face and in the way that she was swaying. Her blouse had only two buttons that were buttoned up, showing a lot of cleavage.

I grew slightly irritated that she was standing there in front of my man in such an indecent manner. And it didn't help that the hymn of her little, tiny miniskirt was riding so high that I could see the bottom of her ass cheeks. She wasn't even wearing panties.

I shook my head. "Fix your clothes, you look like a hooker."

Re-Re laughed at me and rolled her eyes, then she went to the couch, sat down, and fired up a blunt that was in the ashtray. Her eyes were on Sheik, watching him with sensual eyes that made me angry.

I told my sister, "You don't need anymore to drink!"

Sheiks eyes were soft and loving. We gazed at each other, drawing in each other's eyes as though we were submerged into each other's soul.

His voice was mellow. "Come here."

I went to him, embraced him, and he kissed me tenderly. As I held him, I thought how extraordinary special I felt. I was relaxed and happy.

Sheik asked, "How are you doing?"

"Great." I reached down and zipped up his zipper. "What about you?"

He chuckled. "A little tipsy." He asked, "What's going on out there?"

"Everyone is happy as can be." I told him about the naked girl dancing on the piano.

He chuckled and said, "That has to be Shante."

I described the girl to him, and he nodded. "Yeah, that's Shante. She's Crook ex-girlfriend. Speaking of Crook where is she?" He glanced at his watch. "She should've been here." He asked, "Did you meet a few of the guys?"

"I met everyone out there. Some of them twice."

Sheik nodded towards my sister. She had fallen asleep, her head resting on the back of the couch, her mouth wide open as a light snore escaped her mouth.

We both laughed.

Sheik's phone vibrated on his hip, and it was evident that it was an important call because he excused himself and took the call out on the balcony.

I had just pulled myself a drink when Crook walked into the office. She was wearing a cream-colored Prada sweat suit and Timberlands on her feet.

I sipped my drink and smiled. "Hey Crook."

She gave me a look of disdain, glanced at my sister, and shook her head. She asked me, "Where's my big homie?"

I pointed to the balcony.

She asked me, "Do you know how to roll?" She held up

a Cohiba cigar and a sandwich bag full of weed.

I shook my head. "No, Sheik usually rolls for me."

"All you're good for is fuckin' and suckin' hunh?" She smirked. "A damn shame. Clown bitch."

I frowned. "You're so mean."

"I eat a mean pussy too. Do you want to find out?" She cracked up laughing.

I shook my head in disgust and glanced at Sheik standing on the balcony. His face was covered in stress as he argued with someone on the phone. I found it fascinating that he was talking in fluent Spanish.

A few moments later Sheik walked through the French-doors. Crook paused rolling the blunt and they did that friendly hug thing that they do when they greet each other. Sheik then took a seat in the chair behind his desk. I migrated to his lap, my arm over his shoulder.

Crook sat down beside Re-Re and plucked her ear. Re-Re jumped awake looking around, her eyes frenzied like she was about to attack someone.

We all laughed at her.

Re-Re yawned, stretched and moved close to Crook.

Re-Re smiled and kissed Crooks cheek. They shared a quick tongue kissed and then Crook went back to rolling her blunt.

Re-Re said, "That power nap did me good. I had to rejuvenate myself."

Sheik laughed a little. "About an hour ago my brilliant counselor and C.E.O. of Andrews Enterprises was in the middle of the living room doing a striptease to Lil Wayne's song 'Lollipop'."

Re-Re spoke a sheepish. "I made a damn fool of myself."

Sheik chuckled. "Your big sister was taking it off while dropping it like it's hot."

Everybody laughed.

Sheik teased, "Next time you decide to strip for a room full of people at least get paid."

Everybody cracked up with laughter.

Crook looked at Re-Re and said, "Baby next time we're

going to charge a thousand dollars per head."

Laughing, Re-Re punched Crooks arm. "Baby that's fucked up. You probably would try to pimp me like that."

"Taking care of you ain't no cheap task." Crook said while lighting the blunt. "This bitch spent over fifty grand of my money the last time that we were in New York."

Re-Re smiled. "You're the nigga of the relationship aren't you. A big boss balling, right?

"For sure."

Re-Re kissed Crooks cheek. "I'm a high maintenance diva."

Crook blew out a large cloud of smoke. "As much as we pay you for your salary you need to be treating me every now and then."

Re-Re nodded. "No problem. Miami next weekend. All expenses on me."

I said, "Yeah she's definitely drunk."

We all laughed

We sat around smoking a blunt while sharing a ton of laughs. Twenty minutes later we were strolling down the hallway to join the party. Hand in hand Sheik and I made our rounds through the party, everyone worshipping Sheik as if he was God almighty. He was their king, and it was so obvious that they feared and respected him. For the first time in my life, I felt powerful and invincible. God-like. It was incredible.

After a couple of hours, the laid-back party turned into an all-out club atmosphere everyone dancing while the DJ rocked the house. Sheik and I were relaxing in a plush recliner, cuddling while watching the S.F.C. get their party on.

I kissed him gently on the lips and asked. "What's on your mind."

"You."

"Me?"

"Yeah."

"What about me?"

"I'm sitting here thinking how I can wake up to you every morning for the rest of my life."

Grinning I said, "That's sweet."

"It's the truth."

I nodded. Kissed him.

He said, "I can't imagine any reason strong enough to make me want to live a day without you at my side."

"The feeling is mutual."

"I want you to become a permanent fixture in my life."

I was silent. He ran the tip of his fingers over my cheek and kissed my nose. Then we shared a passionate kiss. We kissed so long that I feared that he swallowed my heart.

He said, "I love you."

"I love you too."

"There are two mistakes a man can make along the road to true love." He paused a moment as he gathered his thoughts. "Not going all the way with it and not starting it."

"What are you talking about?"

He hesitated a moment then said, "In order to discover new lands one must be willing to lose sight of the shore for a very long time." He got up and went to a knee in front of me.

The music stopped. Everyone's attention was on us.

My heart began pounding and it felt as if my breath was slipping away. I fanned my face with my hands.

Sheik gazed into my eyes, love beaming. He cleared his throat. "I live by the motto, *leap and the net will appear.*"

I nodded.

He said, "Miss Willow Hope Harrison will you spend the rest of your life with me?"

Tears of joy began flooding my eyes. I nodded and spoke a breathless, "Yes, yes I will spend the rest of my life with you."

The applause and cheers were deafening as he slid the ring on my finger.

He whispered in my ear. "Until death do us apart?"

I whispered back. "No. Beyond death. Eternal. Forever."

"Forever and a day?"

The thunderous clap of three gunshots quickly seized my attention.

My peace, my heaven on earth, was shattered by the malicious intent of someone's ambition to assassinate my fiancé, the king of The South First Commission. I helplessly watched as Sheiks body absorbed a few bullets.

What the fuck!

Mayhem and pandemonium broke out next.

Screams!

Yells!

More gunshots from different sounding guns. Everybody was scattering, running for cover, guns drawn.

What in the hell is going on?

It took only a moment to realize that Sheik was hurt badly. He was slumped on the ground, unconscious.

Automatic weapons were being fired all around me.

Who was the enemy?

What was going on?

I managed to dial *911* and then ducking bullets that were whizzing by I went to attend to Sheik.

Suddenly darkness enveloped me as a piercing sharp pain clutched the left side of my head.

The last thing that I remember was Crooks voice yelling, "SFC to the death!" Then what sounded like a machine gun spit out nonstop rounds of pure terror.

I lost consciousness.

THE END
OF
BOOK ONE

BOOK TWO OF THE TRILOGY COMING SOON

COMPLIMENTARY FREE CHAPTERS FROM THE AUTHORS

AUTOBIOGRAPHY

The Unfolding: Evolution of the Apex Predator by Pertelle Gilmore
AVAILABLE ON AMAZON & Kindle

Introduction

Swift as the wind. Quiet as the forest. Conquer like the fire. Steady as the Mountain.
—Sun Tzu

"Shoot him in the face," whispered Ru. "Don't let that nigga get away." His whisper now a frustrated growl. "Nigga I know that you ain't scared. Shoot that nigga!"

At the tender age of fourteen I was about to shoot a man for the first time. While my peers were naturally enjoying life with the sprightly spirit of young teen ambition and adventure, I was moments away from adopting the role as the Grim Reaper.

Ru tried to snatch the gun away from me while snarling, "Let me show you how to do it nigga! You done froze up! Scared ass nigga…."

With a hard push to his shoulder I whispered a calm, "I got this."

I was not about to shoot this man because I wanted to. I was about to shoot this man because I *had* to. He had victimized me two weeks prior. A grown man, an adult, had preyed upon a skinny, fourteen-year-old kid. He had victimized me with a housing project full of people watching. Right there in the ferocious trenches of Prospect Projects. If

I did not shoot him then I would be considered food to everyone. This means that I will be considered weak, easy prey, a proverbial meal for all the beast of the environment. As a brand-new crack-cocaine dealer I would never have a chance. Once word got out that I let someone rob me and I did not retaliate then even frail, weak crackheads would try their hand at robbing me.

I knew that this had to be done. Ru knew that I had to do it. The streets knew that I had to do it. Or else!

The imminent victim of street justice was completely unaware of the hunt. Oblivious of how close death was to him. He was running from car to car serving crack-cocaine to souls in search of amnesia from whatever reality was afflicting them.

Glancing over my shoulder at Ru I can barely make out his tiny silhouette. The night was starless, a thunderstorm washing the city's mean streets. The towering trees that line the streets are conveniently blocking the streetlights. Darkness is our ally. Always has been. Especially when executing justice to a washed-up gangster that mistakenly robbed the wrong youngster.
He never seen it coming…

Swift as an orca slicing through the turbulent sea pursuing a great white shark.
As nimble as a feline pouncing on its favorite prey. As focused as a Seahawk on the dive prepping to hit the ocean at max speed to
recover a herring; as determined and relentless as a lone wolf hunting an elk in
the dead of winters frigid clutch, the young predator pounces on his first prey.
The first of many…
Pop! Pop! Pop! Pop! Pop!
* * *

Shaky John's Advice

PERTELLE GILMORE

Be where your enemy is not—Sun Tzu

When I was a tender eleven years old, I received the greatest pearl of wisdom that I've ever received in my life. On the train tracks an old wino named Shaky John once told me, "Boy there is always three sides to the truth. Your truth, the other person's truth, and THE TRUTH. Always stand upon THE TRUTH. Fuck all the rest of the bullshit acting like THE TRUTH. The world loves lies imitating THE TRUTH. Why? Because most of the people are cowards lacking courage to face reality (THE TRUTH). Yeah, youngin THE TRUTH is the way and the light. YOU are the way and the light. The way because your path will lead many. The light because your brightness will illuminate that path for them. I know your pedigree. You come from good stock on both sides of your family. You are a different type of dude Gilmore, way different than them knucklehead dudes your age. Youngin' always walk in THE TRUTH. No matter the expense, be you. When you are THE TRUTH, it is lonely. Why? Because TRUTH repels falsehood, and the great majority are counterfeits living false realities because it is comfortable for them. You are destined to be a king. And youngin' as you go through the painful process that all TRUE kings must go through remember that THE TRUTH is the only thing that will sustain your sanity. Be THE TRUTH. Don't ever forget that and you are guaranteed greatness. Forget that shit and die slowly like me."

***

What you have in your hands is my understanding, my interpretation, MY PERCEPTION, my truth, my life. THE TRUTH has no partners. It stands alone. It represents itself and stands by itself. It needs no support. This is YOUR truth, MY truth, and THE TRUTH.

I am sharing my deepest thoughts and views on life, the ever evolving philosophy of an Apex Predator. This book isn't exact science nor is to be ingested as a meal of scientific or historic facts. Though I discuss various historical and scientific topics and how I perceived how they affected me and my Black community it is only relayed through the filter of opinion. This means that everything that you'll read is my own personal opinions, interpretations, perceptions, and views on life and its countless facets. Whatever is read is from me, by me and a part of me.

My heart is laid bare in this duet of honesty and explanation. May you receive the words of this open epistle with clarity and sound mind. May you step into my world and travel with me, leaving a naturally judgmental spirit behind. May my experiences, strengths, weaknesses tragedies, triumphs, growing pains, and sincerest hopes, aid you in gaining an understanding of me and my generation, my peer group, my comrades, us who were nurtured in the womb of the so-called 1980's crack cocaine epidemic.

The word Amerikkka is used in place of the United States of America. This intentional and subversive misspelling of the word America is to etch a remembrance of the White Supremacy foundation of this country. The White Supremacy order that is the heartbeat of this country in the present moment. The KKK are the prototype and in my own opinion have evolved so effectively through well led strategic maneuvering that now they have become invisible to the naked eye. Now they are not your typical white southern hillbilly cracker with the pink face and pristine pointy hood. Now they are the smiling Ivy League graduate with a law degree and a New Englander accent sitting on a judge's bench dishing out hordes of time to Black men.

Lynching has moved from the swamp to the courtroom. Amerikkka definitely made sure slavery never died. It just morphed into what we have termed the *projects* and *prisons*. Thus, the Amerikkka is used as a reminder of the White Supremacy face behind the mask. It is a mocking tribute to the White supremacy institution, that established, sustained, and continually maintains this order of colonization and domination here on the shores of my native Red brothers.

The three K's winks at the Klu Klux Klan, the poster child for white terrorism and supremacy. This was done because of the familiarity of the organization in the consciousness of all generations in regards and relation to the White Supremacy Order. In the hood they are consider the O.G.'s (Original Gangster) of the White Supremacy Order. Under the proverbial umbrella of this KKK stands every single organization, institution, ideology, militia, and movement that embodies this rule and dominance of the White race. The cradle of this White Supremacy Order is the United States thus the three KKK's are used to remind of that truth.

The word jungle is used extensively throughout the book and whenever you see it, I am exclusively referring to life in the hood, the ghetto, the projects. Merriam-Webster Dictionary defines a jungle as, "a place of ruthless struggle for survival." Anybody who has ever spent any substantial time, lived in, or were born and raised in this relentless environment knows and understands that it certainly is a place of ruthless survival in the fullest context of the phrase. Me the product of this unrelenting domain of constant battles bear witness of it being a ruthless struggle for survival.

In the jungle creatures of predators and prey exist on a landscape of unceasing, subtle, and overt hunts. In this realm the furnace of affliction is always at its max, incinerating the hopes and dreams of babies yet to be born. In the jungle, the animalistic, the lower self, the beast, manifest itself in the various personalities of the people. Just like the jungles of Mother Africa the concrete jungle here in Amerikkka births and is home to lions, gazelles, elephants, chameleons, apes, snakes, hyenas, wild dogs, etc. Though these animals are not physically roaming the pavements of the concrete jungle, they exist as the personality types of every single person that lives there.

Wolves, (gangs) roam in packs in every hood. Poisonous snakes (sly, cancerous people), slither through the maze of streets and corners their venomous spirit injecting the fangs of manipulation into the weak and gullible. Chameleons, (deceptive, cunning,) move in and out of every circle picking up seeds(information) as they expertly take on the colors(personalities) of the terrain (whoever is present).

In the jungle there are twelve primary personality types that coincide with the characteristics of various animals from the jungles of the Mother Land. And everyone of them has invested into the unfolding of yours truly. This will be further expounded upon in the forthcoming book titled *The Jungle*. Yet during the meantime it is imperative to understand the term beast, which I use extensively and exclusively in reference to man's lowers self.

It is my personal belief and opinion that humans own two SELVES that abides in the soul of man, as the soul of man. The soul or heart, both synonyms used interchangeably in theological thought, in essence is what we call the mind today. Our mind is the home of our belief system, opinions, intellect, seat of our emotions, and personality. The core of who we are, this unique soul, is the sum total of these two selves, which I recognize as the lower-self and the higher-self.

The lower self is the barbaric, animal-like beast which is profoundly embedded in our inner network of survival instincts. Its innate function is to persist, endure, and persevere in a realm of treacherous savagery. The lower self is hardwired to endure the harshest of conditions and despite insurmountable risks and peril, it rages on until either success or death is accomplished. A fatal trait when unchecked.

This lower self is the foundation of who we are. The beast is what compels us to feed ourselves and indulge in our sexuality, the two most basic drives of man. The beast primary purpose in life is for our fight or flight reflexes, and our sexual appetite and will to consume food for nourishment, for energy to battle in the jungle. The lower self is the being inside of man that is a slave to mental death and power. This inner creature is easy to lead to destruction but difficult to lead to its rightful ascension into a productive union with its counterpart, the higher self. When and if this union occurs the soul of the individual becomes godlike with every aspect of its nature seamlessly executing survival intelligence at its highest level.

The higher self is in complete contrast to its

counterpart, the lower self. The higher self is supreme intelligence. It is the seat of our intellect and the Supreme Mind that governs our cunning decision-making. It is the rational, highest aspect of consciousness. The Apex Predator acquires empirical knowledge of how to unify the duality of the soul, both selves, and uses this awesome weapon to conquer world after world, ascending to the pinnacle of the food chain. This Cain to Abel dynamic that the writer of Genesis allegorically and eloquently relayed to us is the superpower of the conscious person who initiates the process of self revolution.

At its apex, the higher self is godhood which is the utilization and execution of our intelligence at its highest frequency. Jesus said it when he told the people, *I and the Father are one.* The war daily, well more accurately, the war every second of our lives is between these two internal selves. This duality is what makes us human.

The beast is what produces death and carnage, devouring prey for meals and for the elimination of competition. The beast is pure instinct, pure emotion, utilization of the five senses solely for identification of danger. The beast is the animal in us. It is the animal that beseeches our will to survive and thrive in a place of ruthless survival.

May this gift of me explaining the science of the jungle according to my interpretation be a revealing, insightful, and a helpful tool for your personal toolbox of understanding.

By the time I reached the age of sixteen I was debatably the most feared man walking the streets of my city. The fear was purposely and meticulously cultivated and instilled within the hearts of everyone with a ceaseless flow of vicious, seemingly unpredictable acts of violence. And no one was exempt from this wrath. And no one was exempt from the fear.

Seasoned adult gangsters and drug dealers, my former gods, that I blindly and zealously worshipped, all bowed to the will of this young, up-and-coming beast. Everyone bowed. The cries and pleas of grown men, who were certified hitters, apex gangsters, of their respective hoods, floated through the city as common as a lingering trail of cigarette smoke. But that's to be expected from anyone who stumbles into his home after a night out with the fellas to discover his wife and kids duct taped on the bedroom floor with a masked shooter in all black toting the biggest gun he has ever seen. It is enough to tame the wildest, most ferocious beast. Thirty years later I have had retired officers approach me and confess how for years I had the entire Charlottesville Police Department terrified.

The Unfolding: Evolution of the Apex Predator had its informal origin in the filthy, mice infested basement, holding cell of the Juvenile Court building downtown on East High Street in Charlottesville, Virginia. The cold, damp chamber was reminiscent of a castle dungeon. The stench of urine was as thick as fog, a consequence of my peers carelessly pissing on the floor rather than in the stainless-steel toilet in the corner of the cell.

At fourteen years old I sat balled up in a fetal position on a cold, unyielding steel bed frame without a mattress. Fear gripped my every breath as my tiny body shivered from lack of warmth and my enormous fear of the unknown. Seasoned juvenile delinquents who had been in and out of the system were raucously sharing war stories about their past residencies upstate in juvenile prison. This was my first time. Loneliness, fear, anxiety, depression, a longing for home, and anger all were wrenching my gut. The pains in my belly were almost unbearable. I needed relief of some sort.

I was next to go in front of a judge infamous to everyone in the Black community of the city. Us Black folk were aware of her unjust, racist tactics and unfair sentencing when it came to Whites and Black's. Her warfare was waged behind a bench, every judge's shield. Her weapon was the laws of this racist Commonwealth of Virginia. Yes, we all knew of her strict enforcement of the intimidation, terrorization, castration, humiliation, emasculation, and subjugation of our young Black boys.

There was no way that I could make it through the

terror dome, as my peers had nicknamed upstate juvenile prison. I needed solace. Assurance. My silent prayer at once muted the clamor of my dungeon. Words began to formalize in my adolescent mind, and I whispered them continually until the bailiff came and retrieved me for my first court appearance. I did not know it at the time, but a coping mechanism was birthed in my frightened heart that morning. A mechanism that would aid in the maintenance of my sanity through my turbulent thirty-year reign as the apex predator of my ecosystem. The mindful technique and defensive tactic to minimize the overwhelming and tortuous stress of my very own self-imposed afflictions was born in a pissy dungeon full of captured junior beasts.

My life thus far has taught me that in my darkest moments comes the light of opportunity, brightly beaming with the potential to learn and grow into my purposed life.

Death and life are in the power of the tongue:
and they that love it shall eat the fruit thereof.
—King Solomon

In the beginning was the Word. Life birthed in my heart, hope birthed in my soul, light birthed in my spirit with the utterance of the words of my deepest sincerest thoughts and feelings. The creative force of the Word manifested itself from a set of chap lips with a bloody cut from the fight I had had just hours ago at the detention center. Those words are as follows:

God's Shank

As though a merciless curse torments my life
For always, now, and forevermore
Like my plight is somehow God's knife
That joyfully pierces everything that I adore.

There was no plan with these repeatedly uttered words. My only intent was to quiet the chaos inside of me. Two things cannot occupy the same space at the same time.

It is a law of physics. I discovered to replace the torment of stress with melodious words expressing my current reality. It was a form of venting and decompressing. It was not intended poetry but instead a personal rap song to cease all the noise, internally and externally.

Those words helped me to understand the power of changing my present feelings, emotions, thoughts, and circumstances with the mere utterance of organized syllables and words and sentences, phrase, and songs. This spoken word had only one requirement for it to be effective and that was it had to be based solely and specifically on THE TRUTH. The truth shall set you free!

God's Shank vented my heart and souls' anguish of against will. It's a revelation of my faith in a higher power by acknowledgement of what I perceive is God's intentions for placing me in a cage. Life at this time of my life was full of rebellious teenage energy as I tried to figure out this new way of life in the crack culture. This poem was me speaking to the universe my first sentiments of feeling like life was too much to endure. The mere mention of a curse is a proclamation of my initial acceptance of being hunted and touched by misfortune as a punishment for something.

My journey of using words as a medication of immense therapeutic value began in the year of 1990. This book was informally born over thirty years ago in a decrepit court building that rested in the heart of a section of the city called Court Square. This sprawling acreage that sat only four blocks away from the treacherous Garrett Square Housing, the hood that I would eventually takeover, was a complex of three different court buildings equipped with multiple courtrooms. The imposing fortress where a ridiculously high number of years are handed out daily to a predominantly Black male population in the form of prison sentences is designated a historical site due to its use as the premier slave auction block of Charlottesville.

There is no coincidence or accidents. Everything is purposed in life. The slave auction block was still the slave auction block and here I was about to be auctioned off to a plantation of immense treachery named Hanover Learning Center.

Over the years I jotted down poems and essays for purposes of venting and healing. I would write on anything, receipts, napkins, sticky notes, composition notebooks, my skin, and basically anything that I could use when I was inspired to write. All these poems and short essays were meant for me and my eyes only. But as I kept finding them in various boxes and totes that hold decades of my life spent in prison, I began reading them and feeling empowered at a time of my life when I could not see past the day.

Life was quickly slipping away from me as I tried to live a 100% legit life free of any illegal gains. I was working two full time jobs, sleeping only about two hours a night. My weight, health and sanity were falling as quickly as a two-dollar whore's panties. I sat and chronologically ordered every poem and essay to the best of my abilities. What I discovered was awesome! It had the potential to be a great book of poetry.

I was amazed as I read my thoughts and feelings over the course of almost four decades. All my selves, the evolution was unfolded right there before my eyes, haphazardly sitting all over a coffee table. The divine providence of fortune was setting the stage for greatness in my life, in the lives of those that I love, and in the lives of every soul that will be touched by the spirit of these honest, revealing words of my soul.

A full autobiography will be released in June of 2023 if the Creator permits. During the mean time may *The Unfolding* give you a taste of what is to come. These poems and short essays are from my perspective of life from birth until around the age of seventeen. An overwhelming majority of the content is specifically centered around the ages of twelve until the age of seventeen. As us males know, this is the incubation period where we fashion, mold, and solidify our personalities into a protective battleship that guides our every thought, word, or deed. Who I am today, yesterday, and tomorrow, my life's philosophy, which is the steering wheel of my life, was molded and stamped over those five years of constant war.

The Black youth, my generation, raised during the crack epidemic of the 1980's and 1990's, during the professed drug war of President Ronald Reagan, are arguably the most vilified from lack of understanding of who we are. Especially the young Black male, public enemy number one. The jungle is what nurtured us. The question that needs to be asked is Who created this jungle? Here is my interpretation of it told through poetry and short essays of my life story.

Welcome to the Jungle!!!

Predator or Prey

In the midst of chaos, there is also opportunity
—Sun Tzu

From the moment we are discharged from our fathers' loins we are in a race and a battle to reach a place that promises life, the awaiting egg of the woman. Out of 100 million sperm only ONE will have the honor of life. The losers destined for a murky death absorbed by the woman's body, a meal of amino acids and pure protein which is transformed into energy for the woman to nourish the new seed growing inside her womb, the sole VICTOR of the most important battle of life.

I can only imagine the hectic, urgent, and violent scene. Just the thought of that war going on as the most sacred and important act of creation is taking place holds me in complete awe. That entire process is our introduction to the world as we are to know it for our entire time on earth, a continual war, battle after battle. Something always trying to us from existence on every level of our lives. From the micro to the macro, we are in a battle for our lives.

Micro consisting of microbiological organisms, bacteria, and viruses, trying to invade our bodies, feed themselves and kill the host. The macro consisting of people that you host inside the inner depths of your heart and consider them loved ones striving to "KILL" you spiritually, emotionally, psychologically, mentally, financially, morally, and tragically sometimes even physically. Everyone of these battles shapes and forms our personality and identity much like the blacksmith hammering metal on the anvil. Either we grow stronger by every battle or learning experience or we are weakened or even worse destroyed. Thus, we get the clichéd statement, "Anything that does not conquer us will only make us stronger."

What is shaped by life's battles is our will, our beliefs, our lenses of life and most importantly these battles shape our morals, values, and principles which are the rudder that steers our every decision. And this is the process of evolution, the adaptation of intelligence to stimuli in the environment where it abides. This is the realm where we learn survival skills which ultimately leads to where we live on the food chain. Either you evolve into predator or prey. There are no hybrids, no mixed species. Either you are one or the other. Either you are feasting or getting feasted on. You are either hunting or being hunted. ONE thing for certain and two things for sure, once you STUDY this disguised textbook on life, uncut and raw in its truest form, you will see life completely different. Sort of like Neo in the movie *The Matrix* when he took the red pill. His eyes were opened, and he saw life how it truly existed. Now it is your turn!

PUSSY

Women are the most charitable creatures, and the most troublesome. He who shuns women passes up the trouble, but also the benefits. He who puts up with them gains the benefits, but also the trouble. As the saying goes, there's no honey without bees.
—Niccolo Machiavelli

In the jungle pussy is the most precious commodity. There is no other facet of the jungle that causes more successes or failures for males than pussy. These successes are manifested by the male's pursuit of it's awesome delights. He does whatever it takes to fulfill his unceasing and bestial appetite for the nectar of eternal sweetness. He was built to fight and fuck, or in less crude words, his entire physical being, the animal in him, was built to procreate and protect his life and the life of his family unit by all costs.

His sexual drive instinctively compels him to extensively study the female to identify her likes and dislikes, pinpointing what species of animal she is and every detail about her god of choice, which in the jungle usually translates into a vice of some sort. Customarily the female's god or vice is the pursuance of wealth, no matter the species, because of growing up in less than favorable and unfortunate environmental and home conditions. This is always caused by the financial struggles that afflicts the overwhelming majority of the jungle's inhabitants.

The male after careful study of the female is enlightened with this awareness and sets his mind, his single-mindedness, and firmness of purpose on obtaining wealth. But this feat cannot be carried out by the beast alone. What separates the alpha from the typical male of the jungle is the alpha's ability and capacity to merge the beast and the god inside of him. When this transpires and he acquires the **overstanding** of how to effectively utilize this art it almost guarantees that his journey to get what the female defines as wealth will be successful.

The pursuance of pussy has created more drug kingpins, gang leaders, and underworld executives than every other aspect of the jungle combined. But on the other side it has produced more cemetery plots, headstones, and life sentences in prison than every other aspect of the jungle combined.

For as far back as I can remember the female sex has always played a vital role in my life. From my upbringing being nurtured by many strong Black women learning the ways of the most beautiful creature ever created all the way to my attraction to a creature so sublimely diverse and uniquely fashioned. The wonderful landscape of the female body with its curves and valleys, crevices and perfect imperfections of favor and flavor has always piqued my interest and curiosity. The explorations of this curiosity has placed me in the beds of many women, so different in appearance yet so alike in their desire to explore sex without constraints.

Every person is a freak, no matter what they believe or say. Sexuality plays an especially significant role in the world of human development. We are created through this act. We owe our entire existence to the sexual union. And an act so intimate, encompassing the buried desires of the participants, releases emotions, feelings, and thoughts that are primal in origin. Animalistic, carnal, and beastly to say the least.

I know from my own individual experiences that if the right setting is provided, laced with elements of personal fetish and fantasy, mixed with a hefty dose of comfort and relaxation, then usually a freak will be born. Provided with the aforementioned in abundance, the woman, at first inhibited and frightened to reveal her true sexual identity will lose her inhibitions. The birth of this new facet of her existence propels her on a journey to reach the pique of her personal sexuality. All the subliminal messages of sex and sexuality that has been accumulated by her soul over her lifetime culminates in a single awareness that part of her fulfillment in life rest in embracing her true sexuality, which the world calls a freak.

When that *ahha* moment flashes inside her heart of heart's she begins to focus on getting hers too. She makes sure that she is no longer merely a giver of sexual pleasure, which is her learned role from that perpetual cycle of handed down lessons.

When her true sexual identity is revealed to her outside of the secret confines of her bedroom, where she masturbates to whatever tickles her fancy, it is only from the interaction with another freak. Sex with anyone else will be unfulfilling, inadequate, and mediocre at best. But when two people get together who have embraced that freaky side of themselves, they create and experience magic together. Body quaking orgasms. That mind blowing orgasm that makes you dizzy, high as the clouds. Those uncontrollable quakes rising your body from the bed like you are possessed or something.

When this realm is touched then sex becomes an art rather than an act. And with this art the now sexually uninhibited woman has a revolution of internal dialogue where every utterance is a question of how can she go higher. How can she support this new level of sexual freedom? All the wasted sexual moments flash in her mind. She ponders how all these years her sexual selflessness should have been sexual selfishness. But like everything in life she knows that time and aging produce wisdom. If she takes care of her body and soul she will ripen and will grow and evolve gracefully and powerfully.

Time ripens the soul. That is why, middle-aged, and older women make the best lovers. They have been through the stages of development and have endured the many sexual lessons of other's as well as themselves. This woman is the sole controller of her sexuality. She does whatever will make the sexual episode a monumental moment in history. Because she knows and understands that if she feels good, she will operate better in every other aspect of her life.

The mature woman who has bear hugged her inner freak and perfected the art of sex has always been my sexual partner of choice. Alphas love a ready-made freak. Sex becomes an immense joy, an integral part of the mature freaks lifestyle. She becomes the best freak. She becomes what every true God of the jungle desires, a certified freak.

All women are freaks. Oftentimes they just need a little help bringing it out. A freak is a woman or man who has developed and matured beyond the self-taught shame of holding back sexually because of fear of judgment. That is all it boils down to, a fear of judgement. And this fear cripples the opportunity to experience sensations aligned with what she desires, what makes her touch the moon and quake like a violent earthquake.

Sexuality begins young though. The development of the sexual personality begins to fashion itself in the exceedingly preliminary stages of life. Well at least for me and my elementary school classmates it did.

My earliest memory of a sexual experience is at Greenbrier ElementarySchool, the white school in the affluent white neighborhood where we were bussed to from the 'hood. I could not have been more than five years old when I began my journey of sexual adventure. A young pretty girl from Rose Hill, a working class, black community, similar to mine, that bordered my neighborhood, was my first introduction to sexuality and my immense delight in the female's body.

At recess on the playground, we had a small cove that was connected to the school building where us kids would spend time together away from the scrutiny of the teacher's gaze. I recall that this girl and I never really communicated. We were in the same class and were always around each other, but we had never said two words to each other. We would just stare at each other and smile. She was very pretty, like a Black china doll. Her best friend was a friend of mine from my neighborhood, another pretty girl who I secretly had a crush on. And I remember she came to me one day and told me to meet them both in the cove at recess. Immediately my heart started thumping as nervousness and anxiety ripped through me. What did they want to meet for? As time dredged on my young mind wandered and wondered.

At recess, the girls beat me to the cove and were waiting when I got there. The strangest thing happened then. One that baffled me for a long time. It was understood between us two practical strangers that we were here for only one reason and that was for the "oochie-coochie," as we called it then. And while our mutual friend looked out, without a single word spoken, our only exchange was a smile.

I pulled down my shorts exposing my tiny little ding-

267

a-ling and she came over and started licking me all down there. Not sucking but just licking and lapping everywhere. I remember it feeling so good, a tickling sensation. She did that for a few minutes then stood and lifted her skirt. Following the removal of her panties I returned the favor. But the only thing different was that what she had down there was uniquely awesome.

I remember the episode vividly, her smell, the slight hints of urine, the saltiness of her, the way she jumped my face like she was trying to smother me. This meeting became a normal occurrence throughout the remainder of the school year. The three of us meeting in secret. The only thing that changed over time was that all three of us used to partake in it. Taking turns. Where did these urges come from? How can children so young know this type of sexuality? I don't know about her, but I can tell you about me.

Bulk Orders/Wholesale Orders for
books please contact at:
pgilmoresolutions@gmail.com
Or
(804) 471-3737

About the Author

Pertelle "Khalil" Gilmore is the founder and former Executive Director of The B.U.C.K. Squad, a non-profit focused on reducing gun-violence by de-escalation and conflict resolution. He is also the former Senior Coordinator of the LOCUST Therapeutic Community; where he was awarded with several accolades for his exemplary service and innovative techniques in changing the trajectory of incarcerated men lives.

Equipped with over a dozen Social Skill Certifications and a Valedictorian graduate of the prestigious University of Virginia's Darden School of Business Entrepreneurs Program he spends his days investing in the community that he once destroyed by mentoring at-risk young men, teaching and training conflict resolution and de-escalation, and lecturing about the importance of mental health awareness along with a great variety of other lectures on social justice, criminality, etc. His lectures and seminars are dynamic and life altering. Bookings for Violence Interruption Training, lectures, and/or seminars: **pgilmoresolutions@gmail.com** or **(804)471-3737** Pertelle loves to hear from readers. Visit at Facebook: Pertelle Khalil Gilmore.

PERTELLE GILMORE

PERTELLE GILMORE SOLUTIONS
Educational and informative lectures and seminars.

MOTIVATIONAL
1.Success is a lifestyle.
2.Breaking destructive cycles.
3.The Art of self mastery.
4.Excellence is not a goal it's a lifestyle.
5.The Art of survival.

CRIMINALITY AND THE CRIMINAL ELEMENT
1.Gangster-Thug: Mind of the master street predator.
2.Domestic violence: The perpetrators mind state.
3.The convict's mind: Prison politics.
4.Habilitation and Rehabilitation: There is a SIGNIFICANT difference.

YOUTH ISSUES
1.Peer pressure.
2.Bully's.
3.Who am I? -My identity.
(MIDDLE SCHOOL AND HIGH SCHOOL)

GANG PREVENTION AND AWARENESS
1.Battling the enemy of our youth's future"

*CHURCH -FAITH BASED-Dynamic Bible Studies, seminars, and workshops.
CUSTOMIZED LECTURES FOR CRIMINAL JUSTICE CLASSES.

WILLOWS WAY

Schools, colleges and universities, corporations, private groups, churches, adult, and juvenile correctional institutions.

Certified Violence Interrupter Trainer

FOR BOOKING CONTACT AT: (804)471-3737
pgilmoresolutions@gmail.com

10% Commission for all who help get bookings for lectures and seminars.

PERTELLE GILMORE

A c k n o w l e d g m e n t s

Special mention to my sister Tiffany Smith. My behind-the-scenes biggest supporter. You are a special kind of person sis! Thank you for being such a great friend and sister. And a fabulous mother to my nephews Antwan, Alijah, and Jaheim.

Made in the USA
Middletown, DE
04 December 2025

22186917R00157